I0818607

THE WORST OF STAINS

Henry Neville Summersett was baptized on June 23, 1774 at Hadleigh in the county of Suffolk. Nothing is known of Summersett's early life except that he was a self-taught man with a love of literature and the plays of Shakespeare. When Summersett's father, an inn-keeper in Ipswich by profession, was declared bankrupt in 1792, the 17-year-old apparently set out for London to try his hand at writing in order to support his parents. His first novel, *The Offspring of Russell*, was published anonymously by the Minerva Press in 1794 and is an impressive debut written in the popular pseudo-historical Gothic vein. Two more novels followed, both published by the Minerva Press, *The Fate of Sedley* (1795) and *Probable Incidents; or, Scenes in Life* (1797); the latter was the first to feature his name on the title page. *Aberford* (1798) was something of a departure from the first three novels, being a short picaresque novella featuring a large amount of Summersett's poetry.

Three major Gothic novels followed, *Mad Man of the Mountain* (1799), *Jaqueline of Olzeburg; or, Final Retribution* (1800), and *Martyn of Fenrose; or, The Wizard and the Sword* (1801), which boast some of Summersett's most memorable characters and gripping plots of damnation, revenge, murder and unspeakable horror. During this productive period, Summersett also wrote two novels of individuals struggling against adversity in a hostile world, *Leopold Warndorf* (1800) and *The Worst of Stains* (1804). Critics had always been dismissive of Summersett's novels, and it appears that he left London after 1804 to pursue other literary ventures, publishing volumes of poetry and penning plays that were performed in provincial theatres. Summersett's final novel, *All Sorts of Lovers; or, Indiscretion, Truth, and Perfidy* (1811), perhaps his best, was published by the Minerva Press and is a humorous and detailed study of life at the start of the nineteenth century.

Summersett's later life remains a mystery. Archival research reveals that a Henry Neville Summersett married at Spalding in Lincolnshire in 1813; however, his date of birth is listed as 1778. There are also no records to indicate Summersett's year of death and place of burial, although in 1818 he appears to be residing in Nottinghamshire and working at the Southwell theatre.

Steve Orman is an Associate Lecturer in the Department of English & Language Studies at Canterbury Christ Church University. His research interests lie in the early modern period and the long eighteenth century.

By Henry Summersett

The Offspring of Russell (1794)
The Fate of Sedley (1795)*
Probable Incidents, or, Scenes in Life (1797)
Aberford, or, What You Will (1798)*
Mad Man of the Mountain (1799)*
Leopold Warndorf (1800)*
Jaqueline of Olzeburg, or, Final Retribution (1800)
Martyn of Fenrose, or, The Wizard and the Sword (1801)*
The Worst of Stains (1804)*
Happy at Last, or, Sigh No More, Ladies: A Comedy (1805)
Maurice, the Rustic and other Poems (1805)
All Sorts of Lovers, or, Indiscretion, Truth and Perfidy (1811)
Happiness in Retirement: A Poem (1812)
Ferdinand, the Slave of Passion (1818)

* Available or forthcoming from Valancourt Books

THE WORST OF STAINS

A NOVEL

BY

HENRY SUMMERSETT

"OUT, DAMNED SPOT!"

TWO VOLUMES IN ONE

EDITED AND WITH AN INTRODUCTION AND NOTES BY

STEVE ORMAN

VALANCOURT BOOKS

The Worst of Stains by Henry Summersett
First published London: Dutton, 1804
First Valancourt Books edition 2014

Published by Valancourt Books, Richmond, Virginia
Publisher & Editor: James D. Jenkins
http://www.valancourtbooks.com

ISBN 978-1-941147-15-3 (*trade cloth*)

Set in Adobe Caslon 11/13.5

CONTENTS

EDITOR'S DEDICATION

This edition is dedicated to Maria, Greg, my dad Robert, my mum Karon, my brothers Matthew and David, my nan Marie Jones, and in memory of Victor Jones.

INTRODUCTION[1]

Henry Summersett followed up *Martyn of Fenrose; or, The Wizard and the Sword* (1801) with *The Worst of Stains* (1804). Like the former novel, *The Worst of Stains* was printed for R. Dutton of Gracechurch Street, London and contains some of Summersett's most emotive and tortured characters. Published originally in two volumes, the novel could be found in at least a couple of circulating libraries in London and Scotland at the start of the nineteenth century before falling into obscurity.[2] The novel was never reprinted and we are fortunate that it has survived at all; only one copy is known to be extant and is housed in the Corvey library in Germany. *The Worst of Stains*, whilst bearing some similarities with *Martyn of Fenrose*, features a Preface which makes explicit the link between the two novels. Summersett had fared badly at the hands of the periodical critics who had lambasted his previous literary offering as blasphemous, with one reviewer feeling compelled "to throw the book on the floor" half way through his reading.[3] As usual, Summersett responds with fighting talk, writing in the Preface to his new novel that in order to make the characters believable to the reading public, certain extremities in language must be employed. He writes that every "passion has its peculiar language", and *The Worst of Stains* is certainly commendable for its rich exploration of the passions

[1] As this Introduction reveals details concerning the plot of *The Worst of Stains*, readers may wish to consult it after they have finished reading the novel.

[2] The novel could be borrowed from the following circulating libraries: "Aberdeen Public Library, Broad Street, Aberdeen. (Catalogue: 1821); Robert Kinnear's Circulating Library, 29 Frederick Street, Edinburgh. (Catalogue: 1808); A. K. Newman and Co.'s Circulating Library, Minerva Office, 32 & 33 Leadenhall Street, London. (Catalogue: 1814); Richards's Library, Queen Street, Cheapside, London. (Catalogue: 1807)". See *British Fiction 1800-1829: A Database of Production, Circulation & Reception* (http://www.british-fiction.cf.ac.uk) for further details.

[3] *The Critical Review*, Volume XXXIII, September 1801, p. 112.

of anger and jealousy that permeate the novel. Summersett's new literary offering received at least one positive review, with one critic writing, "THIS is, alas! a romance of real life; it is an interesting, impressive, and truly moral tale".[1]

The first question that the reader may ask after beginning reading the novel, is, what exactly *is* the worst of stains and who does it relate to? Summersett's literary technique often utilises such methods of intrigue to maintain the interest of the reader, who is often led to make assumptions about characters that later prove to be misguided, whilst at the same time allowing for his characters to act as real human beings guided by circumstance and opportunity. When the reader first learns of the plight of Ann Pownall, seduced and then abandoned by the rakish Captain Berrington to give birth to a bastard child, the reader may well believe that the worst of stains is the stain of illegitimacy, that is doubly destructive, not only for the heavily distressed mother but also for the unborn child. Such a reading is amply supported by the chilling moment early on in the novel when Ann attacks her young son William with a pair of scissors; an attempt to destroy the living reminder of her previous sin and the polluting stain that is left both on her fragile body and insensible mind. The worst of stains could also apply to the soul of Captain Berrington, for the many injuries and injustices that he causes over the course of his wicked life. Berrington senior's soul is stained, as he repeats a list of his crimes to his terrified son William, which include murder, blasphemy, and breaking the ties of wedlock. It is a horrifying moment in the narrative where the reunion of father and son occasions so much despair and hatred, with Captain Berrington, in a Faustian fashion, painfully acknowledging that his stained soul is destined for Hell.

The list of characters fitting the subject of the worst of stains continues when we consider that Lady Augusta's disastrous marriage to Colonel Heyland results in her own body being stained, not only with a bruise occasioned by the despicable actions of her husband, but also by his open infidelity. Lady Augusta, of course,

[1] *The Imperial Review*, Volume 2, May 1804, p. 143.

is also haunted by her bearing of an illegitimate child residing in Italy, and her suffering is great in the second volume of the novel. The seemingly innocent and close friend of Berrington, Russel, is a character who also demands attention with relation to the worst of stains. Russel's villainy in destroying the happily married life of Lorina and Berrington for his own few moments of pleasure, whilst posing as the virtuous guarantor of truth, is still shocking to readers visiting the novel today.

It will probably have become apparent by now that many of the characters in Summersett's fascinating novel are "stained" in one way or another. The final two characters, Berrington and his wife Lorina, both embody the worst of stains afforded by the author. Lorina's moment of adultery, totally unexpected by the reader, is a problematic moment in the narrative. It is problematic precisely because of the ambiguity that surrounds the actual act of sexual intercourse. Summersett is, as perhaps is to be expected with regard to censorship, quiet on the moment of triumph in Russel's seduction. But reading between the (absent) lines the reader can plausibly assume that this is no conventional tale of an innocent wronged woman seduced by a rakish and unstoppable evil man. There are no hints of violence or a struggle as Lorina appears to act willingly in the moment of adultery. There are no signs of dissent from Lorina, perhaps not only because of her jealousy, but also because she seems inspired to obtain "revenge" on the supposed infidelity of her husband. Lorina's act of adultery therefore is refreshing in a literary context as she willingly embarks on a moment of passion with Russel, only to be immediately haunted and disillusioned once the experience has ended and the severity of her actions dawns upon her. Lorina is a complex character however, and despite the pangs of jealousy that drive her to distraction and are later preyed upon by the odious Russel, there have been cracks appearing in her relationship with Berrington. The couple both have their fair share of secrets that they consciously choose not to share or discuss with each other, and there are certainly suggestions from Summersett that after the birth of their first child, the couple do not engage in intimate sexual relations with each other; initially because of

Berrington's absence in the army, before the extreme feelings of jealousy poison Lorina's mind and convince her that her husband has been unfaithful to her with the beautiful Lady Augusta.

Summersett finally decides that the worst of stains is reserved for William Berrington. After hearing directly from Lorina about her infidelity, the reader is totally unprepared for the visceral carnage that ensues. The shattering of Lorina's skull with the bar of iron, launched at her by her enraged husband, is both sickening and unexpected. Summersett revels in the gory details, increasing the uncomfortable tone of this moment of rashness and brutality in the moment where the now mad Berrington kisses his wife, only to recoil in horror when her blood stains his lips. The worst of stains, it appears, is murder. In fact Berrington's callous murder of his wife and later, of Russel, and the spots of blood that remain on Berrington's hands, are a permanent reminder that his soul is stained and a sign that his own damnation is inevitable. Such a moment, where bloodied hands are stained with sins irremovable, echoes Shakespeare's play *Macbeth*. The play, a favourite of Summersett's, is crucial at the moment where Berrington destroys the harmony of his little world. Hands stained with blood, and suffering from severe psychological distress, Berrington encourages the reader to recall the quotation that Summersett chose to adorn his title page with, "Out, damned spot!"[1] The quotation, spoken by Lady Macbeth in a state of madness, reflects the fact that phantom spots of blood stain the hands, never to be removed. Berrington, of course, before the fight with Russel, *literally* has spots of blood staining his hands.

Summersett undoubtedly saw similarities between Macbeth and Berrington and Lady Macbeth and Lorina, probably from the occasions where he would have seen the play performed in the early-nineteenth-century theatres. As A. R. Braunmuller observes in his commentary on stage productions of *Macbeth*, "Kemble followed the Garrick line (Macbeth sympathetic and/

[1] *Macbeth*, edited by A. R. Braunmuller. The New Cambridge Shakespeare, Cambridge: Cambridge University Press, 2012, V.i.30.

or weak, Lady Macbeth the strong instigator of evil acts)".[1] Berrington is certainly perceived as a weak individual by Lorina, and it is her own act of adultery that brings out the savageness and the very worst of him, similar to the power-relationship between Lady Macbeth and Macbeth. William Berrington becomes a murderer, just like his father, and in a moment which is grimly reminiscent of his mother's suicide by drowning in the river near the Fellers residence, he commits his body to the waves of the sea to succumb to the same fate. Such an act, both for Ann and for young William, also functions as a last desperate attempt to achieve absolution, with the hope that submergence in the cold water will finally cleanse both body and soul of the "worst of stains". The tragically dark tone that dominates the last few pages of the novel is only somewhat alleviated by the re-emergence of Robert Fellers, who manages to comfort the sorrows of William and Lorina's child, and taking the boy into his custody, does offer the slightest of glimpses of hope to rise. However, such small comfort is quickly quashed by Summersett, who in an authorial intervention to provide his own comments on the sign of the times, writes an incredibly bleak closure to the novel which criticises the moral laxities of the times. The fact that Summersett primarily addresses women in these closing paragraphs is more indicative of his intended readership of the novel, rather than an outright misogynistic attack that seemingly alleviates men from the blame of adultery.

The influence of Shakespeare is again apparent in Summersett's novel. Whether it is the anxiety surrounding supposed adultery in *Cymbeline* (1610), or the faithlessness of friends in *The Two Gentlemen of Verona* (1590), Summersett adopts and revises Shakespearean themes to provide a fresh exploration of a range of intense emotional experiences. It is the subject of jealousy, however, that is central to Summersett's novel. Summersett had previously explored the theme of jealousy in *Mad Man of the Mountain*, *Leopold Warndorf*, and *Martyn of Fenrose*, but it is *The Worst of Stains* where the subject receives extended treatment.

[1] "Introduction", *Macbeth*, The New Cambridge Shakespeare, Cambridge: Cambridge University Press, 2012, p. 107.

Even though Shakespeare's *The Winter's Tale* (1611) has much to say about jealousy, Summersett turned to *Othello* (1602) for inspiration on the maddening destruction of jealousy and spousal murder when writing his own novel. The happiness of Othello that is destroyed by Iago is explored in Summersett's novel via the characters of Berrington and Russel. Whereas in *Othello*, is it supposed infidelity that drives Othello insane and culminates in the murder of Desdemona in bed, Summersett's novel presents an actual case of adultery that is brutally punished with a horrific violence *before* Berrington turns mad. If anything, it is the character of Lorina who more closely resembles Othello in *The Worst of Stains*, with Berrington's wife driven to insanity when she first suspects her husband of having an affair with Lady Augusta. Othello's "proof" of Desdemona's guilt is a fatal misconstruction; hidden out of sight and out of ear shot, witnessing Iago talking to Cassio, Othello believes that he sees Cassio admit to having a sexual relationship with Desdemona. Lorina, on the other hand, also falls victim to misconstruction. Entering at the moment when her husband is kneeling and kissing Lady Augusta's bruise on her arm, Lorina has her own ocular proof of her husband's infidelity, and like Othello, she asks questions to her spouse far too late for a resolution to become a possibility.

There is one last curious incident that may reveal a further literary debt in the writing of *The Worst of Stains*. When Summersett mentions Teresa Pancha in his novel he undoubtedly reveals his interest in Miguel de Cervantes's novel *Don Quixote*, the first part of which was published in 1605 with the second appearing in 1615. In particular, Summersett appears most interested in the story of Cardenio that appears in the first part of Cervantes's novel, for reasons that will become apparent below. The story of Cardenio focuses on a wronged lover, Cardenio, who believes himself deprived of his lover Luscinda after praising her beauty and giving poetry he has composed about her to his friend, Don Fernando, who in turn, attempts to seduce and marry Luscinda. Driven to madness, Cardenio runs away and takes up residence in the mountains. Anybody who has read Summersett's novel *Mad Man of the Mountain* will realise that the latter novel shares much of the story of Cardenio. This is where the borrowing becomes curious, as Summersett was undoubtedly aware of, and excited by the fascination of Shakespeare and John Fletcher's lost play, *The History of Cardenio* (1613), based on Cervantes's tale from *Don Quixote*. Crucially, Lewis Theobald had written a play entitled *Double Falsehood, or, The Distressed Lovers* that was first performed on the 13th December 1727 with the claim that the play was written originally by Shakespeare. Debate has raged over the years as to whether Theobald's play is indeed Shakespeare and Fletcher's play revised or a literary fraud, but the play was popular in the eighteenth century and it is possible that a young 17-year-old Henry Summersett could have seen a performance of the play at the Covent Garden theatre in London in June 1791, and he had evidently read it.[1] Certainly Summersett revises ideas from Cervantes's tale including the fact that Lorina reads love poetry penned by Russel and Westdale himself refers to Berrington's wife by the name of another Shakespearean heroine, Imogen. The name Lorina is also phonetically close to the *Double Falsehood*'s Leonora—pronounced Le'nora[2]—providing further evidence that Summersett was fascinated by the play's staging of false friendship and the baseness of human desire.

It is fitting that two hundred and ten years after its first publication, Summersett's engaging novel can once again be read and enjoyed by a whole new host of readers. Summersett may well have been forgotten and ignored since the first half of the nineteenth century, but the characters and their shocking fates in *The Worst of Stains* should help to rebuild the impression of Summersett as a diverse and talented writer.

STEVE ORMAN
Canterbury

April 25, 2013

[1] *Double Falsehood, or, The Distressed Lovers*, edited by Brean Hammond, Arden Shakespeare, London: Methuen, 2010, p. 113.
[2] *Double Falsehood, or, The Distressed Lovers*, edited by Brean Hammond, Arden Shakespeare, London: Methuen, 2010, p. 179.

ACKNOWLEDGEMENTS

I am extremely grateful to Dr. Dan Cadman of Sheffield Hallam University for his time and kindness in assisting me with a research query, and also for his friendship. Finally, my thanks to Jay at Valancourt Books, who aided me in my initial searches concerning Summersett's novel.

NOTE ON THE TEXT

This edition for Valancourt Books uses the first and only printed edition of *The Worst of Stains*, from 1804. Only one copy of the novel is known to exist and is housed at the Corvey library in Germany. In accordance with the editorial policy of Valancourt Books, I have remained faithful to the text as printed in the first edition, including Summersett's penchant for using "your's" and "her's", instead of "yours" and "hers". However, the original edition contains a significant number of printer's errors, which have been corrected for this edition. On the facing page is a complete list of the original edition's errors and the corrections made for this edition.

Volume I

p. 8, l. 8: "Alas! Alas!] "Alas! Alas!"
p. 8, l. 16: Ods' heart] Od's heart
p. 8, l. 23: adversity:"] adversity."
p. 10, l. 10: to night] to-night
p. 20, l. 8 seing] seeing
p. 23, l. 16 thoughlessly] thoughtlessly
p. 30, l. 16 heighth] height
p. 35, l. 5 add] and
p. 37, l. 16 boys] boys'
p. 39, l. 13 cried Robert."] cried Robert.
p. 42, l. 24 heart.] heart."
p. 55, l. 12 Mr] Mr.
p. 55, l. 15 god] got
p. 87, l. 2 castle-hunting] castle-haunting
p. 87, l. 10 to day] to-day
p. 87, l. 19 to day] to-day
p. 88, l. 4 you] your
p. 89, l. 19 strangers] strangers'
p. 93, l. 1 illeberality] illiberality
p. 93, l. 6 He] he
p. 104, l. 5 cencerned] concerned
p. 119, l. 12 Winstanly] Winstanley
p. 120, l. 1 Winstanly] Winstanley
p. 133, l. 15 assuance] assurance
p. 135, l. 23 Pownal] Pownall
p. 158, l. 7 desirious] desirous
p. 181, l. 18 ecnomiums] encomiums
p. 187, l. 16 you] your
p. 191, l. 2 Pownal] Pownall
p. 192, l. 2 Pownal] Pownall
p. 192, l. 10 kindom] kingdom
p. 193, l. 16 Pownal] Pownall
p. 196, l. 16 wish] with

Volume II

p. 1, l. 8 faught] fought
p. 5, l. 12 admistered] administered
p. 16, l. 12 prowed] prowled
p. 17, l. 22 pilgrimage.] pilgrimage."
p. 18, l. 24 abondoned] abandoned
p. 34, l. 4 franticly] franticly
p. 36, l. 1-2 at at] at
p. 41, l. 10 bis] his
p. 66, l. 1 you.] you,
p. 67, l. 12 oscasionally] occasionally
p. 80, l. 9 principle] principal
p. 87, l. 22 are"] are."
p. 125, l. 11 interupted] interrupted
p. 136, l. 10 wae] was
p. 141, l. 14 it.] it."
p. 152, l. 1 b] be
p. 178, l. 10 "What?—'] "What?—"
p. 186, l. 5 and] "and

THE

WORST OF STAINS.

A NOVEL.

BY HENRY SUMMERSETT.

IN TWO VOLUMES.

VOL. I.

"OUT, DAMNED SPOT!"

London:

PRINTED FOR R. DUTTON, GRACECHURCH STREET.

1804.

PREFACE.

THO' it may be hereafter said that the style of this little novel has no merit, criticism shall not make me acknowledge the design to be bad. My hero acts with a degree of manly propriety, while he is supposed to be under the influence of reason; when removed from it, I am not to be censured for either the words or manners of the character. His speeches are sometimes wild, his actions furious; but the reader, in those passages which are strongest, must regard the supporters of the scene, and not the inventor of the tale.

While a man's brethren take him kindly by the hand, and smile in his face, he is a creature of gentleness; but if he see an assassin's knife aimed at his heart, he is by turns the agent of fury and revenge. Every passion has its peculiar language: Love uses the sweetest words; Hatred mutters deeply; Murder franticly talks of perdition; and Madness is more horrible than the wolf that howls amid the darkness of night.

I should not have troubled the reader with this preface, had not a certain class of men put upon me some false accusations.* Our novels have, within a few years, assumed a dramatic appearance; and the food of the theatre has ever been to me palatable. The curses of Lear, the execrations of Macbeth's wife, and a hundred vehement maledictions in Shakespeare, Otway and Rowe, have been admired in the closet, and applauded on the stage.* But if any thing of this nature should be traced in a novel or romance, it is vulgarity, it is *blasphemy*, and the author is treated with no mercy by the periodical critics!* Mild correctors are certainly deserving of thanks; but those who would coarsely mangle with their wit and satire, are only entitled to that peculiar notice which we might give to a butcher in one of our public markets, who, unoffended by the effluvia and corruption produced by the means alluded to by the Prince of Denmark, indulges himself in dog-day jokes and wretched sarcasms.*

THE AUTHOR.

THE

WORST OF STAINS.

GABRIEL FELLERS was the sexton of a village in the eastern part of England; and his deceased father and grandfather had filled the same office before him. Simplicity and honesty were the characteristics of this humble family: They had ever been respected by the inhabitants of the parish; their conduct in life was pointed out, as being worthy of imitation; and Gabriel was happy in the notice of the rich, and in the friendship of the respectable.

He was, at the time of the commencement of this tale, in the fortieth year of his age; and during one half of that time, he had summoned the righteous to the house of God; attended every baptism and wedding: and assisted in laying the worn-out villagers in the bed of eternal quiet. His stipend was but small, and such as would not solely support himself, his wife and son, the latter of whom was only in the second year of his age.

But heaven had given him strength to work, and, likewise, an inclination to perform it. He was the village carpenter; and, in rearing the mansions of simplicity, no mean architect. Being fond of activity, he undertook the care of the gardens belonging to the parsonage, and also those of several of the opulent farmers; but this employment was followed in the more leisure hours; and his own little plot not only produced savoury herbs and substantial vegetables, but likewise blushed with the roses of summer.

The benevolence of Gabriel's heart was often the panegyric of the villagers; and he was always ready to perform those little offices of kindness, which he was enabled to do. Mary Fellers, the sexton's wife, was nearly ten years younger than her husband. She had all the simplicity, all the humanity, and all the charitableness of her partner. The state of her house corresponded with the neatness of her person; and the mild smiles of her face cheered the hearts of those who entered at her door. Mary was neither a village prattler, nor an encourager of gossips. She attended to her household duties, to her husband and child; and owing to the remote situation of her dwelling, she was not subject to many interruptions.

One evening this worthy pair were sitting over their wood-fire. The month was March, and the wind blew very cold. Their chairs were drawn close to the hearth, and a bottle of sweet wine stood upon the table. Each of them had drank a glass, and the cork was carefully replaced, in order to preserve the remainder of the beverage. Mary's child was asleep: Gabriel had just finished a chapter of the bible, (for it was Sunday,) and they proposed to sing the evening hymn, and then retire to their bed. Mary's voice was not destitute of melody, and Gabriel was esteemed a very able leader of the choir. But their religious song was made more sweet by the unaffected piety that shone in their eyes, which were often turned towards that Power, whose goodness and glory they were extolling.

"Surely," said Mary, ceasing to sing, "I heard some person call at the gate. Hark!—" They listened, but the wind alone was noisy. "I was deceived," continued Mary, "for I thought I heard some person call."

They renewed the hymn, and had nearly sung another verse, when it was no longer doubted that a voice came from the garden-gate. Gabriel concluded that the business of the unknown was of a parochial nature. The night was dark, and the wind boisterous. The sexton put a candle into his lanthorn, and walked down the path that led to the gate. He asked who was there, and, before an answer was given, saw a woman of very genteel appearance. She was leaning across the paling, as if for support; but she languidly lifted up her head, and enquired whether Mary Fellers resided at that house. On being answered *yes*, the stranger expressed a wish to speak to her; when Gabriel, not a little surprised, unbarred the gate, and led the feeble visitor to the tenement.

Gabriel held the door while she entered, and Mary rose to receive her. She was in a travelling dress, and her face was concealed by a black veil, which she wore on her hat. She drew near to the sexton's wife, caught hold of her hand, and pressed it.

"Oh, Mary! Mary!" were her first words, which came from her in agony. Mary did not immediately recollect her voice, for it was changed from its natural tone by her sobbings. The villagers were both in amazement: The stranger asked Mary whether she had forgotten her, who replied that she did not remember ever to have seen her before.

"I do not wonder at it," she replied, "for misery has greatly changed me since we parted. But look at me again: Perhaps the traces of what I have been, may call me back to your memory."

She lifted her veil: Mary fixed her eyes upon her pale face, and, with a faint scream, exclaimed, "Dear God of heaven! Do I not see my good young lady, Miss Ann Pownall, with whose family I lived at Wexford-Hall? Surely, surely it must be so."

"I am almost ashamed to confess I am that person. You knew me good, happy, innocent—But now—Mary, Mary! my heart is bursting with grief!"

"Dear madam, be comforted," said Mary; "sit nearer the fire, for you must be very cold. And why are you wandering in this dark night, and in this lonely place, without a companion? Bless me! I dare scarcely trust my senses to see you in such a situation. What, what can have befallen you?"

"Ask me not: My reason is not perfect; and that topic would lead me into madness. I have a request to make to you and your husband; and, knowing the goodness of your heart, I think you will not refuse me."

"And what is it, madam?" said Gabriel; "I shall be happy to serve a lady, of whom I have heard Mary speak so kindly. Tell me what it is?"

"I have suffered much affliction lately: I have been reduced in fortune, degraded in—— My entreaty is, that you will let me die in your house, and afterwards lay me with decency in the earth."

"Die!" exclaimed Mary.

"Die in my house, dear lady!" said Gabriel: "Live in it fifty years; at least till God shall be pleased to send comfort again to your bosom, and peace to your mind."

"O, how my heart thanks you!" cried the wanderer: "But I shall not long be a burthen to you. There is a disease that preys on me; and it will rapidly send me out of the world, in which I shall not struggle to continue."*

"Do not talk thus," said Mary: "If you are unhappy, and I can make you otherwise, I will strive, morning, noon, and night to do it."

"Alas! Alas!"

"And if you have been unfortunate, young lady," rejoined Gabriel, "I have a house that shall shelter you, as long as you like to continue in so lowly a dwelling. Your fare will be humble; but what of that? The bread of honesty is more grateful, to my palate, than the costly viands of vice. Od's heart! Do not droop. Tho' I never saw you before, I have often heard of you. Mary, put another billet on the fire; bring out the cold fowl, and warm a glass of wine. Cheer up, young lady. Tho' I have ever lived in the vale of quiet, I have a mite of compassion for those who are exposed to the tempests of adversity."

The eyes of Ann thanked him most eloquently: She had not the immediate power of speech, and her languor was still great. She took a little of the refreshment that was offered her, for she confessed she had not tasted food before that day; she could, however, swallow only a few mouthfuls, tho' Gabriel pressed her to eat more. Mary prepared a bed for their unexpected guest, who was anxious to repair to it. She wished Gabriel a good night, and followed Mary up stairs.

The violent storm of grief, which had been with pain and difficulty suppressed, now forced its way. She threw her arms around the neck of Mary, and moistened her affectionate bosom with her tears. "For the sake of heaven, dear madam," said Mary, "do not take on so sadly: It makes my heart ache to see you so much distressed. What can have happened to bring you into this condition?"

"Oh, that question! That searching question!"

"Compose yourself; pray do compose yourself. I will not now

ask you the cause of this distress and misery. I beseech you to calm your troubled spirits, and to trust to the mercy of God. The ills under which the good and innocent labour——"

"I am neither good, nor innocent! Oh, that I were!—I am not innocent—I am vile; yet, Mary, indeed I have been very unfortunate. But press me no further to-night, and do not think too hardly of me. You know what I have been, and shall know what I am. Good night! And when you address yourself to God, implore his forgiveness in my behalf."

"You torture my soul," said Mary; "You are too unwell to be left alone; I will come and sleep with you."

Ann opposed this: Mary kissed her cold hand, and, wishing her repose, went down to honest Gabriel, whose wonder had not subsided.

Mary's looks were sad and melancholy; she placed the warming-pan on the hearth, and burst into tears. Gabriel's heart was, likewise, softened; and he began to talk compassionately of their new guest, having previously shut the door that opened to the stair-case, lest Miss Pownall should hear the conversation.

"What, in the name of wonder, Mary," he said, "could bring the poor thing to this place, in such an unseasonable hour. Indeed I am astonished, and know not what to think of it. Young, beautiful, and innocent; wandering in a remote part of the country, without a friend to assist her. What can this possibly mean?"

"Indeed, Gabriel, I know not; and she appeared too ill to answer such questions herself. She is, as you say, very young and beautiful, but nothing like what she used to be; and I fear, Gabriel——"

"What do you fear, Mary?"

"That she has been led into indiscretion."

"It cannot be: there is not an appearance of such a thing."

"I doubt, Gabriel, it is so, however; for she confessed that she is neither good, nor innocent."

"Mercy on me! Is it possible? Not innocent; she never went willingly into error; I dare swear she never did."

"Ah, Gabriel! I fear the poor thing's heart is almost broken. I have not seen her before these three years, and that was about two months before her father's death. I lived in the family sixteen years; Squire Pownall was a good-tempered man, but sadly extravagant; for he spent all his fortune, and left poor Miss Ann little to depend upon. Mrs. Pownall had been dead about a twelvemonth; she was a sweet woman, and every eye in the parish wept for her death. I thought her daughter would have expired with her; for, you will remember, I was there at the time she left this world. Ann hung upon my neck—she cried—she fainted many times; and it could scarcely be said that she lived. Nobody could comfort, nothing quiet or make her cease to lament the fate of her beloved mother.

"She was, at that time, the loveliest girl I ever saw; her beauty was spoken of around the country, and yet she possessed not a spark of vanity. She was, likewise, thought to be very sensible; and the goodness of her heart was the common talk of the villagers. O, dear! O, dear! I never suspected that I should see her in this sad state!

"After the squire was dead, the park and house sold, and while the creditors were scrambling for what they could get, my poor young lady went to live with an old maiden sister of her father in London, or somewhere near to it, and I saw her not from that time till this hour. We must leave her to unravel the mystery; and in the mean time, Gabriel,——"

"I will cherish her, Mary, as if she were my own child; and use my poor means of relieving her sorrows. If she has stepped into error, I am sure she never trod the broad path of vice."

The sexton and his wife then retired to their chamber. Mary went into the room in which Miss Pownall lay, and found her still waking and weeping. But she requested her humble friend to go to her bed; and told her that, in the morning, she hoped her agitated spirits would find tranquillity.

Neither of the cottagers enjoyed much sleep during the night. As soon as it was light Mary went softly into the room of Miss Pownall, and, undrawing the curtain with a gentle hand, discovered that she was asleep. But the momentary gaze of Mary filled her with sorrow; and when she looked upon the death-like figure which lay before her, she thought it could not be the once-blooming Ann Pownall, whom she had formerly known. She again carefully shaded the bed, and went down the stairs, making as little noise as possible.

Gabriel had occasion to go into the village; and, during his absence, Mary employed herself in preparing a more than ordinary breakfast for her guest. The sexton returned in about two hours, and at the same time Miss Pownall left her chamber. The salutation of the villagers was so warm, friendly, and sincere, that it almost overpowered the visiter. It brought a faint bloom upon her pale cheek; and she looked as if she thought herself undeserving of their kind attention.

There was in her a fixed melancholy, which the joint assiduities of Gabriel and Mary could not dissipate. It seemed a confirmed sorrow; the effort to look composed was very feeble; and the tones of grief were so habitual, that she was unsuccessful when she endeavoured to change them. Gabriel, who possessed one of the best hearts that nature ever formed, and whose understanding, tho' not enriched, was not a mean one, did not express any curiosity to have her account for her distress. He rather endeavoured to divert her own thoughts from it; and the affectionate Mary was not less assiduous in this respect.

Miss Pownall was not insensible of this attention, and she secretly thanked them for it; but she was conscious that there must appear much mystery to the honest villagers. To keep them long in ignorance was not, however, her intention. She had a melancholy story to tell them; and to divulge it soon seemed to her highly proper. But she had not power to give it to them immediately; a faintness came upon her whenever she thought of it, and it was too painful to ruminate upon.

In the course of the morning, she renewed the subject of her abiding in their house, and hoped that it would not occasion them much inconvenience. Harbouring a strong presentiment of an early death, she did not suppose that she should long reside with them. She was equally afflicted in body and in mind; and tho' this world contained little to take pleasure in, she often shuddered when she thought of eternity. Sometimes she wished to combat her maladies, and to re-establish her health; and at other times, she considered peace lost to her for ever, and the world unworthy of her regard.

The honest friendship of Gabriel, and the tenderness of Mary, partly alleviated her present sufferings; and she was grateful to heaven, for permitting her to find her last resting-place with this virtuous pair.

They had finished their morning repast, and Gabriel, who was two hours beyond his usual time, was going to his work, when Miss Pownall rose hastily, and informed him that she had something to say to him. She crimsoned as she spoke, and Gabriel turned back again. "I left London precipitately," she cried; "and my reasons for doing so you shall hereafter know. Soon, very soon, will I divulge the secret with which I labour. My motive for coming hither was, principally, to hide myself from the world, from the cruelty of man, and from the pitiless reproaches of my own sex. I would, hereafter, live and die known only to you. It certainly is not possible for you to conceal my being here; but let me entreat you not to mention my name, which, even in this retirement, might be remembered. If any person should see and make enquiries concerning me, speak of me as——a married woman—or rather as a widow. Oh, God! To what a state am I humbled! It is frightful—Mary, I cannot bear all this affliction: it is too much for my heart. But, discarded by the world as I am, forsaken, ruined, and abandoned, give me your love and support; and during the short remainder of my miserable existence, I will not cease to bless you."

She threw herself, almost fainting, into the arms of Mary, whose heart was swelling with sorrow. Gabriel raised her gently, and mildly smiled upon her. He assured her of every service, that was in his power to perform; entreated her to divulge no secret, which she thought best confined to herself, and promised to use the utmost caution in speaking of her.

Somewhat revived by these traits of honesty and affection, she raised her head and thanked him; but, in order to conceal the agitation of her countenance, she almost immediately put her face to that of Mary's child, who stood by her chair.

Gabriel heard nothing in the village, relating to the wanderer;

and, from the silence of the inhabitants, he conjectured that her arrival had not been observed. To attempt to seclude her from all notice he knew to be folly; but he was somewhat puzzled for a probable tale; and such was his idea of moral rectitude, that he almost shrunk from the telling of a falsehood. The youth, beauty and sorrow of his new inmate, troubled his honest and affectionate heart; and he vowed to be the friend of the poor sufferer.

When he returned, he informed her that her arrival had not been remarked; and on enquiring how she had discovered the place of his residence, to which she was a stranger, she told him that she dismissed the chaise, in which she had travelled, at the entrance of the village, and afterwards employed an husbandman in shewing her the sexton's house.

She had not been in the parish three days before the gossips began to talk of her. She was first seen by a farmer's wife, on whose report many other inquisitive dames came to visit Mary, merely to have an opportunity of seeing the young stranger. She had taken the precaution of making her appearance as plain as possible; and, borrowing some mourning of Mary, she entirely laid aside her travelling dress. Seeing the inquisitiveness of her neighbours, Mary thought it best to bring Miss Pownall before them, and to mention that she was her sister, who had recently buried her husband, in a distant part of the kingdom.

Mary, who was not less conscientious than Gabriel, blushed a little when she told this untruth. Her virtues were known, and her veracity had never been questioned; the visiters, therefore, pitied the unfortunate Miss Pownall, and endeavoured to console her for her late loss.

These were trials for the stranger, which she could scarcely support. Her heart was filled with sorrow, and the hectic of shame frequently spread itself on her cheek. Dissimulation she had ever held in abhorrence: But dissimulation in a case like hers was terrible—it was a varnish on guilt, too glaring for the eye of the anguished penitent.

Village curiosity being gratified, Ann Pownall felt less embarrassed in appearing before the parishioners; accompanied by Mary, she would sometimes walk on the heath; and, when the weather was calm, by the side of the water. But her health growing every day more delicate, she at length declined this little exercise, and almost entirely secluded herself in the uninterrupted cottage of her humble friend. Her anguish and misery increased; and the state of her mind began to appear alarming. Sometimes she was silent and desponding, scarcely heeding what was said to her, and vague in her replies; but this torpor was often followed by involuntary starts and exclamations, and frequently by such words and actions as betrayed a deranged mind.

Tho' Mary was half terrified by these prognostics, she, as well as Gabriel, endeavoured to soothe and comfort her, to bring back her wandering imagination, and to divest it of its terrors. They called in the surgeon of the parish, who entertained very serious apprehensions for the patient, and apprised her supposed relations of her imminent danger. Another month wore away, and appearances became more alarming; her appetite was quite gone, her cheek bloodless, her eye hollow, and her voice feeble.

Mary hung over her, and prest her to her bosom; and Gabriel frequently went from her in tears. Had an hundred crimes been attached to her, the sexton, strict in principles as he was, must have forgiven her, when he viewed her affliction, her misery and distraction. Her pregnant state was now visible, and the period of her delivery not far distant. All was still a mystery to the cottagers; but Ann Pownall, one morning starting from a reverie, and wildly seizing the hands of Gabriel and his wife, desired them to listen to the story that she had to tell.

The cottagers soothed her, before they allowed her to begin it: They listened to the tale of her undoing; wept, trembled for her; took her to their bosoms; protested that they would be friends to her and her unborn babe; and, in conclusion, Gabriel, whose tongue had not teemed an oath for many a year, in the name of God thoughtlessly cursed the seducer of Ann Pownall, who sunk apparently lifeless into his arms.

Her hours of perfect sanity after this day were but few. Her imagination was on the rack; but the kindness of Mary would sometimes recal her ideas, and give her a temporary easement from distraction. The task, however, was often too much for the sensibility of the sexton's wife, who could not bear to see the woman whom she had fondled in her childhood, gradually decaying under misery, pain, and insanity. Both she and Gabriel had solemnly protested, when her mind was more free, that they would never give her up to her friends, and they intended, most strictly, to observe their promise.

The surgeon did not now attend her; she could not be prevailed on to see him, nor would she be persuaded that the state of her health needed any medical assistance. Languid and weak as she was, Mary could not deter her from wandering in the churchyard, which she would traverse every evening, and mark out the spot in which she wished her body to be laid. Mary never left her alone in these moments of delirium; and Gabriel endeavoured to prevent her roving as much as possible.

At length she was delivered of a child: It was a boy, and there was a probability of its surviving the wretched mother. Her mind was still disturbed; but she spoke little, and seldom addressed herself to any other person than Mary, who was surprised at her existing under such a complication of afflictions. She would scarcely suffer the infant to be taken from her, even for a moment, and would allow only Mary to nurse it. Mary fondly hoped that the sufferer would soon regain composure of mind, if not bodily health; but in this she was disappointed; for the maladies which troubled both were rooted, and the appearance of dissolution became more strong and palpable.

Gabriel was distressed and unhappy; he could scarcely bear to look on the injured creature, and her incoherent language made him most miserable.

Mary frequently endeavoured, by talking of the most relative matters, to bring reason again to the mind of Ann Pownall. One morning, as she was sitting with her, she renewed the task, and, looking in the face of Ann, asked her if she did not know her.

The answer was, "No."

"And do you not remember your father?" continued Mary.

"No."

"Nor your dear, your beloved mother, who died in your and in my arms?"

"Yes—No—"

"Recollect yourself. Do you not remember Captain Berrington?"

"Who?"

"Berrington, the father of your child."

"My child?" cried Ann, with a wild laugh and shout.—"And pray what do you call my child?"

"This dear little infant! This smiling innocent! Take him to your heart. Kiss him."

"There, there, there! Why he smells sweeter than the rose that I plucked yesterday in the garden."

"Kiss him again—Think who he is—Do you not love him, Ann?"

"Love him?—Oh, yes, yes, yes!"

"And what would you do for the cherub?"

"Do? Look."—She hastily snatched up a pair of scissors, and wounded the throat of the child with them. Mary shrieked aloud, and tore the bleeding infant from the arms of the maniac; and the terrified Gabriel, who happened to come in at that moment, ran for the surgeon.

"God of heaven!" exclaimed Mary; "would you murder your child? would you destroy your infant?"

"I thought it had been the natural child of Berrington; and it is better to die than to be called bastard. Thinking thus, I—I—Who am I?—Oh, I remember all! Murder! Murder and blood!"

She fell on the bed and fainted. Mary could give her no assistance; for the wounded infant screamed at her breast, and she was half dead with terror. It was a quarter of an hour before Gabriel and the surgeon arrived; and, in the mean time, the fear and misery of Mary were dreadful. The wound of the child was first examined, and found not to be dangerous; and the blood being stanched, the infant became more tranquil. They then directed their attention towards the unhappy mother, who had waked from her swoon, but not regained a particle of reason.

She seemed insensible of every thing that had happened, and looked unmeaningly on her friends. Nothing could induce her to speak, nor did she take any notice of the child, which Mary carried out of the room, and consigned to the care of a cottager's wife, who lived not far distant. The tranquillity of Gabriel and his wife, after these frightful traits of madness, was wholly disturbed; and though, for several days, the paroxysms of Ann did not return, yet the villagers could not remain in peace.

They had promised never to deliver her up to her friends; but Gabriel now suggested that to be the most proper thing which could be done. Mary, however, asked him in what manner they should then be regarded by those people, who had been told Ann Pownall was their relation. Gabriel was much perplexed, and knew not what to do; he afterwards resolved to keep her in his house another month, and then, if no happy alteration should have taken place, to apprise her aunt, with whom she had formerly lived, of her residence and distressful state of mind.

She now appeared to be sunk into a state of torpidity; she never complained of pain, scarcely ever spoke, and was not desirous of seeing the child again. She became so mild and unoffending, that Mary was no longer fearful of her; and she yet hoped to see the beams of reason once more irradiate one of the loveliest faces that nature ever formed.

Mary would sit and weep, while she gazed on the unfortunate Ann; and even sob aloud, when she reflected on the injuries and sufferings of a woman, whose heart she had believed to be incorruptible, and who was journeying to the dwelling of death, before she had hailed twenty summers. It was almost too much for the sexton's wife to bear, and her health, in some degree, began to fail; still she gave Ann Pownall the most constant attention, and regarded the infant with as much love as she did her own offspring.

Owing to the mildness and settled melancholy of Ann, she had been suffered to pass several nights alone, care having been first taken to remove every instrument with which it was probable she might injure herself. But Mary one morning went into the room, and, to her agony and astonishment, discovered that she had found means to escape, by dropping from the window, which was only an inconsiderable height from the ground.

Mary's shriek, on finding the room empty, brought Gabriel

to her; and the apprehension and distress of their minds were equal. As they had not heard the smallest noise in the night, the insane must have effected her enlargement with much cunning, there being only a thin partition between the two chambers.

"God of heaven!" exclaimed Mary, with terror, "my thoughts and fears distract me. Fly, Gabriel, round the village.—Pursue her: seek for the poor, unhappy creature, and bring her to me again. Oh, most unfortunate being! God shield thee from danger!"

Gabriel departed from the cottage; and, to the distress of Mary, he was absent several hours. Accompanied by a party of villagers, he made a general search and enquiry after the fugitive, of whom, however, he could learn nothing, no person having seen her. On his return he threw himself into a chair: his knees beat violently against each other, and the paleness of his face frightened his distressed wife, who burst into an agonizing flood of tears, on learning that he had been unsuccessful.

No discovery was made of the lunatic for three days, owing to which the affliction of Mary was so great, that she was confined to her bed; and the voices of her honest neighbours could not comfort her. On the fourth morning the fate of Ann Pownall was no longer a mystery: Her body was found by a miller, in a river about two miles distant, and brought to the cottage of the unhappy Gabriel.

The noise made by the peasants, who had borne the body, reached the ears of Mary. Entertaining a hope of seeing the wretched girl again, she left her chamber hastily, and reached the room just as the corse was placed on the floor. The sight was horrid—she prest her agonised head, and, uttering a shrill scream, fell swooning on the body, from which the terrified Gabriel removed her as soon as possible. The remains of Ann were carried to the chamber which she had occupied, and three days after committed to the earth with funeral rites, there being sufficient evidence for the coroner to determine on her insanity.*

Such was the end of Ann Pownall, whose beauty and mind had been the admiration of every person to whom she was known. She fell the victim of seduction. What the number of her crimes was, and how far she was frail above other women, will be shewn hereafter. The corruptions of villany; the insinuations of hypocrisy; the sensuality of affected love; and the alluring sentiments of false honor, induced her to the performance of an act, to think of which was afterwards madness. The sense of her crime was too acute. She looked on the virtuous, and wished for their reputation; she beheld the vile, and fancied that she contemplated objects less base than herself. The privacy of her guilt was no consolation. She thought each eye scrutinized and taxed her with infamy; and her shame was as great as if her actions had been blazoned, and made the sport of a thousand tongues. These reflections and suspicions were too weighty for her brain, the consequence of which was a total deprivation of reason, and lastly of life.

Mary Fellers recovered her health but slowly. The recent circumstances had struck deeply at her heart: The villagers were concerned to see the effect which the death of her supposed sister had on her; and Gabriel feared that the consequences might terminate seriously. At length, however, her constitution improved; but the depression of her spirits was still great. She talked of little else than the fate of Ann Pownall; and sometimes, in the fulness of her grief, she wished that heaven would send a speedy punishment to the seducer and murderer of the unfortunate girl.

She took the little orphan home, and regarded it with as much love as she did her own child. Gabriel was no less fond of it; and, while they bewailed the death of its mother, they vowed to protect and comfort it.

"We will rear, and teach him to walk in the path of honesty," said Gabriel; "his abandoned father shall not know of his existence; and, in lowly life, he may be good, virtuous, and happy. Contentment can make the state of labour a golden one—sometimes superior to that of wealthy inactivity. Poor little fellow! What a face of loveliness he has! I will be his father; you, Mary, must be his mother; and when he is grown up to manhood, he may bless, comfort, and support us."

"I think he has the features of his mother," said Mary, with a fond gaze.

"He is a sweet infant!" cried Gabriel, kissing him. The child, as if sensible of the endearment, smiled in his face. He kissed it again, and again; and the tender-hearted Mary burst into tears.

At the age of five years, William Berrington, (for so the deceased Ann Pownall, previous to her insanity, had desired the child might be called, if it should prove a boy,) was an engaging little fellow. He possessed fine health, good spirits, and a heart filled with the minor virtues; and there were qualities in his young mind which spoke much of ability. His countenance was interesting to every beholder; his short brown locks curled around his blushing face; there was a brightness in his eyes which almost fascinated; and whenever he went into the village he had a hundred kisses stolen from his red lips.

Vivacity never formed a merrier wight,* nor one less offending in pursuing the objects of his mirth. Every hour was fraught with pastime, except when the face of Mary was shaded by gloom. He would then suspend his sports, and, climbing her knee, look earnestly in her face till he drew from her either a tear or a smile: If the former, he encircled her neck with his arms, and put his face into her bosom; but if the latter, the unrestrained laugh would force its way, and his eyes exhibit all the force of his rapture.

The son of the sexton was his constant companion: Robert Fellers was a fine boy, and scarcely inferior to William Berrington. His spirit was not so great, nor his vivacity so lively; still his mind was as good, his heart as humane; and he lost very little in a comparison between him and William. The two boys were the chief comfort of the sexton: He viewed them as lovely plants, which promised abundance of fruit in the days of their summer; and Mary's pleasure rose sometimes nearly to ecstacy, when she encircled them both in her maternal arms.

Hitherto Gabriel had been their only tutor; and, in his leisure hours, he had taught them to read a little in the bible. Robert, however, was the better scholar of the two; and could read, at least, four verses, while William was toiling thro' one. The difference of the boys' ages made their humble preceptor think justly of their abilities. He neither over-rated the promptness of the one, nor censured the backwardness of the other; but being willing that they should receive greater advantages than he was capable of bestowing, he sent them both to the village school.

The progress of the lads was still unequal; and Robert gained more praise and rewards than William, who made no great advancement in the road of learning, during a period of two years. Gabriel beheld this with concern; but it was removed when he saw the expression of the boy's face, and noticed his quick perception and shrewdness of remark, which frequently made him appear superior to the calm and methodical Robert.

It was about this time that the rector of the parish departed from the world. His virtues had not been many, and his death did not occasion much regret. The rectory was a good one; and no person could possibly have made a shilling more annually, than the late receiver of the profits. He was very conversant in the law of tithes, and willing to shew, by proofs of "holy writ," that he was entitled to them. The rich rectorial* produce he placed in his coffers, in which he likewise seemed to shut up his soul. Charity and beneficence he would talk of, in the pulpit; but in his own house was seen the sorry parsimony of a childless bachelor.

Gabriel communicated the death of the rector to Mary and the boys, about half an hour after it had happened.

"I am sorry to hear it," said the sexton's son.

"I am not at all sorry," said William: "I hope our next parson will be a better man."

"I do not think the doctor was a very bad man," cried Robert.

"I'll tell you," replied William, "what *I* think he was."

"What do you think he was?" enquired Gabriel.

"A hypocrite, uncle: And, I am sure, a hypocrite cannot be a good man."

"What makes you think he was a hypocrite?"

"The last time he preached he spoke these words in his sermon: 'The noblest feelings of the soul arise from the doing of good actions. If we cheer the wretched, the joy is ours; if we feed the hungry and clothe the naked, the joy is also ours. The prayers of the widow, and of the orphan are sweet; and the smiles of gratitude as lovely as the rays of heaven.'"

"Dear me!" exclaimed Mary, "I recollect the very words."

"Tell me, my dear boy," said Gabriel, "how you kept this in your mind."

"Why, I liked the words; so I repeated them a good many times, and when I got home, I asked Robert to write them down for me."

"My sweet fellow!" cried Mary, with a maternal joy, while she traced the beauty of his poor mother in his face.

"Some few days after," continued William, "I met the preacher near the parsonage. Poor Robin Barlow's wife was telling him of the misfortune of her husband, in breaking his leg; and of the distressed state of herself and children. But her story did not move his heart; and his face was almost as black as his coat. 'Do you think,' he said, 'that I can relieve every body? I cannot do it: the parish must make you an allowance, otherwise you and your children must go into the work-house, till your husband can follow his employment again.' Poor Robin's wife wept sadly; and the parson walked away, without even saying he was sorry for her misfortunes. I could not help repeating to myself, *the noblest feelings of the soul arise from the doing of good actions*; and I turned into another path, because I would not move my hat.* Had I not been afraid of his anger falling on you, uncle, I would have spoken that part of his sermon aloud, in order to see whether he could blush at his own hardness of heart."

Such talk as this always delighted Gabriel: It convinced him of the superior understanding of the boy; and he almost lamented that the poor little fellow was doomed to obscurity. But William himself harboured none of these regrets, nor was it then probable that he ever would. His was true happiness: His volatile spirits led him into mirth and gaiety, and caused him to participate in all the village sports and festivities.

One evening, however, he returned home, earlier than usual, and without his companion, Robert. There was an agitation in his young face, and his colour was not so good as it had been on his leaving the cottage. He placed himself silently in a chair, and put his hand upon his forehead, while tears were rising in his eyes. Mary and Gabriel were both present, and they noticed his distress. Somewhat alarmed they anxiously enquired whether he was unwell, and he assured them he was.

"What ails my dear boy?" said Mary, drawing him gently to her bosom. Gabriel, likewise, asked him the occasion of his dejection.

"I have a pain," he replied, sobbing.

"Where? where, my child," cried Mary.

"Here: at my heart."

"Dear, heaven!" exclaimed Mary; "how you alarm me! Run, Gabriel, for the doctor; and tell him to come immediately to the assistance of my dear boy."

"Stay," cried William, rising; "you, uncle, perhaps would do me more good than the doctor. You can tell me——"

"What? what can I tell you, William?"

"Whether that which I heard, just now, in the village be true."

"And what have you heard, my child?"

"That my mother—My poor, poor mother——"

"My dear, agonised boy!"

"That she drowned herself, soon after I was born. Is it true? Was it indeed so, uncle?"

He placed himself between the knees of Gabriel, and looked in his face. The blood seemed to leave the sexton's cheeks; and he turned his eyes, most expressively, towards Mary. William caught the glance, and again urged the question. Gabriel could scarcely speak, and the grief of Mary made her speechless. "Yes, it is true," cried the poor boy; "I see it is true. If she be dead, she is, I know, happy and in heaven; and yet I never thought, while I was walking on the banks of the river, that my dear mother was drowned in it. I shall see her face, when I again look in the cruel water."

For two or three days the fate of William's mother seemed to affect his young mind very sensibly; but as the impressions of early age are soon effaced, his sorrow ere long lost its force. Still there were moments in which he would forego all amusements, in order to talk with Mary of his parent; and he never passed the river without speaking tenderly of her, and bewailing her destiny.

The new rector of the parish arrived at the parsonage; and

Gabriel went immediately to pay his respects. The clergyman came from a distant part of the kingdom, and had never before been in the village. On the sexton's return, his wife and boys eagerly enquired his opinion of the divine; and William seriously hoped that his actions, if not his words, would be better than those of the late incumbent.

Gabriel said it was almost impossible to give any thing like an opinion of the parson's character; but he informed them that he was a middle-aged man, of manners seemingly gentle; and that his face bespoke much goodness of heart. Robert was satisfied, and he made no further enquiries; but William wanted to know more, and expressed great impatience to see the stranger. In the evening he loitered about the parsonage some considerable time, with the hope of seeing the new inhabitant; he was, however, at length obliged to return home without being gratified.

Early in the morning of the following day, Gabriel told the boys that the Rector was gone out for a walk, and pointed to the path he had taken. William immediately rose and seised his hat: "Come, Robert," he cried; "let us go and contrive to meet him."

"No," replied the sexton's son; "my master promised to give the writer of the best copy to-day two-pence; and I will try to do it, before I go to school."

"Never mind," cried William; "I will give you two-pence to go with me; and then, you know, you will get the money, and save yourself the trouble."

"Aye, William, but I value my master's praise more than the money."

"Dear me! What good will that do you? I hate to be praised to my face; it always makes me blush. Will you go and see the parson?"

"No: I shall see him on Sunday."

"On Sunday! Why there are four days to come before Sunday; and I am sure I could not wait so long. Good bye, Robert! I hope your master will call you good boy, and set you up for the lads' admiration. Bye, Robert! Mind your fine strokes and your tittles; and above all see that your master's copper be good."

Robert, without being moved to either mirth or anger, began

his task; and William pursued the path that had been pointed out to him by his supposed uncle. A fleet pair of legs soon brought him in view of the object of his search; and he continued to walk after the Rector, but at some distance, for the space of half an hour. At length William drew nearer to him; and once or twice faintly saw his face, which, on the first glance, was pleasing to his eye, for it certainly had none of the austerity of the old rector's.

William now came close to the parson, and stealing another look, made his most respectful obedience; which was returned by a motion of the head, and by a smile that filled the boy's heart with a secret pleasure. Much gratified he was walking on, when the Rector called to him; he turned round, and, blushing like the summer rose, looked up to the stranger's face.

"Pray," said the Rector, "can I return to the village, if I take the path that runs behind yonder grove?"

"Yes, sir," replied William; "but being a stranger, you will probably find it difficult, as it takes you thro' a coppice, in which there are several turnings. I am, however, going that way; and will, if you please, direct you."

"I thank you, my good boy. Do you live in the parish?"

"Yes, sir; my name is William Berrington, and I am the nephew of Gabriel Fellers, the sexton, who was at the parsonage last night."

"Indeed!—And your parents—Do they reside in the parish?"

"No, sir;" replied William, somewhat dejectedly.

"Where then, my good lad?"

"In heaven," answered William, raising his fine eyes up to the smiling clouds. Tears started into each of them: they were noticed by the Rector, who gently took the hand of this child of sensibility, and enquired whether he had lately been made an orphan.

"Oh, no, sir! My father died before I was born; my poor mother went after him while I was an infant; and went so shockingly——My uncle has taken care of me ever since: He loves me as much as he does his own son, and I ever will love him."

The Rector laid his hand on the boy's shoulder, and gazed earnestly on his face. It was a look which discovered admiration and affection. The words, "and went so shockingly!" touched his heart; but he made no further enquiry, as he saw the extent of the young villager's sensibility. It was upwards of an hour before they reached the parish; and in the latter part of their conversation William gained the heart of the Rector, who, at their parting, invited him to come to the parsonage in the evening, and at what other time he liked. The invitation was accompanied by a present, a shaking of hands, and a smile of affection. The money was not at all regarded by William; but the actions filled his heart with pleasure, and spread joy over his face. He entered Gabriel's cottage with gaiety, and found there the sexton, his wife, and his son, the last of whom had returned disappointed from school, owing to the master of it being obliged to go out on particular business. The whole party eagerly enquired what he had been doing in so long a time, and what was the occasion of his absence.

"I have seen the Rector," cried William.

"I am sure," said Robert, "your trouble has been greater than your gain."

"And so has your's, Robert, or you would have brought home the two-pence. But I have seen the Rector; walked with him; talked with him; shaken hands with him. He gave me this money; and in the evening I shall go to him at the rectory. Now what is my gain, Robert?"

Gabriel and Mary expressed joy and surprise. "But is all this true, William?" enquired their son.

"Pray, Robert," said William, colouring, "did you ever—*could* you ever prove me a liar? I will talk with you no longer."

"Nay, nay, William," said Gabriel; "I am sure Robert did not mean any harm."

"He doubted my truth."

"Indeed; I declare I did not."

"Did you not? Give me your hand then, and take this shilling. Aye, but you shall though, or I'll not make it up with you."

"Well, but the Rector, my dear boy!" said Gabriel.

"Is the best and sweetest tempered man I ever saw. If you had only heard of how kindly he spoke to me! I am sure he will listen to poor Robin's wife, and relieve her too."

"What did you talk about?" said Robert.

"Fifty things, and almost fifty people."

"Bless me! that is very strange. I never can say only yes and no, to a person with whom I am not well acquainted. If I speak five words, I am afraid of saying three too many."

"And yet you can run thro' the multiplication table," said William, "before I get to six times seven. But you shall go with me in the evening, and see the Rector. I will tell him that you are my cousin Robert? and then, I know, he will give us both a welcome."

"Dear William, I would not go for a guinea:* I am sure I should not know what to say." Both Gabriel and Mary thought it proper for William to go alone; and in the evening, with high spirits, he accordingly set out for the parsonage, and was soon taken to the Rector, who received him with true pleasure. William felt no timidity; and his eyes sparkled with vivacity when he seated himself by the side of the Rector, who laid aside a book, in order to notice his juvenile companion.

As the evening was particularly fine, it was agreed that they should have another ramble. They accordingly went from the parsonage, and took a different path to that which they had trodden in the morning. They passed thro' the church-yard: William loitered behind a little, and stooped to the ground; and when the Rector asked him what he was after, he answered that he was plucking a nettle from the grave of his mother.

"I shall root up every weed to-morrow," continued the boy; "and I and Robert Fellers shall cut a new bramble, and put it in the place of the old one. We also intend to plant some violet roots around it; and my uncle says it shall have a new turf."

William did not look at his companion, but gazed at the grave, while he was speaking. The Rector led him gently away, pressing his hand, and smiling upon him.

The boy grew in the favour of Mr. Lavington, who discovered in the little, obscure individual, qualities which it would be cruel to neglect, and a fertility of mind that was worthy of an early cultivation. William was free as the west wind; and as gentle too. He was most respectful when he addressed Mr. Lavington; but there was neither embarrassment in his speech, nor bashfulness in his looks. He always listened attentively to the Rector, whose words he seemed to treasure in his mind. His information was that of a man, rather than a child; he spoke of the wealthy and poor parishioners; and contrived to bring Mr. Lavington to the hut of Robin Barlow.

The cottager was still confined to his bed, by his broken limb; his wife was in sickness; and poverty and want were discoverable in their five children, who stood around their unfortunate mother. William looked at the Rector, and his meaning was known. An enquiry was made into their means of subsistence, which were stated to be only a scanty parish allowance, and the trifling and uncertain donations of the charitable few.

"We are more indebted to the uncle of William Berrington, your reverence's sexton," said the poor woman "than to the richest person in the village; for he has given us food in the moments of want, and even assisted in clothing one of my naked children. William, too, has——"

"These are fine little boys; are they not, sir?" said William, turning the tenor of the woman's discourse; of which modest artifice the Rector was sensible. Mr. Lavington praised the children; commiserated the state of the afflicted rustics, and assured them of relief. He then took the hand of his companion, and departed.

"And does this man bear a good character?" said Mr. Lavington, when they were at a little distance from the cottage.

"An excellent one, sir: So good, so harmless! He never got drunk, and always went to church on a Sunday. I remember, about two years ago, I ran a thorn into my foot, as I was walking in a harvest field. Robin left his work; took me on his back; and carried me nearly two miles; and when I cried out with the pain, he looked so sorrowful, that he seemed to feel it himself. I will ever love him for the kindness of his heart."

"And I will soften his present distresses," said Mr. Lavington.

It was almost dark when they reached the parsonage; William supped with the Rector, and afterwards returned to Gabriel's house. As he was going away, Mr. Lavington assured him that he should expect to see him every day, and that he could not come too often. The boy was elated; and Gabriel, his wife, and his son were told of all the virtues and kindness of the new rector.

Mr. Lavington was a widower, and without children. He lost an amiable wife, some few months after his marriage: This circumstance caused an habitual pensiveness to hang upon his features; it also softened his manners and his mind; and tho' many years had elapsed since her death, his memory dwelt on her, and melancholy would often arise while he was thinking of his irremediable loss. As his affections had rested solely on his wife, he renounced the idea of ever entering into another marriage contract.

His mind was slightly tinctured with enthusiasm: To soften his anguish, he applied himself to literature, and cultivated a poetic talent; this reduced his misery to a regret, which sometimes was poignant, but more frequently sober and calm. In the morning he seemed to converse with the mild sharer of his past felicities; and in his evening rambles, he would fancy that she wandered with him, unseen, among the rural shades. He often wasted the nightly taper, in praying for her peace in the world of spirits, or in praising her virtues and lamenting her flight, in a manner of which the purer mind alone is sensible.

Gabriel Fellers came to the parsonage on the following day, in order to speak of some parish business, which being adjusted, Mr. Lavington introduced the subject of his acquaintance with William Berrington, and made some enquiries respecting him. The sexton repeated the general story, tho' he felt, as usual, a repugnance in deviating from truth. The Rector acknowledged an additional love for the boy, when he heard of the calamities of his mother; and he spoke of him in high terms of commendation to the sexton, who listened to them with inward delight.

From that day William was a constant visiter at the rectory, at which place he spent more time than at Gabriel's cottage. His love, however, for his earliest protectors did not abate, but rather increased; and he thought it not easy to repay their numberless kindnesses. He went no longer to the village school; Mr.

Lavington had undertaken his education, and the progress of the pupil was most pleasing to the instructor. Robert Fellers could still puzzle William in figures; and still write a fairer copy: But he could neither read with so much propriety, nor speak with so much accuracy; and the rules of grammar appeared not only perplexing, but useless to him.

Mr. Lavington had been in the village about two years, when William became an inmate at the rectory; which was the cause of much joy to the sexton and his family. The boy had increased in beauty and in understanding; his heart was stored with goodness, and his actions endeared him to every person. He seemed to be wholly essential to the happiness of his patron, who beheld him with those sentiments which must have filled the mind of Beattie, in viewing his ideal minstrel.*

William never failed to go once in each day to the sexton's house. The smiles of Mary were still dear to him, as was also the love of her husband. His affection for Robert was unabated; and he had not three dearer friends than those at the cottage. They listened to his conversation with delight; and Mary would often wipe away the tear of remembrance, while she was attending to what he said. The stripling looked forward for honors and respect; he relied on his own powers and abilities, and cast an enthusiastic eye on the distant prospects of life.

"If prosperity should reward my exertions," he said, "what joy it will be to make you, my dear friends, the first partakers of it. You, aunt—I know not what I can do good enough for you."—Mary kissed him.—"My uncle shall repose himself in his old age, and close his many days of virtue in peace."—Gabriel encircled him with his arms.—"And my friend, Robert, shall have an equal share of my purse and of my heart!"

"Thank ye, dear William!" replied the sexton's son; "but I hope I shall do well enough in the world, and not want your purse. I shall be put apprentice to a carpenter next week; and, I dare say, after I have served seven years, I shall find enough work in the village as long as I live."

"Good heaven!" exclaimed William; "you surely will want to see the world, Robert?"

"No: I want to see no more of it than I have already seen."

"Astonishing! Why you were never twelve miles from home in your life."

"Yes, but I was though. I went to the county town a few days ago, and that is twenty miles you know. I hope I shall never go so long a journey again, for I was greatly tired."

"Still, Robert, you must have seen something to please you, even there."

"Indeed I did not. I saw a great many people running, and heard them say to each other, 'We shall be too late: We shall be too late.' I ran as fast as they did, and was soon near a gallows, on which a man was hanged for murder. I shuddered while I looked at him! On returning, I learnt that there was something else to be seen. I again took to my heels, and, mingling with the crowd, saw the skin of a wretched woman whipped off her poor, lean back, because she had stolen a breast of mutton. Her cries pierced my heart! My body smarted every time the lash fell on her."

"I am glad I was not there," said William, shrinking.

"I am sorry that *I was*," said Robert. "The wretch shrieked, bled, and fainted: The mob laughed, hooted, and swore; and yet she looked three parts starved. I could not forbear weeping: A butcher's boy cursed me for a barn-door fowl; and a lame beggar, to whom I had given a penny, stole my handkerchief out of my pocket. Two fish-women were fighting with bloody noses; and, at a little distance, a fine-drest lady was drinking gin and eating ginger-bread with a black trumpeter. I then said to myself, if this be seeing the world, I hope I shall never leave my home again."

"Indeed, Robert, the objects you met with were disgusting. It was owing to the execution of the murderer that you saw such a disagreeable assemblage; and yet, Mr. Lavington says, it is possible for us to learn lessons of morality from the actions of the vicious. But your journey can scarcely be called a peep at the world. O, how impatient I am for the arrival of September, when I am to accompany Mr. Lavington to London."

"Well, I own I should like to see London myself," said Robert: "I dare say the king and my lord-mayor are worth looking at."

"And after that," continued William, "we shall go to Westmoreland,* and spend a month there. What delight it will give me to climb the rocks, of which I have read; to see the earth fathoms beneath my feet; the torrent rushing from the precipice; and the wide sea stretched before my eyes! Shall you not envy me, Robert?"

"No: I confess I should like to see a man of war: But as to rock-climbing—level ground and no danger for me."

"There are few things in which you and your cousin entirely agree," said Gabriel. "Yet you never quarrel. I hope God will be with you both, and prosper your undertakings."

"Amen!" said Mary; "Heaven bless my dear boys. And, oh! that William's beloved mother could join in the prayer."

"Unhappy for me that she cannot!" cried the son. "Good night."

"Do not go yet, William," said Mary.

"Yes, I must go now," he replied, while he partly concealed his face. "Good night, dear friends!"

"Have I—Have I pained my beloved boy, in speaking of——"

"No—Not much. And yet, you know, my mother—Blessings on you all!"

The clock struck eight when William left the house; and nine before he entered the parsonage. The intervening time had been spent near the turf that covered his mother.

The season wore away. William went to London; visited the rocks and lakes; and returned again to the village. The pleasure he had experienced he communicated to Gabriel and his family; and the lively manner in which he spoke of what he had seen, and his animated description of the beauties of nature, made even the quiet Robert wish that he had been of the party.

Several years more went over: William was now nineteen; Mr. Lavington still in health; and Gabriel, Mary and Robert were all well and happy. The Rector's affection for his young friend was as ardent as it had ever been. He viewed him with pleasure and pride; his beauty and understanding were admired by his instructor, who intended to shape his fortune to the education which had been given by him.

The prosperity of William did not make him proud; he would still look into the cottages which he had visited in his earlier days; and his humanity and affability were the subjects of a village panegyric. Mr. Lavington once intended to send him to college; but he found that his absence would occasion him much regret, and therefore put aside the project. William scarcely wanted any further instruction; for his present education, owing to the assiduity of the Rector, was such as would enable him to engage in any profession.

He had read the best authors; conversed on the matter of the historian; and wandered delighted thro' the paradise of poetry. For the last species of literature he professed an admiration; and he had for it a talent, which he endeavoured to improve. Mr. Lavington wooed, and not unsuccessfully, the muse; he favoured the propensity of his pupil, and their little pieces were occasionally shewn to each other, tho' they wrote merely for amusement, and were not always careful in their constructions and polishings.

One morning they exchanged papers: William opened that which had been given to him, and read some lines his friend had written on the preceding night.

"The last visitation of *my* muse," he cried, "was not so serious as your's. A modern poet, and one whom I admire, has said that, poems are generally read with one set of feelings.* This, however, is disputable; for the true lovers of poetry, (and few readers who are not real lovers will toil thro' a volume of verses,) are susceptible of many of the passions, and alive to the very sentiments which filled the writer himself. What would become of the popular ode of poor Collins, if our feelings did not undergo a variety of changes?* When you first put that poem into my hands, the finest sensation I ever experienced was occasioned by the abrupt ending of the song on Hope. I no longer beheld the goddess; no longer heard the music of her voice, or the prolongations of echo: But I saw the frenzy of revenge, palpably saw it; and the loud blast of his "war-denouncing trumpet," seemed to thunder in my ear.* Can the Bard of Gray be read with the feelings which must attend the perusal of his beautiful elegy?* Ignorance herself could scarcely repeat the words, without catching a spark from the former, or feeling the pensiveness of some of the stanzas of the latter. But here is my poem, sir: If it were in print, I do not suppose it would be long from the chandler's shops of the metropolis.

---

*SONG OF AURORA'S ELDEST-BORN.**

Come, airy sisters, sport with me,
No longer thus inactive lie;
Be blithesome, merry, gay and free,
Expand your wings, and let us fly.

O, slumber not! the western heaven
Is crimson'd by the sunny ray;
The flocks are o'er the mountains driven,
And, hark! I heard the shepherd's lay.

Come, rosy sisters! Smiling band!
And ere the earthly blossoms close,
We'll steal with cunning, unseen hand,
The odour of each blushing rose.

The wild thyme and the purple bell,
That deck the skirts of yonder heath,
The lilies of each neighbouring dell
Shall yield to us their sweetest breath.

The envious fays,* who dare not peep
Until their small torch-bearers shine,
Will o'er the pillag'd flow'rets weep,
And for their balmy loss repine.

Haste, haste! I long to belt the hill,
On which eve's star is seen to dawn;
To wing my flight near yon bright rill,
And flutter o'er the mossy lawn.

Wandering in the lonely glen,
  The toil-worn rustic wipes his brow;
Unseen by grosser, mortal ken
  Sweet sister-spirits, gently blow!

We'll make the tall pines softly bend,
  And rock the hidden nightingale;
The music of our lyres we'll send
  Thro' hamlet still, and quiet dale.

Hyperion* fades—He smiles no more—
  The light-wing'd swallow shoots along;
But what like us can boldly soar,
  Or what like us its flight prolong?

The glance of love, the ray of mind,
  Enthusiasm's darting eye,
Are slow, when we our zones unbind,
  And thro' our kindred regions fly.

Astraeus'* children, follow me,
  For in the bowers of yonder grove,
The strains of earthly minstrelsy
  The mortal heart with rapture move.

Oft plaintive is the poet's theme,
  But now his harp is turn'd to joy?
See, starting from his blissful dream,
  He clasps the muse, no longer coy.

She yields ————

"You see it is only a fragment," said William: "While we keep or poems in our cabinets the critics cannot snarl at us. If we look not for reputation we shall escape censure. Fame and money are the two only inducements of authorship. I do not think that I shall ever seek for the former in the press; and the latter——"

"Shall never be to you a motive for scribbling," said Mr. Lavington: "But come; the morning is most inviting; let us ramble a little."

They left the parsonage; and sought for the pleasantest walk. The infant spring was smiling; and the earliest flowers were peeping out of the earth. They were passing a small tenement at which Robert Fellers was at work: It had been unoccupied some time, and when William enquired who was coming to reside in it, he was informed that it had been lately purchased by a lady in London, who was expected down in the course of a fortnight.

As the lady mentioned by Robert Fellers, is a person of some concern in the subsequent part of this history, she shall now be introduced to the reader.

It was a cold evening in April, when Mrs. Gerrald and her daughter arrived at their destined habitation. An unexpected reverse of fortune had forced them to a retreat from the metropolis, which had been their chief residence for several years. As Mrs. Gerrald entered her village house, an obstinate tear started into her eye; but she blamed herself for suffering it to fall, in the presence of her daughter, who was a girl of mild and interesting aspect, of the age of seventeen. Mrs. Gerrald viewed her apartment attentively, and discovered in it so much neatness, that she soon expressed her satisfaction to her daughter.

"I think, my dear Lorina," she cried, with an affectionate smile, "that we may find *some* happiness in this retirement. Do *you* not think we may?"

"I do not doubt it," replied Louisa;* "unjustly persecuted as you have been, I think you will here find a return of that peace, which the villany of mankind has nearly ruined."

"Hush, hush, my dear girl! I suffer principally by the tardiness of the laws of my country. But all may be well by and bye. Hope still clings around my heart: Shift that solace from the bosoms of the unfortunate, and they are wretched indeed!"

After eating a slight supper, they retired for the night; each with a stronger appearance of happiness in the face, than the disagreeing heart possessed. In the morning Lorina arose earlier than her mother: She again examined the house, which she found sufficiently commodious; and tho' it consisted of only a kitchen and two parlours, she felt no sorrow when her thoughts wandered back to her late mansion in London, and to the gay circle of her former friends.

Having viewed the interior, she walked into a small garden, neatly laid out in the front of the house, where she found many of the earlier flowers, just beginning to shew, by putting forth the verdant bud, and unfolding the silken leaf, that they had braved the rigour of winter. The landscape around was simple: But it was pleasing to the eye of Lorina; and tho' it boasted none of the strong features of nature, she considered it by no means devoid of beauty.

After half an hour's ramble thro' the adjacent meadows, she returned to the house, and employed the time, until her mother was risen, in emptying a box of clothes, which had been sent by her from London. While Mrs. Gerrald and her daughter were taking their morning repast, the latter described whatever had interested her in her stroll. Her mother was, or affected to be pleased with Lorina's talk; but a cloud of anxiety hung upon her brow, which her child would not openly notice, tho' she secretly mourned that she could not banish it.

"I am gratified, my dear girl," said Mrs. Gerrald, "that these rural scenes promise to be pleasant to you. I am not yet, nor can I immediately expect to be, perfectly tranquil in my mind. But the events of a few months may probably dissipate the care, which it is natural for me, in my present situation, to harbour; and then I may participate the luxuriant pleasure of summer, and share with you, peace and felicity."

"Heaven grant it!" cried Lorina with fervor.

"But I must not be too sanguine in my expectations," said Mrs. Gerrald, thoughtfully: "Probably I am condemned to years of suspense, and difficulties beyond number. My property, you know, is wrested from me by relations—shame on the word!—who live in luxury and splendour; and who are, I suspect, actuated more by malice, than the desire of lucre. But why do you weep, my Lorina? I still have to boast of one consolation: Inclined as they are to complete my ruin, my little annuity is placed far beyond their malignity."

It is necessary to give a still more explicit account of Mrs.

Gerrald, and of her present embarrassments. She was the widow of an officer, who had been dead about eight years, and who was the only son of a gentleman of reputed wealth and respectable character. The fortune Mrs. Gerrald brought her husband was not very considerable; but a proper provision was made for her shortly after her marriage. The senior Mr. Gerrald was snatched from the world by an apoplexy; and the premature death of his son, which happened six months after that of his father, involved the widow in much mental distress.

Altho' Mr. Gerrald had been a man of good principles, he ever displayed a passion for ostentation; and it was evidently his wish to be thought of more consequence than any of the neighbouring gentlemen. His family was very ancient; and the quartering of his arms spoke no little distinction. Having only one son, his views respecting him bordered on the extravagant; but the clandestine marriage of the Captain destroyed his hopes, and shaded his bright expectations.

His love for the Captain, was as great as his veneration for the "canonized bones" of his ancestors; and wounding as this unexpected incident was to his feelings, he was not sufficiently obdurate to reject the solicitations of his son, when, with his bride, he asked for the parental blessing. The fortune Mrs. Gerrald was intitled to, was little more than three thousand pounds; but this scantiness did not preclude her from the enjoyment of a handsome provision, which was made chargeable on the estates of Mr. Gerrald, whose greatest consolation was in discovering, that her blood was not of the impure plebeian nature; and that she was, (in what degree it could not easily be ascertained,) related to an Irish peer.

The suavity and complacency of her mind and manners destroyed every prejudice; he introduced her to all the families which he thought worthy of notice. The house was now too inelegant and incommodious; various and expensive additions were made; and not content with having a new coat of varnish cast over the arms on his carriage, one of the most polished vehicles was sent for to London, with all possible expedition.

The sentiments and actions of man are strangely variable;

with little knowledge of himself, he is less known to his fellows; and what he calls rooted determinations, may be put to flight by a momentary impulse. Mr. Gerrald now lived in a manner which had recently appeared disagreeable to him. His gloomy state was changed into splendour: His old domestics were pensioned for past services; but supplanted by lacqueys. His boasted hospitality was succeeded by modern profusion, and six months of every year were dedicated to the pleasures of a town life.

The Captain, delighted with this alteration, often applauded his father for making it; he spoke of the noble acquaintance it procured; of the respect and submission it commanded; and of the universal reputation that it brought to him. Nothing could be more congenial to the gay disposition of young Gerrald. He was incessantly in search of pleasure; and he generally found it. His fond wife beheld his happiness: she participated his amusements, and did not doubt but that their indulgencies were limited to their fortune.

Eight years passed in this manner, a part of which had been spent in France, and all the parties remained well and happy. The two that followed were dedicated to retirement and economy; and the elder of the Gerralds stated his reasons for the change. His expences had greatly exceeded his income; a considerable mortgage encumbered his estate; and the appearance of his affairs was somewhat alarming. His son was astonished, and his daughter miserable; but he assured them that two or three years' seclusion would effectually remove every embarrassment.

During the first mentioned term, however, a continual gloom hung on the old gentleman's countenance. He afterwards became less grave; a legacy of four thousand pounds devolved to him, with which, joined to the accumulations of his late frugality, he intended to take off part of the incumbrance.

The person to whom the mortgage had been made, was a Mr. Winstanley, the brother of the deceased Mrs. Gerrald; a man who was esteemed very rich, but whose character and disposition were not altogether amiable or prepossessing. He was in the habit of visiting the family, and always well received by his brother in law; but neither the Captain, or his wife, held him in great estimation, and they could very well have dispensed with his society.

Mr. Gerrald was suddenly taken ill; he almost instantly quitted the world; and his body had scarcely been interred a month, when Mr. Winstanley came down to the hall, and stated his claim to the petrified son of the deceased. The mortgage deeds were produced; the original sum was half the value of the property; and the several further advances, and accumulated interest, amounted to more than a fourth part of it. Captain Gerrald was almost chilled to death, when this account was opened to him; a faintness at first overpowered him; and his brain was afterwards nearly agitated to madness.

"Merciful heaven!" he exclaimed; "has no part of the mortgage been discharged. Recollect yourself, sir. Have there been no payments?"

"None, sir: My demand is just such as I have stated it."

"Impossible!" cried Gerrald: "I will not believe it. Did not my father recently pay you a considerable sum of money?"

"He did, sir. About two months ago I received of him six thousand pounds."

"And why, sir," demanded Gerrald, "was not this acknowledged on the back of the deed? Answer me that?"

"Be not so peremptory, young gentleman," replied Mr. Winstanley; "the money then paid was in discharge of a debt, long due on his bond, which was cancelled in the presence of his steward and my attorney. If you look among his papers, you will probably find the instrument; and the first mentioned witness will speak to you of the circumstance."

"He is dead! He is dead!" cried Gerrald, franticly.

"Indeed! so soon after his master? But the attorney is living: He did business for your father, as well as for me. He lives in the next town; dispatch a servant for him, and I will wait till he arrives."

"For God's sake torture me no more at this time!" cried Gerrald; "it is too much for my brain. Delay saying any thing more on the subject for a month. I will inspect the papers of my father, and then write for you to come down again."

Mr. Winstanley attended to this request, and returned to London. The wretched Gerrald discovered the bond; interrogated the attorney; and found that circumstances were as Winstanley had stated them, which would consequently bring ruin on him. He was no philosopher: His looks, his words, and his actions, were those of a maniac; he cursed the infatuations of himself and his father; and terrified his wife by his vehemence and execrations.

At the end of the month, Mr. Winstanley again wrote to him, respecting his claim; stated his present want of money, and expressed a desire of having it immediately raised, by the sale of the estate. Gerrald solicited further time, and it was refused: This had a dreadful effect on him; his reason was almost destroyed; his health entirely broken; and in less than three months his body was resting in the vault of his ancestors.

Mrs. Gerrald could scarcely support her affliction, or bear the weight of her grief. Winstanley soon took possession of the estate. The widow obtained the personal property; and having paid the private debts of her father and her husband, she went with the poor remainder to London. All that could be done with her present fortune was, to purchase two annuities, of sixty pounds each, for herself and her daughter, who, in the moments of sorrow, was a solace and blessing to her unfortunate parent. The settlement made on her marriage was found to be defective in a particular point; and all her claim now vested in Mr. Winstanley, a man whom she despised, and whose honesty she strongly suspected.

She declined all manner of intercourse with him. She thought him a villain; but, owing to the sterility of evidence, dared not to express her suspicions. She knew him to be callous and inhuman; and when he once called on her in London, she refused to admit him; and desired that he would never again attempt to see her.

She was almost weary of the world; her despondency increased daily, and her health declined. She remained a long while inactive in her affairs, but was afterwards prevailed on to file a bill in chancery against Mr. Winstanley's claim. Her solicitor flattered her of obtaining some redress; three years, however, she was kept in suspense; the suit was still going on, without a shadow of early termination, and all her comfort rested on the monotonous jargon of the lawyer.

It was at this time that she determined on leaving town; she accordingly quitted her habitation, and travelled, with her beloved daughter, to the little mansion that had been purchased by her. She and Lorina endeavoured to fortify their minds against the worst mischief that could happen; and they would often speak of the probability of their claim being set aside, in order that they might not sink under oppression, if it actually terminated unsuccessfully.

Mrs. Gerrald's house was not far distant from the parsonage. Berrington was wandering past it, the second morning after her arrival; and looking over the fence of the garden, he saw Mrs. Gerrald walking in it, and caught a faint view of Lorina, as she went into the house.

The appearance of the elder stranger was extremely interesting; a kind of autumnal beauty hung upon her face, and there was an unstudied dignity in her deportment. Exceedingly pleased with her aspect, Berrington looked at her again; their eyes encountered; he modestly withdrew his, and went back to the parsonage, where he found Mr. Lavington, to whom he immediately spoke of the stranger he had seen, urging his good old friend to introduce himself to her.

This was done with so much warmth, that the Rector smiled, and told him he could scarcely believe the lady was of the age which had been hinted to him, or that there was not some other great attraction.

"On my honor," said Berrington, "she is the only magnet; there is, I believe, a young lady——"

"Aye, I thought so: a young lady, eh, Berrington?"

"Whose face, I assure you, I never saw."

"But whose beauty, perhaps, you have already heard commended."

"Indeed I have not. Whether she inclines to the Venus, or the Medusa, is yet a mystery; for I saw only her back."

"But then you saw a grace, a symmetry; an air, a dignity, a——"

"Stop, stop, my dear sir! Whither are you going?"

"Going! Why this is only the beginning of a heroine's description. What would the ladies say to our novellists, if they were laconic in such affairs? They are absolutely more important than silver moons, and castle-haunting spectres. Fye, fye, Berrington! Check the fancy of an old man, and one who, on such subjects, *professes not talking*."

"O, you mistake your abilities, sir," said Berrington, "for, indeed, you seem deep in romance. But shall we go and see the ladies?"

"Not to day: I have an engagement."

"To-morrow, then?"

"To-morrow? No. I meet the captain at the citadel."

"The next day——"

"Is Sunday; and I hope we shall see them at church."

"At church? I would rather see them at their house."

"And rather to day than on Sunday?"

"Yes, if it could be so ordered; but I cannot introduce myself, and so——"

"And so, and so, put on your hat, and I will bring you before them in half an hour."

"Indeed!"

"Aye, indeed. Really, Berrington, it is delectable to play with your enthusiasm. A small sprinkling will not allay the heat of your imagination; and your fancy beats down the fences, and gigantically strides over the boundaries, of argument. But, jesting apart, I like the picture you have drawn; and if you have, presumptuously, aimed too much at the Titian,* I will not quarrel with you."

The friends left the parsonage; and, after purposely prolonging the walk, Mr. Lavington brought his companion to the house of the stranger. They were admitted, and shewn into the parlour; and on being informed that Mrs. Gerrald was at home, the Rector desired she might be told that he wished to pay his respects to her. She almost immediately came to them; and her appearance corresponded so well with Berrington's description, that Mr. Lavington was not, in any degree, disappointed.

Divested, for the present, of anxiety, her countenance shewed much placid sweetness; and the slight embarrassment that she felt, on coming before the strangers, was soon removed by her good breeding, and the easy habits of polite life.

Mr. Lavington apologised for his early visit by saying, that it was a custom with him, to introduce himself to every person, who sought for a residence in the village, in order that the circle of his acquaintance might be increased, and the pleasures of society better known to him. The reply of Mrs. Gerrald evinced a good understanding; and she confessed that she was both pleased and flattered by his attention.

They were discoursing on general topics, when Lorina entered the room. She had been walking in the meadows, which lay at the back of the house; and not being apprised of the strangers' visit, she was much surprised on seeing them sitting with her mother. Roses seemed to be thrown on her face; for she had entered very abruptly; and she felt somewhat awkward, while her mother was making her known to Mr. Lavington and his friend.

If any thing could be said of beauty, which had not been said before, a description of Lorina's person should be attempted; but as the thing is scarcely practicable, it will only be affirmed, that she was generally called a lovely, and, by some who dealt in the superlative, most lovely girl. Of her charms neither the Rector, nor Berrington, were unconscious; and the fertility of her mind was discovered in the conversation that ensued.

Mr. Lavington was a man who did not possess many prejudices; tho' his mind was cultivated, there was a considerable degree of simplicity in his character. He contemned pride; he despised affectation and parade. Living in retirement as he did, he was not unaware of the arts of the world; and each succeeding day brought him proof of its hypocrisies.

Once in every year he was accustomed to go to the Capital, which he always beheld with mingled sensations of admiration and disgust; and from whence he was soon glad to fly, in order that he might again range in those wide and green ways, which the feet of guilt seldom imprinted. When he regarded the immense city on the better side, viewing its literature, its sciences and manufactures, both his heart and understanding were gratified. But the deformity exceeded the beauty: Vice stared him in the face; drunkenness reeled before, and prostitution leered around him. Objects loathsome and obscene plagued* his heels with professional cant:* Neither the clattering of horses, nor the thousands of noisy wheels, could sink the voices of blasphemy; and, meek and charitable as he was, tho' he encountered those whom nature had designed for men, yet he felt a repugnance to acknowledge that such they were.

He looked not with either a sour or puritanical eye, on the manners of the fashionable world; but they were generally such as he could not approve. He found the aged, as well as the youthful, striving to be eccentric and admired; mothers emulating their daughters; and women who had come into the world as early as himself, simpering, with exposed bosoms and purchased hair, in the places of public resort.* Perhaps his prejudices, in respect to town habits and characters, were a little too strong; and some lovely readers, who are accustomed to shew themselves in the Park,* or at the opera, may think that he was a very crabbed and censorious little old man.

When he first heard that the cottage had been bought by a lady, who, with her daughter, was coming from London, he anticipated none of the pleasures of society. He believed that retirement could have but few charms for those who had moved in morning crowds, and fluttered to nightly shews; and thought it very probable that he should soon see a girlish widow of fifty, and a younger thing, made up with flowers, feathers and rouge.

On finding them so very different, he was highly pleased; and he reproved himself for the illiberality of his disposition. He saw in Mrs. Gerrald no small degree of worthiness; for there was, evidently, sincerity in every word she spoke. He regarded her as the future companion of his unemployed hours; he judged, by her countenance, that she had true piety in her soul, and that she would, among his simple people, most truly serve her God, and praise the name of his Son.

Berrington was very willing to believe in the merits of the mother; but he addressed himself more particularly to her beautiful daughter, who possessed a heart which gave additional charms to her countenance. She neither tickled herself for wit, nor dived deeply for sentiment. Her tongue uttered no scandal, and the follies of the world led her not into talkativeness. Berrington found that she was fond of rural scenes, which could not be otherwise than gratifying, to one who often sought the smiles of the pastoral muse.

Neither of the visitors was desirous of leaving the newly-discovered friends; they staid at the cottage nearly an hour; and on their return to the parsonage, each of them spoke in praise of the mother and daughter, who, at the same time, were discussing the civility, and apparent merits, of the Rector and his interesting companion.

Berrington had been so much charmed, at the first interview, that he was impatient for a second; and in the morning of the following day he presented himself at the cottage. The smiles of the inhabitants greeted him; and the eyes of Lorina expressed the pleasure of her heart. The day was come in with mildness and sunshine; this induced all of them to leave the house; and, after walking awhile in the garden, Berrington prevailed on Mrs. Gerrald and her daughter to accompany him to the rectory.

From this period, an intimacy subsisted between the parties; and they spent much of their time together. Mr. Lavington had seen, at first, that Mrs. Gerrald's heart was sometimes weighed down by anxiety; but he generally perceived in her face, a smile which made resignation beautiful. Berrington, also, observed that Lorina was often serious and dejected; still, when her parent's countenance became serene, the daughter looked like one who was truly happy and contented with her fortunes.

It was not long before Mrs. Gerrald told them a short story of her serious calamities; in doing this, she excited considerable interest; and she felt more easy after the disclosure. Those who listened to her, did not merely say that they pitied her: The elder of the hearers not only assured her of his friendly assistance, on all occasions, but wished her to confide in Him, who would, ultimately, scourge the oppressor, and lift up the injured; while the younger strove to bring back the smiles of the amiable Lorina.

From this lovely girl he had no wish to conceal any thing that related to his own little history, with which she was soon acquainted; and she was not long a stranger to the virtues and modest merits of Mary Fellers, in whose habitation she often found a resting place, after a long ramble in a summer's evening. Her mother frequently accompanied her; but sometimes her only companion was Berrington, who possessed the entire confidence of the unprejudiced Mrs. Gerrald.

Nature had formed the places in which they strolled, with a beautiful simplicity. She neither piled the tremendous rock, nor stretched the clear lake; but she bade the purest of rills to flow thro' verdant meadows, and planted groves which, morning and eve, resounded with the harmony of a thousand merry birds.

Those who are fond of rural scenes can judge of the pleasure of Berrington, while, straying with a lovely and modest woman, he viewed the green and sunny prospect, and spoke of his delight to one, whose admiration was equal to his own.

Was it insipid, ye creatures of idleness and dissipation, who, unwilling to leave a corrupt and unwholesome town, spend the purest days of the year, in throwing up the dust of the thronged park, and in sauntering to and fro that famous street, where prostitutes mingle with dutchesses, and pick-pockets with the elder and the younger born of peers; all of whom fashion assimilates, leaving the uninitiated ignorant, as well in regard to their different merits, as to the rank which is awarded them by a weak and enslaved community. But wherefore put a question relative to nature, to those of either sex, who daily, nay, hourly shew that they contemn her principles; and who would readily place the red marks of a harlot on her face, which has ever been no less fair than the lilies of her cooler groves?

Some of my readers may wonder what the young, rusticated pair could find to talk of, in their many serious rambles; while others will believe, that they could not possibly discourse on any other subject than that of love.

But let not Berrington become an object of ridicule, when it is affirmed that, he never openly praised the beauty of his companion's face; that, instead of the tortures of a lacerated heart, he spoke of the creatures which moved around and were allied to him; of history, of poetry, of painting, and, most devoutly, of his God.

He possessed a mind, in which there was little vacuity: In all that he said, there was some degree of interest; and Lorina listened to him for instruction, as well as with pleasure. It was owing to his talents, and goodness of heart, that sorrow and anxiety did not prey on her; for tho' she was more indifferent in regard to grandeur, and expensive amusements, than many women of her own age, yet she was not inclined to forego the fortune about which there was such a serious dispute, and to which she really believed, the unnatural oppressor of her mother and herself had no just claim.

While she attended to the unaffected philosophy of Berrington, she was most conscious of his merits; and it was not long before she began to love the man, in whom she found so much concern and tenderness. But let it not be inferred, from this slight information, that her condition was like that of many a maiden, whose numerous woes and adventures swell the pages of modern romance. She looked for no shades to weep in; spoke no soliloquies to the moon, which sometimes peeped into her chamber; made no little fawn the confidant of her passion; nor wrote pathetic verses,* in order that she might sing them, when she played upon the lute.

She certainly felt that peculiar torment, which is considered as the very essence of love. She believed that, had her mother brought forth a son, she should have valued him neither more nor less than her present friend; and if her calculation was false, she forgot not that she had made it, and kept herself within the pale of discretion.

The adventitious circumstances of birth and fortune, could not influence a mind like Lorina's. She had never been told, even in the autumnal days of prosperity, to expect an union with nobility; and feeling an esteem for Berrington, she wished not to lessen it, by reminding herself of his humble origin, and want of paternal riches. She was not one of the many women, who could love a man for his face, and be indifferent as to his heart. But let it not be supposed she was devoid of that quality which is denominated taste; or that, when she listened to the voice of Berrington, she wholly disregarded the lustre of his eyes, the darker roses of his cheek, or the white teeth which shewed themselves on the parting of his lips.

"Well! And did he feel no congeniality of sentiment!" enquires the young and impatient lady, who has not skipt over this page for the want of an incident.——Madam, I cannot immediately answer this question; but you will, probably, be satisfied very soon; and pray do not think the information less important, for not being brought about by the rescuing of our heroine from the brink of a precipice, the bottom of a river, or the jaws of a wild beast.

A very sincere friendship was established, among the elder and the younger parties; and they were so well pleased with their small society, that we shall not, to enlarge our history, collect the other characters with which they sometimes associated.

The disposition of Mrs. Gerrald was pious and amiable: The past vicissitudes of her life would sometimes still draw a tear from her eye, and a sigh from her bosom. Her excellent understanding did not, however, suffer her loudly to repine; and whenever she found her mind growing weak she sought relief in one who soothed with a tender voice, and administered comfort with a smile.

Her observations on those who were daily around her, often lessened her concern; for, in most of them, she saw happiness and content: Some of the poor husbandmen, indeed, were exceptions; she lamented that, after the severe toil of the day, the owners of the land should suffer the tillers* to go home in emptiness to their hungry babes; and, tho' her means were scanty, she strove to lift up the creatures who writhed under the foot of oppression.

The state of the village frequently caused a conversation between Mrs. Gerrald and Mr. Lavington; and both were pleased with its decencies and prosperity. The nearest country town was, at least, twelve miles distant; and the farmers, few of whom were anxious to step into the class of gentlemen, suffered not their daughters to resort, too often, to the little emporium of fashion and folly. Nobility here was a thing but rarely seen, and much wondered at; for the rural scenery was not spoiled by the summer lodges of quality; and the greatest parts of the contiguous estates belonged to an old lady of a singular disposition, who secluded herself in a manor house, which was suffered by its penurious mistress to fall into decay.

Mrs. Gerrald's love for the spot increased every day; and, whatever her fortune might be hereafter, she had no wish to remove from that place of health and tranquillity. She would sometimes amuse herself by forming little plans for future execution; and, by means like these, she diverted her mind, and kept it free from pain.

Her cottage, in its present state, was neat and comfortable; and if her fortunes were not to be amended, she resolved on keeping it as it was. But, if justice were to be done to her and her daughter, she intended to make some alterations and additions; to seek no more for happiness in the busy scenes of life; and to spend the remainder of her days, where virtue might be best exercised, and God truly worshipped.

The doubts and uncertainties, however, which had long been hanging on her mind, were not soon to be removed. There was still a most tantalizing tardiness in those who were concerned in the law proceedings; and summer again smiled, and winter once more ceased to blow around her, before the arrival of any satisfactory intelligence.

There was an evenness in the lives of the villagers, little suited to the pages of narrative; and tho' Lorina's affection for Berrington strengthened, rather than failed, yet it was too spiritless to please those, who are fond of the extravagant descriptions of fictitious and romantic love.

One evening, after a long and delightful walk, she went with Berrington into the cottage of Mary Fellers, whom she found with the honest sexton; and within a few minutes, they were joined by their son. Robert had ever been one of Lorina's favourites; for she discovered much sincerity in his heart, an equal degree of tenderness in his disposition, and a handsomeness in his features, which was improved by an habitual and unaffected smile.

Lorina respected the whole family; and she loved them the more for their affinity to Berrington. There was, at this time, much embarrassment in Robert, for which neither of the visiters could account. It was evident that he was desirous of speaking on some particular subject, the beginning of which was perplexing; and at length, blushing as he used his voice, he accounted for his hesitation and awkwardness.

"You know, cousin William," he cried, "that I have, for some time past, been the lover of Jenny Bloomfield at the Valley farm; and next Tuesday we are to be married. Her mother has long objected to the match; but, last night, she gave her consent, and desired that a licence might be procured immediately; for she would not have her daughter asked three times in church. Next Tuesday——"

"May God then look smilingly on you," said Berrington, "and add ten thousand happy days to that of your union."

"Dear, dear cousin William! there is so much kindness in many things you say, that, while you fill the heart with joy, you bring tears into the eyes. See, what an effect your speech has on my mother. She weeps—but is it for grief? O, no! I know the cause of it. I am convinced that my choice is approved by all my relations; for Jane is young, pretty, virtuous, and good-tempered. The old lady not only consents with willingness, but also gives her daughter a little fortune. I have, indeed, heard that a London-bred lady would lose as much at a game of cards, and afterwards go merrily home; still it is more than I expected; and every shilling of it shall be reserved for Jane. William, shall I see you on Tuesday?"

"I will be with you early: I will then go to the altar, and, while God is looking on, with an approving eye, put the hand of Jane into that which I now press with true pleasure."

"I cannot bear this, William: You are too good to me."

"And I must not be excluded from the happy meeting," said Lorina: "If the arrangements are not already made, I beg that I may be chosen as one of the bride's-maids."

Rapture sparkled in the eyes of Robert, and he joined with his father and mother, in thanking her for her kindness and condescension. Her offer was instantly accepted; and she left the party even more joyful than she had found it. Mrs. Gerrald approved of the promise which her daughter had made; and Mr. Lavington felt a desire to be liberal, as well as kind, to those whose honesty and virtues were fully known to him.

The nuptial morning arrived; and it was as sweet and fresh as when the newly-created sun shed his beams on the bowers and turf of paradise. Berrington rose early; and before eight o'clock he was at the door of Mrs. Gerrald's house. Lorina was ready to receive him: She met him with a smile, the beauty of which he did not fail to notice; and her snowy robe added to the charms that nature first endowed her with.

They repaired immediately to the habitation of Gabriel Fellers; and there they found the happy Robert and his rosy Jane, whose rustic embarrassment was speedily removed by the affability of Lorina.

The church soon received them: Mr. Lavington officiated with a more than common zeal; and after the mutual vows were ratified, the fair bride, and her fairer maid, received a kiss from the priest, and from each of the younger men.

The day was spent in happiness and pleasantry: A small party of respectable friends was invited, and Mr. Berrington and Mrs. Gerrald were, for a while, among them. The latter, however, did not long continue with the joyful group: Berrington and Lorina walked home with her; but she insisted on their returning immediately to Robert and his bride. They, therefore, left her at the door, from which Berrington departed, with Lorina hanging upon his arm.

Several meadows lay between them and the house of festivity; these meadows were covered with flowers, as well as brightened by the sun; and while they sauntered along, they heard the sound that issued from the village steeple

> "Falling, at intervals, upon the ear
> In cadence sweet, then dying all away,
> Then peeling loud again, and louder still,
> Clear and sonorous, as the gale came on."
>
> THE TASK.*

"Hail, connubial love!" exclaimed Berrington, stopping under the branches of a large thorn, that was covered with innumerable blossoms—"Hail, connubial love, which, like the tree that now shades us from the sun, is sweet, prolific, and full of golden promises! To the scene which I witnessed this morning, I would have collected the philosophers of present times; and, before the altar, enquired of them, whether they then had the temerity to deride the words of the priest, and to prefer the proposed acts, which but few of the sons and daughters of my country will sanction. The poison that was put in the chalice for us, has merely blistered our lips; and we shall yet fully prove, that virtue is a noble antidote. You know, Lorina, that both men and women have, of late, been striving to plant strange notions in the minds of the multitude. The seductive sentiments were first expressed by those, who must long have dealt in licentiousness, over which they spread a rotten veil of false morality; and afterwards adopted by the weak and affected, who loved the thing merely because it was new and preposterous. Having said this, how ridiculous shall I make myself, when I confess to you, that I have admired the projects which I now abhor—that, for a while, in the principles of immorality, I thought I saw the beauties of truth; and panted for a station, in which only guilt and folly could wish to remain. But the infatuation is past; and I am no longer made unworthy, by my own absurdities, of the love of him to whom I owe infinitely more than I can ever repay. Hence, concubinage! Hence, fool-deluding sensualists, who wear the masks of virtue, with depraved and vicious hearts. Give me, God! at some time hereafter, give me a chaste and modest woman, who never listened to the sophistry of the new schools, or, having listened, despises it. I will bestow the love of my heart on her; and my principal aims shall be, to secure the approbation of heaven, and of man; the smiles of my soul's dear partner; the duty and affection of those who shall be by us brought into life. Lorina——"

Berrington paused, and his companion remained silent. He had spoken with irresistible energy; and while he prest Lorina's hand, her eyes were fixed on the turf, and her cheeks became redder than the roses which flaunted in the hedges.

This was the first time of her feeling confusion in the company of Berrington, whose peculiarity of tone, in speaking her name, connected with the preceding sentence, conveyed infinite meaning to her ear. The heart beat to a pleasing tune; and it was with difficulty she could conceal the state of it. Tho' abashed, she was rather inclined to be sorry that Berrington had concluded so abruptly. She wished her virtuous affections to meet with others which were reciprocal; and tho' she was necessarily silent, a renewal of the subject, on his part, would not have been by her regarded as a crime.

But Berrington did not touch again on the embarrassing topic. The pressure which he gave her hand, when he put it through his arm, denoted his mind was not vacant; and as he led her forward, she felt assured that she was in possession of his heart.

They were soon at the house of Gabriel, and the remainder of the day was truly festive. In the evening the newly married pair, with all their friends, retired to a grassy part of the garden, that lay at the back of the parsonage, whither they had been invited by Mr. Lavington, who placed refreshments of various sorts, in the arbours and summer-houses. One musician only dwelt in the village, and he was summoned to the *fête*. His strains, indeed, put none of the trees in motion, nor did they inspire his hearers with ecstacy; but his bow flew over the strings of his instrument; his elbow was nimble; and his sounds caused the dancers to beat the turf with merriment and glee.

Robert and Jane opened the rural ball; and Berrington and Lorina followed next. Their grace and sprightliness were admired by every person present; many a glance was sent, by the smiling maidens, to the handsome partner of Lorina; and her beauty was silently admired, by those who considered her company as a condescension.

Mr. Lavington enjoyed the scene, and seemed to grow young amid the actors of it. The dance ended not till after the moon had risen: About nine o'clock they partook of a rural supper; after which the friends separated, and Berrington went home with Lorina. He declined entering the house with her; but, at parting, she bade him remember his engagement, for he and Mr.

Lavington had promised to breakfast with her on the following morning.

She lingered awhile at the garden-gate; and he, loath to retire, talked to her of the beauty of the heavens, and of the serenity of the groves and meadows. The clock struck eleven: Lorina then wished him good night, and went gaily to her mother. Her mirth, however, was instantly checked; for she found her beloved parent in a dejected attitude, and with tears in her eyes.

Alarmed and terrified, she threw her arms around the neck of Mrs. Gerrald, and enquired the cause of her grief. She was, at first, only answered by a sigh; but when she began to weep, her mother acted the part of a comforter, and smilingly assured her that her indisposition was not great.

"I have had a most severe pain in my head," she continued, "and long wished to be in my bed. But I did not like to go to my chamber till you returned; and I thought you would be frightened if I sent for you. Let us go up stairs, my beloved girl! I am already better: Lorina, you are a physician who can cure my malady even with your looks."

Lorina's apprehension decreased, when she heard her mother speak with such tenderness and composure. They immediately went to their chamber; and after Mrs. Gerrald had performed her devotional duties, she put her hands on her child, and prayed the Almighty to bless her. This was one of her usual actions; but there was, on this occasion, a peculiarity in her manner which almost dissolved the heart of Lorina, who strove to conceal the effect, by turning her head aside.

She slept not till she had several times enquired whether her mother was better; at length, however, her eyes closed, and when she awoke in the morning, she found the object of her late concern standing near her bed. For a moment, she thought her parent looked ill and melancholy; but almost immediately her opinion changed, and she saw cheerfulness take the place of dejection.

It was not till now that she apprised her mother, of the coming of Mr. Lavington and his adopted son; and she had not been in the parlour half an hour when her friends arrived. Mrs. Gerrald was ever glad to see them; but the welcome she now gave them was unusually animated; and she told the elder of her visiters that she met with him most seasonably.

As she did not immediately explain her meaning, Lorina was a little surprised; and Mr. Lavington, while he was at the breakfast table, (which had been brought into the garden,) expressed great pleasure, on seeing the alteration of her countenance, and the freedom of her spirits.

"I confess," she replied, "that I am more at ease, than I have been for a long time; and perhaps, I shall be allowed so to continue. Yet this must appear very strange to Lorina, who, last night, found me in pain and dejection; and probably I may be, hereafter, considered as one who has few real merits and much insensibility. You, Mr. Lavington, will not thus regard me; and surely I need stand in no fear of my daughter."

"What do you mean, my mother? When I forget the love and duty I owe you, abandon me——throw me from your heart for ever."

"And could that heart, my girl, be endured in my bosom, after it had been so alienated? My daughter! My Lorina! My best and tenderest comforter!—Mr. Lavington, I did not wish to make you a witness to my tears; but, believe me, I have little sorrow in my heart at this time. What a vast number of plans is the human mind capable of forming in a few hours! I have been busy since we last met; and tho' my inclination has many times turned towards scenes and persons, which were once well known to me, yet I am now resolved, never to extend my views and actions beyond this village."

"There is something further to be said," cried Lorina, anxiously; "I am sure there is. You have received intelligence——"

"Every hour I receive intelligence of the goodness of God, of which I could wish to make myself more worthy than I have been. In many ways he has enriched me, and placed the means of comfort in my hands. I am contented—I will not dare to ask of Him, why have you done not this, or why has that been suffered? But come, my girl, a little nearer to me; and I will tell you the cause of my late agitation, as well as of my present satisfaction. In your absence last night I received a letter from my solicitor, which tells me that the long depending business is now settled. Check your emotions, Lorina, or you shall not hear another word from me."

"Go on, mother—hesitate not—pray proceed."

"Mr. Winstanley may now triumph: Every thing is in his grasp, and our claim totally defeated."

"Injustice! Injustice!" exclaimed Lorina: "Oh, this is most unfair and shameful!"

"Lorina, you respect not the peace of your mother," said Mrs. Gerrald: "You would drown her happiness with weak and unavailing tears. Yet I ought not to chide you, for I was, last night, in a similar condition; and I trust, that in a little time, your judgment will be a quiet and faithful guide to you. Mr. Winstanley can exult only a few years; you know my thoughts of him, and he may still abhor the foulness of his past actions. We have lost nothing that may not be dispensed with; and, possessing a competency, why should we embitter our lives, by ruminating on the removal of a superfluity. I rejoice that there is yet a barrier between us and poverty. My annuity will supply all my wants; and your provision, my girl, will keep you from those serious difficulties, with which ten thousand deserving people daily struggle.—Smile—be cheerful—believe that you are happy. The fortune which has been wrested from us, might have induced some hypocrite to swear he loved you; and I, perhaps, should have seen you splendidly wretched, and wholly unknown to domestic comfort, tho' to the unthinking world you were a greatly envied object. Talk to my girl, my amiable Mr. Lavington; for you have soothed the sorrows of one who, troubled by them no longer, calls on you to bless and console a creature most dear and precious to her heart. I have a daughter to love, friends to respect, and a God to uphold me in righteousness! Possessing these, I can still smile in happiness, and, with the poet, exclaim

> "Oh, thou bounteous giver of all good,
> Thou art of all thy gifts thyself the crown!
> Give what thou can'st, without thee we are poor;
> And with thee rich, take what thou wilt away."
>
> COWPER.*

"My mother! My excellent mother!" exclaimed Lorina, throwing her arms around the neck of Mrs. Gerrald.

"My noble, my virtuous friend!" cried Mr. Lavington, who affectionately embraced, at once, the mother and her child.

Berrington's feelings were roused; he turned his eyes for a moment from the scene, but almost immediately reverted to the pious Mrs. Gerrald and her lovely daughter. The virtue and resignation of the former, seemed to make the rigour of fortune of little concern; and those who now witnessed her smiles and good humour, could scarcely believe that she had suffered any recent calamity. She proved how much religion was capable of softening the severities imposed on the good by a wicked world; and while her guests continued with her, she not only spoke with fortitude, on the subject that had been listened to with real concern, but also on topics which she knew to be most interesting to her amiable friends.

On the return of Mr. Lavington and his companion, the priest spoke in terms of esteem and admiration of those whom he had just left. He was concerned that injustice bore so strongly on them; but the mental strength which opposed it he could not sufficiently commend.

The task had long been his to teach, in the village church, the doctrine of holiness and morality. Adversity may sweep a monarch from his throne, and hurl the peasant into ruin. The station and quality of the man who meets it, are of little concern; and he who meets it with most fortitude, best deserves the sustaining hand. The breast of the priest was often pained, by the ill chances of the meritorious: The firmness of many he commended; and the weakness of the sick-hearted he endeavoured to strengthen; but in no one instance had he seen a cruel trial borne with such exemplary piety and patience. He loved the creature that could act so nobly: He was speaking of her, almost in every minute to Berrington; and he suffered only a few hours to elapse, before he hastened to her again, lest her strength should fail, and despondency weigh down her spirits.

The kindness of his intentions, she immediately perceived and acknowledged. She was most truly pleased with his society, and proved to him, by the calmness of her conduct, that none of her virtues were affected. Lorina, in the presence of her mother, was tranquil and uncomplaining; but, away from her, she was sometimes uneasy and disturbed, and she murmured at the harshness of the late proceedings.

Several weeks had elapsed, since the arrival of the unpleasant news; and Lorina was, at intervals, very seriously affected by it. She had reared a fabric on high, which the winds of adversity demolished. The quick and glowing blood of youth is not often either impeded, or gratefully cooled by philosophy: What the ear then receives, can seldom find the wide passage to the heart; and Lorina, tho' she loved and respected her mother, did not feel the force of all her noble sentiments.

Berrington continued her companion and friend; but she sometimes looked on him with altered eyes, fearing the narrowness of her present fortune might divert from her the heart, of which she had flattered herself she was once the mistress. In an evening walk he soon told her in what manner he regarded her reversed circumstances; and the conversation passed at a time when the season was mild, and every cloud smiling.

"Indeed, Lorina," he cried, "you think too seriously of your concerns; and I shall not scruple to add, you ought to go further, in order to meet the virtues of your mother. In her face I see looks which would adorn a saint; in your's a degree of unhappiness, which robs your countenance of some of its beauty, and evidently places a burthen on your mind. This must not be: Let me teach and implore you to think differently."

"I elect you for my tutor," replied Lorina, smilingly; "spare me only for this day: To-morrow chide, correct me. If lenitives* are vainly applied, resort to different means, and take from me the friendliness of your heart."

"Oh, Lorina! You must recollect the words that were used by your mother, when she was beginning to explain the misfortune, which she nobly sustained. I could make some part of her speech applicable to the present occasion; but your memory, I am assured, renders this unnecessary. What will you, Lorina, think of me, when I declare that, tho' I felt awhile for your heavy disappointments, I am more inclined to rejoice than grieve, on account of the splendid fortune having been snatched from you, by the crafty Winstanley and his agents?"

"Rejoice, Berrington? Impossible! Why rejoice?"

"You know not how thankful I am to you, for making that enquiry; because it leads to a subject, of which I never had sufficient resolution to speak. While it was probable that affluence would draw you and your mother from these humble scenes, and that you would, allured by the pleasures of the world, lose all remembrance of these fields, these hills, these vallies, aye, and of the obscure Berrington too,—I have often inwardly said, why should I thus regard a woman, who may soon be lifted above me; and who will think of me with cold indifference, when she returns to the gaieties of life, and listens to the adulation of tongues, which for her, at this time, have no praise, no commendation?"

"I cannot applaud your sentiments," answered Lorina.

"But, I know, you will approve of my sincerity. Thinking as I did, I was awkward in attempting to address you: The beginning of my life, and the adoption of Mr. Lavington, are similar to things of which I have read in some of our recent novels. A poor orphan, befriended by a clergyman; supported, educated, beloved by him! The world would say, as a fiction it is stale,—but, ah, heaven! the world can never know the affection, the gratitude, the thankfulness of my sincere heart! Without the protection which I have received, I should not have been favoured with the friendship of Mrs. Gerrald,—I should neither have listened to the familiar words of her daughter, nor dared to speak of my love to her!"

"Berrington!"

"The tide of joy is strong, Lorina: Let it flow! Till now I have suppressed my voice; and would it had been eternally still, if I am to be accused by you of temerity. On the holy power, to whom I am most secretly known, I call, to witness that I love you; and that were you placed amid a thousand women, you should be the only select object. I know not how you will regard this declaration, yet trust that it will not bring on me your enmity. The mystery has long been tormenting to the breast that concealed it; and I should not now have spoken of it to you, had I not previously addressed myself to your mother on the same subject."

"My mother,—Have you, really? What did she say?"

"If my daughter love you, Berrington, and I suspect she does, I have no motives for opposing your affections. But nothing must or shall be done, without the entire approbation of your truest and valuable friend. He knows what is best to be performed in a concern like this, and ought to be the director of us all. The virtues of my girl often fill my heart with joy. I have reared her, like a flower in the garden; and when the storms were abroad, I heeded them not on my own account, and was only anxious for my sweet and delicate charge. You know the littleness of her fortune; and I must insist that you will not speak to her on this topic, without the sanction of him who can never be undeserving of your confidence."

"Well, Berrington," said Lorina; "and——"

"I kissed the hand of this respectable woman, and made a promise, which gave her satisfaction. Within a few hours Mr. Lavington was acquainted with my wishes; and it seemed that I only confessed what he had long since known. The reply of your mother has been stated to you in your own words; and in the same manner shall you be informed of Mr. Lavington's: 'Berrington,' he said, 'I will not keep you in any suspense, nor hesitate in declaring, that I applaud your sentiments and attachment. I wish to see you married, my boy: I would have Lorina your wife, and willingly place her, with these hands, in that capacity. I respect Mrs. Gerrald for the delicacy with which she has acted, and hope to see *her* daughter *mine*, for so she must be, if ever she is united to my son. Berrington, by the sparkling of your eye, I know what is passing in your heart; but be less grateful, for I am planning happiness for myself, as well as for you. The unkindness of fortune towards you, I will endeavour to alleviate; and all that I can do for you shall be permanent. I frequently accuse myself, for not having placed you in some profession. Had I loved you less, you might have been more opulent; but, after I had accustomed myself to look on you; to hear you talk; to regard you as my child, my companion and friend, I could not bear the idea of putting you from me. I know you are fond of retirement—I will buy you the first farm, that is to be disposed of in the village; and while Providence is smiling on your efforts, I will be at hand to witness your gratitude.'——"Such, Lorina, was the proposal of this excellent man; and never did I listen to any thing with more complete satisfaction. Tell me what you think of him."

"My thoughts are similar to your own,—My affection as sincere—My gratitude equally strong."

"And dare I believe that you will cherish my love, and become a joint partaker of his bounty?"

"He is willing to regard me as his daughter. My mother, you say, approvingly listened to you. Berrington, why should this tear start into my eye, when I confess you are in my heart?"

"I will look at it for a minute, before my lips remove it. It is eloquent, and I can judge your soul by its tenderness and purity. Lorina, when I reflected on my humble birth and poor attainments, I was apprehensive lest I should not appear deserving to you. But you bring no maxims from prejudiced society; and nature, who made you fair, has also made you truly virtuous. Thanks, kind and generous friends, to whom my happiness is dear! Thanks, amiable Lorina, for the hopes which you have planted in my nourishing heart! The scheme of Mr. Lavington is good and simple; and the station, in which he intends to place me, I shall enjoy, without listening to the voice of ambition. It is such as my eye previously gazed on, with a great degree of satisfaction. Often have I fancied myself the master of a little pleasant estate; and viewed the uplands in the sun, and the vallies in the shade: my small flocks grazing around me; my plough directed by the hands of strength and industry. I have rambled with Lorina, considering her my wife; seen her point to children, ruddy with health, and playful as lambs; and then heard her say to me, Berrington, these are ours!"

How often the happy Berrington renewed this tender conversation, it will not be mentioned. A female writer, who is always agreeable, has remarked that, "the passion of love, as represented, is certain to be insipid or disgusting, unless it creates smiles or tears."* Doubting our capacity, of the truly comic and pathetic, we shall speak no more of courtship, but continue our history, with the information that, within two months after the preceding dialogue, God was implored to bless the wedded Lorina.

Berrington and his wife chiefly lived at the parsonage; and Mrs. Gerrald believed that her daughter had every possible assurance of happiness. Soon after the union of his favourite boy and girl, Mr. Lavington agreed to purchase an estate for them, of the old lady at the manor-house; but, owing to the singularity of her character, and to the particularities of her ancient and methodical steward, the business met with considerable delay.

Berrington found his present state so blissful, that he sighed not for any other; and, loved by his friends and Lorina, he was almost indifferent, as to the independence in which Mr. Lavington was anxious to place him. Nothing could be more calm or pleasing than the little domestic party at the rectory: The mind of Mrs. Gerrald was no longer vexed by past vicissitudes; and the smiles that sat on her face sweetly proclaimed the triumphs of virtue and piety.

Lorina was the joy of her friends: The affection of her mother increased with the number of her days; whatever she said or did for Mr. Lavington was repaid with love and tenderness; and the eye of Berrington always turned to her with delight. A secluded life could not be vapid to any of them. The busier scenes of the world would not have charmed them like the rural shades thro' which they daily wandered, discoursing on such topics as pleased the ear, and made them to each other still more loving.

Inclined as Berrington had been to call Lorina his own, he, at no time, importuned either of the elder parties; but it was the desire of Mr. Lavington, that the union should immediately be effected: for he did not then suspect there would be any impediment to the business, that was going on between him and the lady of the manor.

Berrington always possessed the esteem of the inhabitants of the parish, with whom Lorina was become a favourite; and as they strolled thro' the fields and meadows they never failed to meet the smiles of friendship and respect. But whenever they entered the house of Gabriel, they experienced something more: they were then viewed as creatures who could not be sufficiently loved; and Mary still often kissed the mouth that had hung on the breast of the miserable Ann Pownall.

Seeing him in a situation greatly above any thing she had thought of, while he was a child, she was frequently inclined to tell him the real circumstances of his birth; and to confess the imposition that had been put on him. But in this she was always over-ruled by Gabriel, who could not conceive any advantages would arise from such a discovery, and who was still fearful of the censures of the Rector and his neighbours.

Berrington had been married some months: Happiness and content were still around him, and Lorina promised, ere long, to put a child into the arms of her adoring husband. Mr. Lavington was pleased to observe her pregnancy; he anticipated the smiles of Berrington's offspring, and hoped to see their innocent sports before her went into the regions of death.

But, while he was calculating these events, he fell suddenly into sickness; and disease rushed upon him, putting her hand upon his cheeks. His mind was disturbed; Berrington raised him in his arms, but was not remembered; and Mrs. Gerrald and Lorina were as strangers to him. Terror seized on all his friends, and his dissolution was hourly expected by them; for the apprehensions of the physician were strong, and he gave them only those weak assurances which cannot cling to the heart. For many days he continued in a most perilous state; but afterwards the fever decreased, and his body grew more healthful, tho' his intellects were still disordered.

It was a most joyful hour to Berrington, when, aided by Lorina, he led his friend and benefactor from the chamber of sickness, and heard him again discourse with reason and tenderness. Mr. Lavington considered them as the appointed agents of a merciful God; and the grateful eyes which he raised to heaven, afterwards fell on those whom he affectionately called his children. The colour of his cheek came back; he talked, he smiled, and seemed reserved for many days of health and happiness.

The season was autumn, and he was impatient to be abroad. On one warm evening, therefore, he was carried into the fields, and placed on a spot from whence a lovely prospect was to be seen, and which was visited by a refreshing air. Many of the villagers passed by; and their eyes declared how much they rejoiced in the recovery of the priest, who answered, even the most humble, with a voice which had never been swelled by the words of pride. His head often rested on the shoulder of Mrs. Gerrald; and Berrington and Lorina stood near, performing many little offices with true pleasure.

"My friend! My children!" he cried; "this is one of the fairest hours of my life. The value of health can be most justly estimated after we have suffered affliction. We then regard the world, like him whom God first created; and the breezes which beat the tops of the pines, and played among the flowers of Eden, seem to infuse themselves in our languid bodies, and to bear up the still languishing spirit. O, I have many debts of gratitude to pay—many praises to bestow; How, Berrington, how, Lorina, shall I reward you for your care and watchfulness?"

"By letting us attend you, as we have done," answered the one—

"And by loving us still!" rejoined the other, putting her arm around the neck of the feeble enquirer.

"You must not treat me in this manner," said Mr. Lavington; "my heart is not yet sufficiently fortified. I am, at this time, almost overpowered by bliss, and cannot collect words enough to make my feelings known to you. So lately on a sick and feverish bed—now surrounded by my dearest companions, and sitting serenely under the smiling heavens! Every object is to me most interesting: The woods did not look so beautiful, even in the days of spring; the golden-tufted fields tell me of the power that is most bountiful; and yon group of gleaners, going down the valley, makes the scene most pleasing and picturesque. Berrington, had I died, what an injury would you have sustained!"

"Oh, an irreparable one! Years would not have made me insensible of it."

"Your answer delights me; but you have not taken my meaning. About two days before my illness, I destroyed my will; because I intended to do something more for Lorina. If I had not recovered my reason, you know the consequences: You would have been left without provision; and all my property would have gone to my quality cousin Lady Augusta Hartley, a woman of whom I know very little, and who would probably blush to confess her consanguinity. Of the sweets of relationship I have not had much experience. You, Berrington, have been dearer to me than the brother who came with me into the world, and who was sent out of it by his own intemperance. When I recollected my precipitancy, in burning the important paper, I wonder I had not relapsed. I would not speak to you before on this subject: but I have sent directions to my attorney, desiring that he will be with me to-morrow morning; and then my dear boy and girl shall be made secure. I feel myself so much amended, that I trust all of you will gather round my hearth in the winter; and that, in the ensuing spring, we shall rove together in the woodlands, with healthful bodies and unincumbered minds. But let me be taken home again, lest I should, after my confinement, too much fatigue myself."

He was accordingly removed to the house; and, for an hour or two, he sat discoursing with the friends of his heart. He then retired to his chamber: When he was in bed, Lorina went to him, and smoothed his pillow; she, at the same time, took his blessing, and afterwards visited him again, and saw him in a slumber peaceful as the sleep of angels.

On the following morning, Berrington gently walked into the room of his benefactor, whom he found—still and cold as the clod that lies on the dead man's grave. The spirits of heaven had been with him, and taken him to the unbounded receptacle, where the virtuous are received by a smiling God. Berrington spoke, and was not answered; his hand touched a cheek which chilled it; and, robbed of caution by his terrors, he flew to the chamber of Lorina, to whom he precipitately announced the circumstance.

Confusion soon reigned in the house: Berrington pulled the bell with violence; and in the course of a few minutes, the servants and Mrs. Gerrald, who occasionally slept at the rectory, assembled to hear the melancholy tidings. The body was again examined; there was full and dreadful conviction, that it was never to feel reanimation; and Berrington threw himself on the stiffened form of him, who had recently anticipated days of peace, and smiling seasons.

He grew almost frantic, and neither his wife nor her mother could give him much consolation; for they had weighty griefs in their own hearts, and were the feeble support of each other. At length he listened to the persuasions of Lorina, and went weeping with her out of the room. The account of the Rector's death was soon known by the whole village; and the sexton, and his family, were the first that came with overflowing eyes to the gate.

Amid so much sorrow, the voice of philosophy was not to be heard. The object that drew forth the sigh, and blinded the sight, had been most virtuous, most amiable; and those who were enabled to think of the event, with the greatest judgment, regardless of the qualities which they possessed, acted like their mournful associates, who had never listened to the language of the schools.

About the hour of ten, a chaise was drawn up to the gate, out of which stept the attorney, who came with the paper, which was to have entitled Berrington and his wife to the fortune of the deceased, no part of which they could now possess. But it was the loss of his friend, not of the property, which he deplored, the restoration of whom would have given him ten thousand times more delight, than if all the gold and gems of the world had been accumulated, and he the only master of the pile.

He could not discourse much on business; but he convinced the attorney that he would act in the concerns with probity and honor; and in the evening of the same day, he wrote to inform Lady Augusta Hartley of the event, and to desire that she would immediately send some person down to the rectory. Being a stranger to the heiress, his letter was laconic; he spoke little of himself, nor even hinted at the frustrated designs of the deceased.

On the sixth day afterwards, her ladyship's agent arrived; he brought a polite letter from his employer, which entreated Berrington to put himself to no inconvenience, and also to write to her more particularly of his situation. As soon, however, as he had followed his friend to the grave, he removed from the rectory; the property which he had ever conceived to be his own, and merely that, he conveyed to the house of Mrs. Gerrald, who, aided by her daughter, strove to cheer his spirits, and to raise him from despondency.

The letter he received from Lady Augusta, certainly demanded an early answer; and as she invited him to be explicit, he thought he was not censurable for sending her the will, which would have defeated her claim. In the course of a week, he heard from her again: In terms which could not have wounded the proudest spirit, she begged his acceptance of an hundred pounds; and desired he would immediately take a journey to London, in order that she might listen to his wishes, and prove herself his friend.

Berrington was surprised by the liberality of a woman, to whom he was totally unknown. He would form no plan, without first consulting his Lorina and her mother; but, being by both of them advised to wait on Lady Augusta, for awhile he absented himself from them; and within a few hours after his arrival at London, he introduced himself to the stranger, at her house in Park-lane. He found her handsome, elegant, and most engaging in her manners. Her affability removed his awkwardness; and his modesty had not to combat with quality pride.

"I must be better known to you, Mr. Berrington," she said; "for the style of your last letter gave me infinite pleasure. I assure you I felt no satisfaction in your disappointments; and as the intentions of your late friend are known to me, I must be allowed to do some of those things, which were to have been performed by him."

"Your ladyship ought first to enquire into my worthyness," replied Berrington with a faint smile, which added to the handsomeness of his countenance.

"I would not be too busy in that respect: Mr. Lavington must have known you well; and tho' he and I were almost strangers to each other, I doubt not that he had virtue and discernment. He was only distantly related to my father; they were never intimate;

and my residence abroad allowed me no opportunity of cultivating his acquaintance. I really am concerned, that he was not more cautious in regard to his will: This expression may induce you to think I am a hypocrite; but when you know me better, I trust you will change your opinion. Had you any immediate thing in view, on the happening of this unpleasant event?"

"Madam, I have not been long married: Mr. Lavington loved my wife, to whom he united me. It was his design to purchase a farm for us."

"A farm! I beg pardon for smiling at your rural plan; but there is something in your countenance and manner that tells me you have abilities for a higher station. Of retirement, however, I can be but an ill judge; for I have been only a poor insect, fluttering my wings among the general ephemera. I have read some things, relative to a country life, with infinite satisfaction; but as soon as I flew to the shades, I found them wearisome, and confessed myself a dupe of the poet that drew me thither. The arts have attracted my regard, more than nature: During my residence in Italy, the works of the masters were daily before my eyes; and I really often gazed on the different landscapes with admiration. So I did on the sweetly smiling scenes of that lovely country! But the pleasure held not: And I protest, rather than live quietly in Arcadia,* I would pierce the interior of Africa, or tie a Siberian sledge to an antelope, and lash it over the frozen seas."

"Habit, Lady Augusta, has made retirement sweet to me; and it *might* have had the same effect on you. But it is the diversity of our opinions, of our customs and pursuits, which occasions the necessary motions in the world. The sea has its venturous merchants, the army its fearless heroes, the senate its unabashed orators, and the man of peace and quiet—such I have seen, whoever protests against—vales, lawns and groves; where he may either gravely discourse with reason, or frolic and sport with fancy. With all my partialities, I am not one who would lay his head on a sunny hillock, and dream away the noons of summer. Wherever I could do good, I would be active, whether in village, or in city; otherwise I should prefer the torpidity of the mole, and think myself more worthily employed, in breathing without thought, and looking without sense. If I have capacities for the world, the world shall have me."

"And I will be your voucher that you have," said Lady Augusta; "but we must talk more on this subject hereafter. To-day I have many engagements, all of which, perhaps, you would think extremely frivolous; and to-morrow I am going a few miles out of town. On the following day you must dine with me; be with me at five in order that we may have an hour for previous conversation."

"Your ladyship's condescension is as kind as it was unexpected."

"What! You have heard evil things of me? Well, let the tongue of slander still curl for venom; neither you nor I have the means of rooting it up. Mr. Berrington, I consider myself almost as your plunderer; and for the unintentional injury you have sustained through me, I must make you amends. Adieu, sir. I shall anticipate the pleasure of seeing you again."

The satisfaction which Berrington felt on this occasion was strong and sincere; since the death of his best friend his features had scarcely relaxed; but now a smile sat on his countenance, and his heart became generously warm. Mr. Lavington often spoke of her ladyship as a mere woman of fashion, and Berrington had expected some exterior charms, but little native worth. With a fascinating figure, however, he found she possessed no mean capacity of mind; and her manner, at their first interview, served to convince him that there was much friendliness in her disposition.

He understood that her fortune was scarcely adequate to her rank; and the world, very frequently, said she had many expensive propensities. This made her liberality a greater merit; and the free and unaffected smiles of her countenance pleased the young villager, better than any feigned concern could have done. He was himself a sincere mourner; and he wished not to see a melancholy face, where the heart was not in unison.

Perhaps it may have been thought, from what has been said of him, that he was fixed in his principles, and steady in his resolutions. But he was not forgetful of the few compliments Lady Augusta had directed towards him; and, tho' not intoxicated with vanity, he was not indifferent to her praises. In the course of a few hours his rural plan seemed to have lost some of its delights; and the activity he now observed, wherever he turned his eyes, seemed to banish many others which had pertained to it.

When he again saw Lady Augusta, he found her friendship increased, rather than diminished; and he believed her purposes were honourable to her heart. After some conversation, which was carried on with sensibility, as well as with spirit, she spoke more relatively than she had done before; and Berrington attended to her with respect and gratitude.

"Altho' since I saw you," she said, "I have participated a hundred pleasures, at least, and been obliged to smile at twice that number of things, which others commended, yet, I assure you, my mind has often turned towards you, whom I must consider as a new and valuable friend.—Already decided! some of those who pique themselves on their caution and sagacity would exclaim. Berrington, I recant not; nor would I dedicate half a century to find the value of a single object. I dine earlier than I intended, which is to please an old-fashioned but respected acquaintance, whom you will meet at table. I shall have only three friends with me; and if I give you over to one, and take the other two to the opera, pray do not suppose that I am regarding my own pleasure, without thinking of your interest. To be plain, the arrangement is made; for, dispensing with your approbation, I have, most strongly, recommended you to the old nobleman, with whom you are to continue after my departure. But the matters of discourse, I must not meddle with at present. He is high in rank and power: If he offers you any kind of patronage, you must answer him as you think proper. You must, however, pardon me for acting in this manner, without your sanction; and if the spur of ambition shall find you impenetrable, you must then take up your pencil, and delineate the path which you conceive will, most readily, lead you to happiness."

"Lady Augusta! My heart is——"

"I believe a very good one. But, hark! My friends are arrived. Come with me, in order that I may introduce you."

She took hold of Berrington's arm, and led him out of the room. Her familiarity was very seasonable, for he was then entertaining some little thoughts, in regard to himself; and the timidity he felt, on being presented to the strangers, was soon banished.

Tho' he had not much knowledge of the manners of the day, he could behave with ease and politeness. Neither bashfulness nor rusticity marked his actions; and Lady Augusta smilingly encouraged him to speak, on many subjects and occasions. Her female acquaintance was lively and agreeable, and the gentleman who came with her, seemed of a congenial disposition.

The person who occupied the other seat, claimed most of Berrington's notice; he being evidently the same to whom Lady Augusta alluded. The name of Lord Seaford he had heard before: He knew his lordship's connections, and attachment to the ruling party, must put very considerable power into his hands; and the countenance of the old nobleman denoted a promptitude to oblige a woman, so lovely and admired as Lady Augusta.

The conversation, during dinner, and after the removal of the cloth, was sprightly and entertaining. The face of the peer brightened into conviviality, as the glass went round; and after the ladies were withdrawn, he told many a facetious story to Berrington.

About nine o'clock, Lady Augusta rang for the carriage to be drawn up, and, thro' compliment, asked Lord Seaford whether he would attend her to the opera.

"I shall see you there, by and bye," he replied, "for I intend to have a peep at the *ballet*. I will take some more wine with Mr. Berrington; with whom I am not sufficiently acquainted. Here I am at home, you know: I honor you with my company only on that condition. But you will be too late for the newly imported Buffa.* Adieu!"

The opera party was immediately rolled away, and Berrington left with Lord Seaford. It was not long before the latter turned to the subject which the former expected. To repeat the whole of the conversation that ensued would be unnecessary: But his Lordship promised to be the friend of Berrington, whose heart swelled with sensibility and gratitude.

His mind occasionally turned towards his Lorina, and he

was not assured, that she would approve of his abandoning the unambitious scheme they had formed together; yet he could scarcely believe she would restrain him from society, when it was probable that he should derive a permanent advantage from it. Lord Seaford did not give any particular promise, but he made many general assurances.

"I am ever ready," he cried, "to shew a respect for the interest of a man of real merit; and you come to me strongly recommended by a woman, whose beauty and disposition alone, thousands at this time admire, and as many envy. She told me some things, relative to your losing the expected fortune, and in a manner which convinced me of her own uncommon disinterestedness. Of those views which may have attracted your notice, I have no knowledge; but if you are inclined to take my best services, you may freely command them. I have been active for his Majesty, and his ministers are not forgetful of it. I have served him, in more than one capacity, and have fought and bled for him, sir. This I speak without vaunting; and, 'tho' I am declining into the vale of years',* I would fight and bleed for him again. Young man, it is not a custom with me to make fine speeches: A jack-daw of a Baronet once grinned at me in Parliament, for mis-placing a metaphor, tho' he was too much of a poltroon, to listen to my justification in the Park. If you can leave your groves and your Sylvias,—Zounds! you are married though—I say, if you are less desirous of ease, and more craving after honor, I will endeavour to find a way for you with my elbow. And now, good night to you. We shall meet again."

Lord Seaford prevented Berrington from expressing any thanks. He left the room immediately, and the villager soon afterwards went to his lodgings, and ruminated half the night on things which he had heard and seen.

Previous to Lady Augusta's going to the opera, she had desired him to be with her the next morning; about one o'clock, therefore, he went to her, and communicated all that had passed between himself and Lord Seaford.

"Having secured his promise," replied Lady Augusta, "you need not fear the performance of it. In his character there are some singularities, to which the over-refined cannot be reconciled; but I know not a man who has more sincerity, or a stronger desire of doing good. Be assured you will not miss the favor, for which he encouraged you to look. My wishes will, I am persuaded, be accomplished; and I hope your advantages will not fall short of my calculations."

"Lady Augusta, I am not to thank you any more; but I never can forget my thousand obligations."

"Drive half of them, at least, from your mind, or I shall never expect you to be entertaining. Fellows with hearts such as your own, if they meet with a few civilities, like the damsel who lost her head on the ice, would fain be chattering, at times when all the functions of less peculiar mortals are quite at an end. Your smile tells me you acquit me of impertinence, though, perhaps, that is treating me better than I deserve. But let me give you my advice on a few matters, which are not altogether unimportant. Considering the promise of your patron seriously, I think it would be most expedient for you, to remove yourself and your wife from the little vale of quiet, and for a while reside in London. Should his lordship find nothing suitable for you; or should he offer any thing that you cannot approve; then return, and fulfil those designs which you have previously formed. In that case, I shall insist on acting as I think proper and equitable. I seriously declare, I will take no mercenary advantages; and if you decline accepting a part of that fortune, the whole of which should have been your own, let it go to those who have fewer scruples; I care not to whom, so it does not feed any of the follies, by which I have been too much distinguished."

The concluding sentence would have sounded reproachingly, had it not been for the exquisite modulations of her voice, and the sweetness of her smiles. Berrington was, in some degree, affected by the speech and manners of this singular woman; and his emotions nearly suppressed half of his reply. For her advice, however, he thanked her; and, to shew his approbation, he proposed to leave town on the following day, in order that he might arrange his little concerns, and apprise Lorina of his new intentions.

The next morning he had another interview, and was closeted

nearly an hour with Lord Seaford, who received him with more cordiality than ceremony. The hopes which had been put into his breast were now strengthened: A fair prospect lay before his eyes, and he was encouraged to look on it.

In the evening he left London; and within four and twenty hours, the airs of his native village played upon his forehead. It was late in autumn, but the weather was remarkably fine. No frost had touched the vegetable world: Tho' the leaves of the trees were yellow, they had not all forsaken the branches, and many remained to be scattered by the northern blasts, which were still to go forth, and by the hail that was thereafter to break the heavier clouds.

The scene was softened by moonlight; and hill and dale appeared more beautiful, than when the sun gave to the world its stronger rays. All was silence and serenity. Labour and sport unbuskined their feet, and sought their beds, at an hour when the luxuries of the modern day were merely commencing.

Berrington on his way, passed thro' the church-yard; his foot nearly touched the turf, that covered the bones of his unfortunate mother; and he afterwards applied his eye to the window of the house of prayer, and looked at the tomb which had lately taken in the body of his venerable friend. This he could see but very indistinctly: Imagination, however, wrought upon his mind; and he not only fancied that he saw the surpliced priest move devotionally towards the altar, but that he heard the name of the Creator, breathed forth by the voice of holiness.

He went forward sighing: The cottage of Gabriel was as still as the church; and it was not long before the little mansion of his love was before his eye. He approached it by the back way, and, in the meadow which adjoined it, saw two figures in black, walking as if the beauty of the night had made them much in love with it.

His wife was leaning on her mother, and he called the former by her name, when, breaking from her companion, she threw herself into his arms. Berrington kissed both of them, and gently chiding Lorina for being abroad, lest she should take cold, he led her into the house.

All that he had to tell was too long for the evening; but he spoke of some things which had happened, and they listened to him with serious attention. Berrington was somewhat fatigued by his long journey, and by his walk after he had left the stage, which turned on the high road, at about the distance of three miles from the village. He, therefore, soon proposed to go to his chamber; when wishing his mother good night, he went up stairs with Lorina.

In the morning he was awake at an early hour, and he rose soon after he unclosed his eyes. It had been a custom with Lorina, to ramble with him soon after day-break; but her advanced state of pregnancy had, for some weeks, caused her to decline it: and she was in a profound slumber when he quitted the chamber.

The husbandman was at work; the fowler seeking his wary prey; and the spaniel rustling thro' the stubble, in search of the persecuted covey. The vallies heard the notes of the blackbird, as well as the whistle of the sportsman, and threw them back again. The scene was beautiful, even to him who was most familiar with it; and, tho' he was not forgetful of his late severe loss, his heart grew lighter as he roved from field to field, imbibing the delicious breaths of morning.

Before he returned home, he pressed the hand of Gabriel and Robert Fellers, and gave his smiles to his supposed aunt, who hung on his neck with joy. They were desirous of knowing what had been transacted in London. He did not, however, explain to them all that had transpired; for he thought proper to be more explicit with those who were most intitled to his confidence, before he was fully communicative with others.

When he reached his own house, Lorina and her mother were ready to receive him; and, at the breakfast table, he told them of all that had passed during his stay in London. The pleasure of Mrs. Gerrald was of a more sober kind than that of her daughter. There was but little strength in her smile; and when he spoke of the great, she shook her head significantly.

"Does not my mother approve of what I have done?" said Berrington.—"Has she any suspicions, any fears?"

"My son," replied Mrs. Gerrald, "if I have some few apprehensions, be assured they cannot shake the affection which I have long felt for you, who are no less dear to me than my Lorina. I have never spoken much of Lady Augusta, but she is not altogether a stranger to me. About five years ago I met her at several places; Lorina, however, was not with me; and her ladyship has been represented as a woman fond of gaming, and of an intriguing disposition."

"The world is slanderous, madam."

"I grant it, Berrington: And Heaven forbid that I should asperse the character of any person. We were formed for the purposes of love, of friendship, and of humanity; and those who consider it not so, are more worthless than the matter of which they were first composed, and into which God has put no spirit. I would neither give wings to the dart of malice, nor send forth the sly insinuation; the greater cruelty of which, I shall not attempt to elucidate. Lady Augusta, indeed, seems to possess much liberality; but the real worth of a gift depends greatly on the merit of the donor. Lord Seaford's promises are such as, perhaps, a thousand ears may have listened to, and a thousand hearts *wished* to cherish, even after they were falling into the sickness of disappointment. His patronage——"

"Is surely worth the trying for," said Lorina, rather impatiently.

"Very likely: Had I been allowed to speak further, I might have said so."

"I am reproved," replied Lorina, bursting into tears.

"For God's sake, why is this, my girl? You cut me to the heart,—Lorina, you must not be cruel to the mother, who regards you with a degree of fondness, which is sometimes too strong for her own happiness. Away with your tears! Put your eyes on my bosom; and the warmth of maternal love shall dry them. Oh, what pleasure is it for me to say, particularly so after the many adversities which have met me in the face, and pressed at my heels,—How joyful, how consolatory to exclaim, I have been cherished by the most dutiful of daughters, and given to an amiable man a true and loving wife! Support me, my children—pray let me lean on you a moment."

"Oh, mother! Mother!" exclaimed Berrington, as well as

Lorina, while they clasped her agitated form, and kissed her cheek.

"I revive, and again am happy. The plant bends languidly beneath the storm; but when the sun breaks forth, it feels its former vigor, and may be said to smile. And so it is with me. Lorina, you never can love your husband too much; never spend too much time in adding to his comforts, and in attempting to secure prosperity for him. What I have said, was levelled at the peace of both. I only wished Berrington to guard against disappointment and insincerity. But should he receive the advantages which are due to his merits, none, none would feel a pleasure stronger than my own. And now, listen to my plan——"

"Speak, my respected mother!" cried Berrington.

"We have seen the best of friends laid in the earth; and his words of wisdom we shall hear no more. His designs are frustrated: Our after plans falling into nothingness. Lorina must not be removed to London, till after her delivery; and I shall retain the cottage for six months, nay longer, in case Lord Seaford does not provide for you. It is necessary you should see more of Lady Augusta, before you accept her offer. Pride is contemptible, when it puts aside the hand of friendship; and it is despicably mean to catch at the high-lifted purse of ostentation. But Berrington knows these things. If you return to the country, we shall again smile, and range joyfully together among these hills and vallies. If we part——"

"Part, my mother! That must not be: Lorina's heart could never endure it."

"The domestic chain is as sweet, and lightly borne, as if it were formed with thornless roses. But there must be a period for its division. With joy does the village mother regard the growth and sports of her progeny. The boys, however, at length rise into men. Farewel! they say to her. Her arms lose them: They range the world; and, looking for happiness and wealth, too often meet with peril, war and death. Poor matron! while you draw the thread at your threshold, or break it, and pause before you take it up again, the fool of vanity, who despises your uninformed mind, sees not the drops of blood which steal from your heart."

"You teach us," said Berrington, "to *see them feelingly.*"

"Indeed I talk somewhat widely of the material subject; and my words, I suspect, are calculated to pain, rather than to sooth. But I never wish to be in the bustle of the world again; and should you and Lorina be established in London, I think I shall visit my sister in Ireland, and spend with her two or three years, should Providence grant them. In that case, I shall have occasion for very little money. My sister is obliged to live with economy; she shall instruct me in her method, and half of my annuity I will appropriate to the use of Lorina's child."

"That must not be," said Berrington.

"But it *shall* be," replied Mrs. Gerrald, with a smile: "For once I will be peremptory. You know not what expences you may be put to; and I will repay myself from the first golden bough that I find in your hand. But no more of this at present: Come, let us finish our breakfast, and walk a little in the garden."

During the week they had frequent conversations on the same topic; and before Berrington had been at home a month he received a letter from Lady Augusta, who entreated him to come immediately to London. Lorina did not oppose his going; for, in regard to his welfare, she was not entirely unambitious; and she thought it was only proper that he should, on every occasion, exercise those talents which she often viewed with secret pride and pleasure.

Berrington scrutinized the face of Mrs. Gerrald, whose peace of mind he most sincerely respected. But of her reflections he had no knowledge; tho' he was inclined to believe that her scruples decreased, and that her sentiments were now more kindred to his own. Recommending Lorina to the care of her mother, and to Heaven, he once more left the village; and it was not long before the fascinating voice of Lady Augusta again came upon his ear.

On the day of his arrival, Lord Seaford met him in Park-lane;* and without any particular ceremony, the old nobleman soon entered upon business. Two proposals were made to Berrington: He was first offered a situation as a secretary to a minister, and then a lieutenancy in a regiment of horse. He pondered: the veteran waited for his decision with impatience; and Lady Augusta, who was present, was not less desirous to hear his choice.

Berrington could bring himself to no determination; he wished to consult his wife and mother, but was informed that, if he made not his election before night, the present chances would be effectually removed from him.

Man sometimes strides towards, and in a moment takes possession, of the very post, which he has perhaps for years avoided. That the rural Berrington should become a soldier, will probably seem to many an inconsistency. For the sword, however, he declined the pen; his decision gave joy to the old patriotic peer, and the smiles of Lady Augusta expressed her approbation.

She now introduced him to many of her acquaintances; and in less than a week he received information that Lorina was delivered of a healthful boy. This intelligence surprised, as much as it delighted him; for he had not so soon expected the happening of such an event. He immediately wrote to her; and his letter was composed while the tenderest of feelings pervaded his breast. Not knowing that she would approve of what he had done, he cautiously withheld it, and only expressed a wish, that the completion of his business might speedily allow him to take his wife and infant boy into his arms.

His commission was soon signed; and Lord Seaford informed him, it would be necessary for him to join the regiment in the course of a month. The affair was now finally settled: To fly from an important station, which he was bound to maintain, he had no wish; but his heart was craving to be near Lorina, and he believed he should be most happy, if the recent transaction were approved by her. Of this, however, he had some doubt.

He had been nearly a fortnight in London, when he left it, in order that he might return, for a little while, to his dearest friends. He bade Lady Augusta adieu: She answered him very feelingly; and it seemed that she conceived they were not soon to meet again, tho' he proposed being in London once more, before he went to the regiment.

With what ecstacy did Berrington raise up Lorina, and look

on her infant! He saw the one returning to health; the other appeared to him a bud, promising of beauty and maturity. Still he had some perplexing apprehensions; and he dreaded to open himself. But, two days after his arrival, he received an extraordinary packet, from the agent of Lady Augusta; and his agitation on reading it was so great, that Mrs. Gerrald, who was with him while he perused it, entreated he would explain to her the cause of his uncommon emotions.

He made a full confession to her: She listened with surprise, and then hung her head dejectedly. Berrington pressed her hand to his heart, and smiled in her face.

"I have been informed," he said, "that the father of Lorina, while he was a British officer, had in his breast a brave and gallant spirit. If living, he would not approve these tears: The husband of his virtuous girl must remove them. I will leave you for an hour—in the mean time, read this letter; and when I come to you again, let there be neither pain in your heart, nor sorrow in your face."

He left the room hastily; and, removing the tears from her eyes, Mrs. Gerrald perused the following epistle.

"It was owing partly to my own awkwardness, and partly to the high independence of your spirit, that I did not render my present occupation unnecessary, by speaking to you on the subject which now employs my pen. I received your farewel about half an hour ago, and shall order this to be put into your hands, soon after you have again pressed your Lorina to your heart.

"Altho' I have, many times, congratulated you on what I conceive to be part of your good fortune, I must here add a wish, that the most flattering of your expectations may be completely realised. I am conscious of your merits: The blind alone will be backward in praising you; and from this hour I shall put your name in the fairest tablet of friendship. I regret that I am not to know your wife; for I dare believe, the woman of Berrington's choice cannot be otherwise than amiable. But to meet her at present there is no chance; and a long time may elapse before you and I shall be permitted to renew our acquaintance.

"Not an hour ago you saw me smile; heard me talk with cheerfulness; remarked the vivacity with which I saluted my visiters. What hypocrisies do we daily and hourly practice! While I laughed and seemed gay, I had pain in my bosom, and no small degree of apprehension in my mind.—In the early part of the ensuing week I shall leave London. I am summoned, by the dearest of all friends, to return immediately to Italy; and my arrangements are made with so much privacy, that I shall probably be many leagues at sea before half a dozen people are apprised of my removal.

"I will give no further confidence to the world, till I am better assured of its merits, its liberalities and discretion. I wish I could have brought myself to take a kinder farewel of you; but my reasons are already assigned, and I will trouble you with no repetitions.

"Friendship has dictated thus far; and now I must turn to business. My solicitor, in the Temple,* whose address you are acquainted with, has received directions to pay you two thousand pounds, which I would have you apply for, as soon as you return to town. This affair has been managed with some regard to delicacy; and the gift is free, kind, voluntary. Accept it, Berrington: Do not dare to put it aside, lest I should forget that you have any worthiness, and sink a noble being into a creature of affectation.

"Those who are in the army find many expences, of which you are not now aware; and I certainly should not have advised you to take the lieutenancy, had I not supposed you would consent to receive from me, the means of better supporting the post of honor.

"I cannot persuade myself that I act so justly as I ought, in retaining the larger part of the property, which came to me so unexpectedly. But I have some knowledge of the spirit that opposes me; and the dread of losing your friendship prevents me from doing what my heart wishes to have performed.

"Adieu, young guardian of England and its king! May the greenest laurels rise before you in the path of glory. I fear not that your eye will turn from humanity, while valor prompts you to pluck them; and, having grasped the warrior's meed,* to form a wreath for your brows, would be a most pleasing employment for the hands of

"AUGUSTA HARTLEY."

Mrs. Gerrald was nearly overpowered by surprise, and so much affected, that the paper fell from her hand. She was almost persuaded, in a moment, that her thoughts had been injurious to Lady Augusta, whose letter contained either a very refined piece of hypocrisy, or the principles of a noble and generous heart.

Unwilling to believe human nature so corrupt as it is frequently represented, Mrs. Gerrald seldom looked for the darker spots; and tho' she had recently considered Lady Augusta as a thoughtless, and somewhat imprudent woman, yet the composition which she now perused nearly reversed her opinion, and established the previously suspected merits of Berrington's benefactress.

The husband of Lorina soon came back again; and he smilingly took up the epistle, enquiring at the same time, what were Mrs. Gerrald's thoughts of it. Perhaps, even then, she had a secret wish in her heart, that he was circumstanced as he had been before his journey to London. Such an one, however, she did not express; and while she encouraged him with a smile, the encomiums she bestowed on Lady Augusta were very gratifying to his ear.

They had a long conversation on the subject; and both of them wondered no less at her precipitate retreat, than at her uncommon bounty. Berrington was concerned for her; and he lamented that a person, who had been so kindly assiduous, in regard to his happiness, should suffer any serious mental distress. His independence filled him for a while with joy; but he wanted to direct his feelings to one particular point, and afterwards was concerned that he could shew none of his vast store of gratitude, to the generous friend who was entitled to the whole of it.

Lorina regained her strength surprisingly; and in the course of a few days, the appointment of her husband was made known to her. Like her mother, her joys were blended with cares; and while she regarded the honors which awaited her dear Berrington, she was not unmindful of the dangers he might be exposed to.

Preparations were now made for their leaving the village; for a fortnight only had to elapse, before Berrington was to join his troop. Lorina proposed travelling, about six weeks after her first confinement; and, at her solicitation, her mother agreed to reside, for a month or two, in the town where the regiment was then quartered, previous to her departure to Ireland. Mrs. Gerrald could not be prevailed on to abandon her project; and, indeed, Berrington did not long oppose it; for he was assured her health would not allow her to follow the army; and the manner in which she spoke of her sister, convinced him that England could not offer her so comfortable an asylum.

The intentions of Berrington were now well known in the village. Some rejoiced, and others were grieved on the occasion. But the emotions of Gabriel and his family can be only faintly delineated. The sexton seemed to think he was going to sustain an irreparable loss: Robert hung down his head, whenever the subject was mentioned; and the eyes of Mary were hourly filled with tears. In the course of a few days she altered surprisingly. Her countenance became wan and dejected; and a thousand times she supplicated him to abandon a scheme which was to her most terrifying.

It was in vain he talked to her of the necessity of the business; for her feelings had been startled; and death and despair seemed to stalk around her, whenever she thought of the agents of the cruel war. Berrington's heart was greatly pained, and he lamented that he could not sooth the sorrows of his humble, but beloved friend, to whom he owed a long contracted debt of gratitude and affection. He opposed gaiety to her grief, but could not create a single smile.

The day previous to that fixed for his departure arrived; and he had arranged his concerns so judiciously, that no particular trouble could arise, in the disposal of his property in the village. The health of Lorina improved so rapidly, and such was the thriving state of the boy, that it was highly probable they would be able to follow him in the course of a fortnight, which was no less pleasing to Mrs. Gerrald, than to Berrington.

He was now going to abandon his native hamlet—To leave

the calmest of scenes, for the most active; and to enter into a profession which required valor, enterprise and fortitude.

The season was now becoming rather severe; and snows descended on the fields, over which he trod to take a farewel of some of his acquaintances. Still a dear, local attachment was in his breast; and as he looked at many things he exclaimed, "These have been mine; at least I have had a property in them, and now I am about to lose them, perhaps for ever."

His spirit, for a while, ceased to blaze; and the words of his friends served not to fan the embers. The prayers of the good, the virtuous, the simple, were all for his happiness. He could not listen to them, with an unaffected heart, and was necessarily silent, when he prest some of the extended hands.

But the severest task was still to come; for he had yet to take leave of Gabriel and his family, and this he intended to do in the evening, as his journey was to commence at four o'clock the next morning, and long before it was light, in order that he might meet the mail-coach.

It was rather late when he went to them; and he trod over the snow, which was beautified by the clear and unclouded moon. He lifted the latch, and, entering, saw Gabriel, his wife and children assembled round the fire. Robert and his father rose, and prest his hands without speaking; but Mary moved not from her seat, and her head hung sickly on the shoulder of Jane.

Anguish occupied the whole of her bosom: Despair fixed her eyes, and gave to her whole countenance an appearance of melancholy madness. Berrington spoke to her, with an agonised heart; and strove to cheer her by clasping her to his breast.

"It will not do, William," she cried; "I am past all comfort, and shall long continue in wretchedness. You are going to leave me—I shall never have you in my arms again—You will be torn away by death, and trampled on in the field of battle. We shall meet no more: And when you are dead, the spirit of your mother will pine throughout many, many a night for you!"

"Oh, for God's sake, forbear!"

"I shall not long survive your loss: I am sure I shall not. My life hangs on you and Robert; and it will perish if any disaster befal either of my children. Then, what dangers will come around you! The cruel sword may, in a little while, pierce you to the heart; or these limbs—O, Lord of Heaven!—these limbs may be blown from your body; ground to dust by the feet of soldiers, and by the hoofs of a thousand horses. I see it all, at this very moment. You are stretched on the earth; your blood flows from the gashes; and your groans bring you neither aid nor comfort."

It was to no purpose, that Berrington answered her with different language; and seeing her face buried in Jane's bosom, he turned towards his other friends, from whom he wished soon to depart, lest he should forget his manhood, and be more deeply affected by the contagion of sorrow.

"In the morning," he cried, "I must be gone; I entreat that neither of you will then be visible, for I find, on some occasions, my heart is a very coward. I go, wherever the supporters of my country may think it proper to send me; but, should a thousand leagues lie between us, my memory will often visit and hang on you with pleasure. Uncle, your hand; and your's too, dear Robert! You have been kind to me beyond example; and when I forget it, let every man abhor and shun me as a monster of ingratitude. We shall meet again——"

"Oh, God grant it!" said Gabriel, putting his hand over his eyes.

"Yes, yes; we shall meet again. After a few years are elapsed, in this very hearth, and while festivity is among us, I may recount to you some of my adventures. Why droops your head, my honest brother? Never let melancholy take possession of your soul, while Jane is so near to you. Your unborn children may yet be the playmates of Lorina's; and as retirement is, at some season, dear to every one, I shall, perhaps, bid adieu to the world, even where first I opened my eyes. But I will cling to the bosom of hope, and trust that many years of happiness will be enjoyed by us. And now, I bid you all farewel——"

"So soon, William!" cried Robert; "half an hour——"

"Pray do not ask me; for the longer I stay, the more reluctant I shall be to depart. Uncle, God bless you! Robert, give me your hand again: You know what I would say. Jane, think of me sometimes, and be with Lorina as much as possible, till her removal. Aunt, my dear, unhappy aunt——"

"Oh, most miserable! Most miserable! Gabriel, it shall be as I said: He must not depart in ignorance. William, I will walk a little way with you; for I have something of consequence to divulge. I must not be opposed: Pray give me my cloak, Jane."

"Speak to me here," said Berrington; "indeed it will be best."

She grasped his hand, and hurried him out of the house. In a minute they were in the church-yard: Mary led him to the porch, and while he regarded her countenance and actions, he feared her mind was really distracted. The grave of Ann Pownall was in view: Mary pointed to it, and then, throwing her arms around his neck, she made known to him the circumstances which had been concealed for more than twenty years.

At first his suspicions of her derangement increased; but she afterwards spoke in a manner that convinced him of her sanity; and having heard her tale, a giddiness seized his head, which rested languidly against the wall. For a minute or two he remained silent: he then, doubtingly, enquired whether she had spoken with certainty, and urged her to give him further information.

"Oh, why am I to lose you, so soon?" cried Mary; "I could now spend whole nights with you, in talking of your unhappy mother. Here are some letters and papers, which formerly belonged to her; and I am sure you will not read them without weeping. You will find what an inconsiderate man her father Mr. Pownall, was; and certainly will not love the character of her aunt. But, her betrayer——Oh, my dear boy! how will your heart be wrung to find that, after ruining the sweetest creature the Almighty ever formed——After corrupting her innocence, and vowing to marry her, he secretly left her in a state of pregnancy, and went out of the kingdom, without even bidding her farewel."

"Oh, inhuman villain!"

"He was such indeed. Good God! I shall never forget the hour in which your poor mother came to us; and I scarcely ever dare think of what followed. So young, and once so innocent! Her death——"

"Spare me for a moment—My heart shrinks within me—Yet, go on."

"Death closed all her sufferings. The tale which I and Gabriel told, to conceal her error, was never suspected; and you alone know it is a fiction. Do not blame me, for keeping the cruel circumstances from you so long. I have ever dearly loved, ever been afraid of losing you; and now the cruel moment is come. And must we indeed part? We must, we must! Come hither to me—kneel by the grave of your mother. Almighty God! as you have admitted the soul of Ann into heaven, I beseech you to make her son your care, and from the hour——"

She fell senseless on the ground, and her husband then coming up, with the assistance of Berrington, he carried her home. The young soldier confessed to Gabriel that he was in possession of the secret; and as soon as he saw Mary reviving, he left the house, and hurried to his own.

He rushed into the parlour, and sunk on a sofa: Mrs. Gerrald was present, and noticing the paleness of his cheeks, as well as the wildness of his eyes, she could scarcely prevent herself from expressing her terror with a shriek. But she drew near to him; and after his head had rested awhile on her bosom, he told her of all he had heard. They perused the letters together, and mingled the tears of sorrow. Mrs. Gerrald knew how to comfort an afflicted heart; she entreated him to go to Lorina; and promised to have some conversation with Mary, on the melancholy subject, after his departure.

The next morning Berrington left the village; and during his journey to London, he could not banish his melancholy. But having reached the metropolis, it was necessary for him to be active; he, however, found very little society while he continued there, for Lady Augusta was on her way to Italy, and Lord Seaford confined to his bed, with a very severe fit of the gout.*

At the appointed time, he joined the regiment at Canterbury,* and was well received by the officers. Within three weeks Lorina and her mother came to him: He met them with joy, and traced all the former beauty and sweetness in the face of Lorina. He was very impatient to hear what Mary had further related, concerning the wretched fugitive; but it did not amount to much, and, with his wife and mother, he often spoke lamentingly of his poor seduced parent.

Tho' he held his father to be a wretch, he was desirous of knowing what had become of him; and there appeared one way only, by which it was probable any information could be obtained. The betrayer of Ann Pownall, in his letters, often mentioned the name of a gentleman, who had since been created a peer, and of him Berrington, in a fictitious name, took the liberty to enquire whether he had, at this period, any knowledge of his former friend. An answer was earnestly requested, and in the course of a fortnight it arrived. Berrington opened it with trembling hands, and found it laconic.

"The person enquired after," his lordship replied, "expired at Paris many years ago. I once called him my friend; but at a later time, found him the most deceitful of enemies. He left the army in disgrace, and after a long and shameful prostitution of talents, which might have been turned to noble and generous purposes. His life was infamous; and he died not till he had suffered, most severely, thro' penury and disease."

Berrington's heart grew sick, as he read these lines; and those to whom he shewed the paper, perused it with similar sensations.

Mrs. Gerrald continued with her daughter nearly six months; she then took a tender and very affecting farewel of Lorina, who, with an overburthened heart, saw her mother begin her journey towards Ireland. The separation was, at first, distressing to both of them; but the one was afterwards consoled by the assiduities of a loving sister; and the kindness of Berrington, the beauty of his boy, and the diversity of the scenes in a military life, greatly soothed the uneasiness of the other.

The incidents which arose in the following year were of little importance. Lorina was, during that time, cheerful and happy; and she received frequent letters from her mother, written in a strain which increased her pleasure. The period of joy, however, at length expired. Connubial happiness was interrupted, and Berrington sent, with the English forces, to repel the French in the Netherlands.*

The sufferings of Lorina, on parting from her mother, had been severe; but when she received the farewel kiss of the agitated Berrington,—perhaps his last kiss—when she saw him fold his smiling boy in his arms, and heard the rattling drum, she sunk into insensibility. On the return of reason she found herself supported by her servant; but the charger on which Berrington had vaulted, was bearing him far away from the distressed Lorina.

As soon as he first heard of the intended expedition, he consulted with her, in regard to the manner of her living while they were separated; and conceived it would be better for her to go to Ireland. To this, however, she was averse; but as the company of her mother was now most essential, she wrote to request that Mrs. Gerrald would, for awhile, take lodgings in London, where they met about a month after the embarkation of the soldiers.

Here they continued several months together, each striving to cheer the sick heart of the other; for the mother's heroism was scarcely stronger than the daughter's, tho' she more carefully restrained herself in her actions, and did not so frequently express what she actually felt.

How lightly are the horrors of war thought of by the multitude! Glorious, is a term often applied to frenzied and brutal actions—If ten thousand bodies strew the field of battle, it is brilliant—And he who wades thro' the deepest stream of blood, shall, most assuredly, thereafter mount a pedestal, and be idolized like a God!—What the sentiments and actions of Berrington were, during several months, it will not here be stated: Of those things we have heard enough; aye, and somewhat too much, says humanity, with a sigh.

Mrs. Gerrald had been more than half a year with her daughter, when she was again summoned to Ireland by her sister, who conceived herself to be slowly dying when she wrote the letter. She was a widow, with few connections; and three daughters, under eighteen years of age, were then lamenting over their sick mother.

This was a new pain for Mrs. Gerrald, whose long tried fortitude and resignation would still be strong. Lorina had nothing selfish in her bosom: She urged her mother to go to the afflicted relict and her sorrowing girls; and, on her departure, bade her consider that she had more daughters than one.

Berrington's wife then removed to smaller lodgings; but her melancholy increased when she found herself in loneliness. Fear was always creeping to and chilling her bosom; and every morning she trembled, lest she should receive intelligence of her aunt's decease, and also of the massacre of her Berrington, her friend, her husband.

END OF VOL. I.

THE

WORST OF STAINS.

A NOVEL.

BY HENRY SUMMERSETT.

IN TWO VOLUMES.

VOL. II.

"OUT, DAMNED SPOT!"

London:

PRINTED FOR J. CAWTHORN, CATHERINE-STREET; AND
R. DUTTON, GRACECHURCH-STREET.

1804.

THE

WORST OF STAINS.

IN the different skirmishes between the French and English armies, Berrington only received some scratches, which were soon healed and forgotten. But he was not always to retreat so favourably; mightier blows were struck, and the vengeance of the enemy fell heavily on him. A desperate battle was fought: Berrington saw many of his associates sink into death; and, engaged as he was, when he stalked over the gaping bodies, he more than once exclaimed, "surely the creator of man loathes the work of his own hands."

The eye of the soldier, it is said, laughs at the havoc of his foes, while his ear opens, not without a sensation somewhat allied to pleasure, to the groans of the dying. Confirm it a lie, dear nature!—It must be false—To rejoice at the most acute tortures; to deride the most dreadful of adversities; to break the noble image of God, and scatter the fragments with curses!—Nature, I call on thee again; proclaim it to be false as the doctrine of devils, or I shall lose all manner of love and respect for thee.

Berrington was separated from his men; his left arm was already wounded, and the nitrous vapour thickening around him, and choaking up his throat and nostrils. A french soldier, designing him a sacrifice, levelled his musquet at him. The aim was admirable! and a heated ball of lead was sent to be cooled in the body of poor Berrington. He fell—he writhed—His enemies rushed over him, as if he were a worm of the earth; and, locking his jaws in agony, he forgot his pain and every other thing.

His eyes were long closed; and when they opened again, he saw only two living objects, an Irish and an English woman, who, having pillaged many of the dead, were now laying their hands on him. They had taken off his coat, the lace and epaulette* of which fascinated them, and also become the possessors of his watch. "It is gold!" said one of them, with great satisfaction. Berrington then shewed some few signs of life; the harpies* immediately scoured away, either in shame or in terror; and in the course of half an hour, the waggoners came and picked up Berrington, who was placed among the dead and mangled, and jolted to the hospital of the town, of which the English then had possession.

The season was rather severe: His sword wounds had grown cold; and when he applied his languid hand to them, he seemed to feel the probe of death's finger. He had been so plundered, that his rank was not distinguished; and no voice remained in him to make it known. He believed he was dying.—On what spot, and among whom, his last groan should issue, was not to him very material.

"Lorina is not here—My boy will never see me again—Fate!—Oh, Berrington, thou art lost!"

These were thoughts, rather than words: He was placed on a bundle of straw, in a temporary hospital; and it was a considerable time before his wounds were regarded. As he lay, agonised and enfeebled, he heard a general voice of wretchedness. The mangled shrieked, and called for the surgeons, who performed their business so hastily, that they were often entreated to return, and stop the bodily gaps, which they had attempted to close. "Come hither, ye promoters of national dissention," said Berrington, inwardly,—"Come hither, and open your eyes and ears."

At length one of the operators approached and recognised him; but he made a motion, with his hand, signifying his wish of not being removed. His arm was dressed, and, after much difficulty, the ball was extracted, tho' a piece of inward flesh was torn out with it. This was going beyond the endurance of nature; and darkness and forgetfulness again sunk on the soldier's eyes and mind.

Restoratives were applied: All that could possibly be administered he received; and in the course of an hour, he saw by his side a fellow officer and friend, of the name of Westdale. He knew him, feebly extended his hand, and smiled, tho' he was filled with agonies. Westdale, throwing himself on his knees, embraced the sufferer, and wept while his arms enfolded the body. He was not, for this, less a soldier. His emotions ennobled him; and it was evident that the devil war had not stript him of humanity.

When his duty drew him from the hospital, he silently prest the hot hand of Berrington, to whom he returned in the evening, in order that he might give consolation where there was so much misfortune. An attempt was made to remove the wounded soldier to a less offensive place; but this occasioned him excruciating pain, and he begged his friends to desist.

On the following day, his sufferings were less acute; still he believed he was dying, and the thought was not to be banished by the gentle spirit that stood over his pallet, blending compassion with grief.

"My battles are all fought," cried Berrington, "and some mother of my country must provide a soldier for the vacuity I am about to make. I shall die, Westdale; and chide me not, for the manner in which I speak of my destiny. Oh! I shall leave such precious things behind—I shall regret them even in heaven!"

"You speak despairingly, my friend."

"My wife! My wife! Lorina, thou wilt never visit my poor grave. Poor girl! Afflicted, miserable widow! How many tears wilt thou shed on the bosom of my boy—How many shrieks of distraction will rend thy throat, when it shall be said to thee, Woman, thy husband has perished!"

"For God's sake talk not thus, dear Berrington! You double the wounds of your enemies."

"Westdale, loving as I do, and separated as I am, I cannot be collected. My feelings are not merely dependent on myself. Death should find me an uncomplaining victim, if the chain he is preparing to cast over me, were not to harrass, and at length destroy, the woman whom God himself taught me to adore. I know her heart—It will grow pale and cold with bleeding. She will soon be without a husband; and, ere long, my boy may be thrown an orphan on the dangerous world. Console her, Westdale, if ever you reach England:——Bid her not despair:—Tell her, it will be a breach of maternal duty, if she does not struggle for the sake of the boy. Tell her—you know the rest—My spirit shall sometimes be near, to smile languidly on your exertions."

The despondency of Berrington was the issue of excessive love. The danger he apprehended did not come to him; and his daily amendment was not more delightful than surprising. In the course of six weeks, and he had previously been removed, he was enabled to leave his bed for the space of an hour in each day, and shortly after carried to another town, in which the English army took their winter quarters.

The best exertions of a noble creature, came from Westdale to Berrington: A brother could not have shewn more solicitude; a friend never felt more sincerely. He was one of those few young men, who, possessing sensibility, and a vivacious spirit, had not been corrupted by the general vices of the military character. He saw the intemperance of his brother officers; heard of their seductions and adulteries; their gamings, their blasphemies——imitative habits of plumed boys, caught from the bold faced veteran——yet he suffered not his heart to go astray, and cherished the principles of honor and humanity.

Where there is true friendship, there must be congeniality of disposition. Friends are part of ourselves, and *they* have property in *us*. It is like one spirit pervading two bodies; and he who feels it not so, must be content with an humbler name.

Berrington and Westdale were soldiers of necessity; which was not forgotten by the soldiers of choice. The secret sneer of the minor debauchee, and the private wink of the countenancing tutor, sometimes travelled to them; and a military wit once said that, previous to their wielding swords, he believed them to have been garret-philosophers, in the pay of the different powers of Paternoster-Row.*

As soon as Berrington found himself capable of taking up a pen, he wrote to his Lorina; and fearing she had seen, in the English news-papers, an account of his disaster, he attempted not to conceal it, tho' he wished the style of his letter to make her suppose, his hurts were not of the dangerous nature that had been reported.

At length he received her answer. The man who brought it to him retired: Casting his eyes around, and finding himself alone, he hastily unfolded it, and——What! A soldier, Berrington, and in tears!

"Berrington!—Husband!—Father of my child; I have been as one tottering on the verge of a frightful pit, into which distraction would have forced me. Wounded, lacerated! Oh, I have calculated your pages, till I found an equal number in my own miserable breast. Suspense scatters more horrors around her, than certainty is capable of producing. She makes pyramids of them: Wherever we move, she places barriers, infinitely above our stride; and we pace our narrow confines, like whirling lunatics in their dungeons, which echo with the shriek, the laugh, and the hollo.

"What rare invention is there to be found in this populous city! Ministers of state will not exhaust our admiration; for a part of it must be reserved for those feathery Mercuries,* who scour the streets of the metropolis, and rend their throats with the sounds of either victory or defeat.

"One evening I was reading the melancholy strains of a female poet, who can impose her own sorrows on us, and shoot those feelings thro' our bosoms, which, if the time of their residence were long, would lead us from grief nearly into idiotism.* I sighed with the muse, and followed her, slowly and in tears. There is a fashionable melancholy, the cost of which amounts to scarcely any thing: We have effusions as common as the wind, and hearts that call on puerility, to express those emotions, which are more pleasant to ridicule, than grateful to sensibility. But the sincerity of grief is easily proved; and I have traced the feverish and sickly mind, till I wondered at its endurance.

"Our boy, my Berrington, was sprawling on the carpet, with his white arms clasped sportively round the neck of a little negro child, who, having lost its mother coming to England, found in the person with whom I reside, a generous and humane protectress. I put aside my book, and turned my eyes on the children. It is, I believe, in derision that planters, and the owners of estates in the Indies, give names to the offspring of their slaves. We call our dogs Pompey, Cato, &c. and an overseer frequently, "for something, or for nothing," beats an Anthony and Cleopatra, or makes a frighted Cæsar fly before his lash.

"Our little black-visaged inmate bears the name of Octavius: Poor Octavius! I cried, thou hast no mother; and thou, my own boy, perhaps no father! At that moment a voice was heard under my window, hoarse as that of Death, when he carries a body down into the earth, and gives it to the craving gnomes.* A horn sounded: "News! Dreadful news! Bloody news from the continent! Bloody news!" Such were the frightful sounds that came to my ears, while I was thinking of Berrington. They seemed ominous. A cold horror ran thro' my frame, when, starting from my seat, I pulled the bell with violence, and the servant girl appeared.

"I desired her to run and buy me a paper: She was gone longer than I wished—I rushed down stairs, and was informed she could not find the vender of political evils. Again hearing the horn and sepulchral voice, I flew out of the house, and made my purchase. I then hastened to my chamber: Read of marches, pillaged towns, and dreadful battles; of prisoners—wounded—killed—Berrington, my Berrington, certainly in the second class, and perhaps since fallen into the third!

"My shrieks brought up the woman of the house. Again I said to the little negro, Octavius, thou hast no mother! To our child, My boy! My miserable boy, thou hast no father! I became almost crazy; and as I felt for you, so would you have felt for me. Consolation was offered; but I could only speak of you, as one from whom I was torn for ever. He was the best of husbands, I exclaimed; the tenderest, the most loving! He would have been a noble parent to my poor boy.——And may be still, said my tender-hearted supporter. I put my hand on her mouth; for my soul was filled with despair, and I would listen to no delusions.

"Hope is a nurse who sometimes props up for one hour, and in the next fills us with sickness. She cannot always be talking to us; and on the ceasing of her voice, we expect never to hear it again: You would say I was garrulous, if I told you what my feelings were on each succeeding day; but I will shew no egotism in that respect, till I can put my arms around your neck, and speak to you of all I have endured, while my cheek finds a resting-place on your's.

"And will that ever be? Are there not a thousand chances against it? Your wounds healed—your health partly re-established—then, in the spring, you will again be led to the field of battle; and probably bleed to death, on the spot where a thousand flowers used to blow, ere peace was frightened from her lamented haunts, by the savage and bellowing war.

"There is a sentiment, mistermed religion—religion justly scorns it—the imbibing of which, I have been told, would prove to me a most delightful solace. I know what is due above, and all that ought to come from me, shall be truly rendered. Reason, however, and not custom, shall make the award: It is the gift of God himself, his noblest gift, and he will applaud the proper use of it. Nothing that I have ever read or heard, can persuade me that, an approving eye sends its rays from those beautiful clouds, which gloriously screen us from glory, to range among the horrors occasioned by obstinate, unruly, and headstrong men.

"The matrons and wives of Rome applied to their deities in behalf of their sons and husbands. But Jupiter could not attend to every solicitation; and the sunny-haired victor of the day, prowled the earth with his broad breast, and gnashed his teeth in death, on the morrow. Tho' they mistook the divinity, I can believe their disappointments were not dependent on the error.

"If ever we meet again, my Berrington, my tears shall wash away my happiness, or my sighs put it on the wing, that shall never more waft towards me, if you do not renounce your profession, and establish yourself in some other. The church? You smile a negation, and I know your thoughts——The law? No, no; the genius of my Berrington, on which Apollo* looks delighted, and which his children record, shall not be extinguished, among those sombrous things of method and self-importance, that dulness is always sure to claim in the middle age, if she make not her demand earlier. Well, then, we will touch on physic—Now can I see the sourness of your visage, and hear you, in the words of old Lear, cry for "an ounce of civet."*

"Take care of your hurts: I would walk the distance that you are from me, only to be your nurse. Your present situation demands great tenderness; yet I am fearful, those who are around you are not remarkable for their gentleness. Remember, my life is in you: Should your spirit fly from you, my own would pine to be wandering after it; and not even the love I bear for my boy could, I think, divert it from its pilgrimage."

Lorina's letter ended not here; it is unnecessary, however, to transcribe the remainder, tho' it possessed an equal degree of feeling, pathos and affection.

Proud of the treasure that he called his own, he frequently spoke of its value to Westdale, who hoped, at some future period, to be introduced to the lovely wife of his friend. He had, with two or three other officers, lately come into the regiment, and Lorina was wholly unknown to him. He possessed an ear for poetry, and an eye for painting: From his various readings, he soon selected an ideal Lorina, fixing on the Imogen of Shakespeare,* the sweetest female character ever designed: and he always spoke of her by that name to her happy husband.

The wounds of Berrington healed slowly; and as he had received them in almost the last attempt, which the English army made to oppose the successful enemy, he was scarcely recovered at the time when the British forces abandoned their projects, and returned in tatters and meagreness, a once noble body, divested of its members, to their greatly mortified country. While he viewed his thin troop, preparing for embarkation, he fancied himself Pluto, counting the shades of his dominion. The sap of manhood had found an aperture, and run to waste, while disease dyed many faces with saffron, and hollowed many an eye.

On the day previous to their entering the transports, Berrington and Westdale, while sitting together, were disturbed by one of the sergeants, belonging to the troop of which the former had lately been made a captain. He informed his officer, that there was a strange man in the company, of whose conduct he must complain. This person was a private, who had lately come from the Austrian into the English army, and who now obstinately refused to accompany the regiment back to his native land.

The evidences of a local attachment, which were seen in almost every face, made this circumstance extraordinary; and, never inclining to an hasty severity, Berrington proposed to see and expostulate with the fellow, rather than allow those who were so proud of office, to exercise their harsh authority. He accordingly went with the sergeant to the refractory soldier, whom he found in a depressed, or as it might have been termed, a moody state.

The autumn of life was come on him; and, in spite of his dress, some former habits were to be perceived. As he neglected to notice the entrance of his captain, as subordinates are accustomed, the sergeant was going to teach him better manners with his cane. The arm of Berrington, however, quickly prevented the chastisement; he rebuked the impetuosity that was designed to please him, and enquired of the soldier, why he disobeyed the general command, which had been with so much pleasure attended to by others.

A strange expression sat on the features of the soldier: It was something between an ironical smile, and a sick look of despair. He answered not to the question; and after it had been repeated, only shook and held down his head. Berrington, rather displeased by his silence, desired him to risque no punishment by disobedience. A flash of indignation then came from the eyes of the upbraided; a proud spirit seemed reviving in his breast, and his ruminations were evidently bitter.

Our young officer regarded the object attentively, and immediately saw a person, who had not always been accustomed to tread the paths of vulgar life. He was now concerned that he had spoken so peremptorily, to one whom malice and affliction might have severely scourged; and he sent the sergeant away, in order that he might shew a respect for the distresses of the mind, which was not, he conceived, to be limited by the subordination of the sufferer.

The conduct which some of his brethren in command would have punished with the lash, operated very differently on the feelings of Berrington. He loved the spirit that was proud, if it ran not into insolence; and the scoff of the soldier pleased, instead of irritating him.

"There is something in your appearance," cried Berrington, "which convinces me a better fortune once attended you. I doubt not that your abilities would be suited to a higher station; and if, on our arrival in England, I can render you any service——"

"Do it in this manner," replied the soldier; "search for my offences; bring me to trial, and sentence me to the bullet. The cord can only tantalize, and I should smile at it. But one little ball, lodged in a heart solicitous of the attack, would make me bless the marksman with my dying breath. When we arrive in England!—Fate, I have courted you in the field; and my only remaining hope is, that you will summon me to you, beneath the waves of a roaring sea."

"This language suits not the condition of a man—A soldier—Who can have taught it?"

"Misery—Misery and despair!"

"Perhaps you have listened to them too eagerly. Though you have repulsed my offered services, you may hereafter have them, merely by bringing to my memory, should I be forgetful, what I have now spoken to you."

"For your good intentions, sir, take the thanks of a heart, which is almost breaking with grief and pride. I have given you some trouble, and am sorry for it. My feelings were hurrying me from my duty; but I will return to it. In my frenzy, last night, I endeavoured to strangle myself. I am, however, now resolved to go to England, with the low-minded brutes, whose hourly insults I am accustomed to receive. I boast of no services done by me; for war, a hot and desperate war, has filled my heart and brain. Too much a wretch have I been, to regard either the happiness or distresses of others.—Sovereignty, rule, empire, were to me nothing—property and freedom, merely sounds.—Religion—if there be virtue in that word, let me not prophane it. I know enough of it to say, I shall die despairingly, and can horror look further than that?"

"Oh, no, indeed!" cried Berrington, entering into the feelings of the soldier:—"May I enquire into your history?"

"No: Your prerogative must not extend so far. I would be forgetful of myself, but cannot. I will not, dare not blazon the million of follies and vices, which have sprung from my actions. Sometimes I sit, as silent and free as inanimation; But it will not long be so: Conscience hurls her brand, with a furious arm, and fires instantly kindle in my breast. Young man, leave me. I am not fond of your species. You may be severe with me, for want of respect; for I was never accustomed to obsequiousness. The brute that left us just now, shook his cane over my head——Villain! I will perform my duty, sir; but, when I reach England, the whole national force shall not prevent my desertion."

"You mean, then, to——"

"Die—Mingle my dust with that of those creatures, who roared and growled in the world; and only increase the race of reptiles."

"Forego the diabolical intention," cried Berrington, "and make provision for your soul."

"Not a word of metaphysics: Not a single word. My arrangements are formed. Attempt not to rouse me from my dream, even tho' the hand of delusion gathered the poppies, which composed the draught she afterwards administered."

The soldier walked away: His head was bent towards the earth, and his arms laid across his heaving breast.

Berrington remained in astonishment; for he had not supposed such a character was to be found in the regiment. The person, as well as the words of the private, was remarkable. When first spoken to, a more than common expression came into his face; and afterwards his features, which were quickly fading beauties, varied with his discourse, and accompanied the painful changes of his mind. His eye could still blaze, tho' affliction had extinguished some of its fires; and his voice was capable of many a melancholy, sarcastic, and resentful tone.

Berrington was musing on the singularity of this incident, when he was interrupted by the re-appearance of the sergeant, who summoned him to a meeting of the officers. He could not, therefore, for the present, search any further into the character of the soldier; but he desired the sergeant to treat him mildly, even if he should seem rather refractory.

In the course of the day, Berrington spoke of him to Westdale.

They had not, however, any opportunity of seeing him till the following morning, when he marched towards the shore with a proud sullenness; and, after the embarkation, he mingled with the thickest group of soldiers, in order to avoid the eye which he conceived curiosity to direct to him.

Berrington, Westdale, and a captain, whose name was Russel, were the only officers on board; and their accommodation was very indifferent. They sailed, at first, with a favourable gale; but it soon became otherwise. A storm separated them from the rest of the transports, and drove them greatly out of their designed course. They were buffeted by the blustering winds; their provisions were scanty, and the men hourly fell into sickness.

At one time the storm was so strong and noisy, that Berrington conceived the danger to be unavoidable. He feared he should never see Lorina again. The agitation of the vessel; the torn shrouds and broken cordage; the waves that sounded horribly in the night, and looked frightful in the day; and the dull countenance of the outworn pilot, seemed to confirm the suspicion. Berrington alternately gazed on the ugliness of the sea, and the gloom of the heavens; and he frequently exclaimed, "My wife, we shall meet no more!"

But the flush of animation soon came across the pale cheek of despair. The elements grew kinder: There was a probability of regaining the channel, out of which they had been driven; the tacking vessel again steered toward the British isle; and their provisions were greatly increased, by a merchantman that fell in with them.

Man is never secure; but his belief of it constitutes the principal pleasure of his life, and is a knotted and generous staff throughout his pilgrimage. The storm being over, no dread was entertained of its return. The sun looked out of a lovely heaven; the gale was fresh and fair; and each big wave separated into a thousand playful ones. Berrington clasped the hand of his heart's dear friend, who, collecting some unexpressed thoughts, smiled and whispered, "We shall yet see Imogen!"

The three officers were long in offering their congratulations; and none of them were more warm than those which came from

Russel, for whom Berrington had a very sincere regard, tho' the amount of it equalled not that which was awarded to Westdale. There was something, in the former person, rather repulsive to confidence; but the latter might have been called brother by the best of men, and trusted by the most scrupulous.

While the storm raged, Berrington had not been indifferent to the men. To the sick he was truly tender and humane; and the extraordinary soldier being among the number, his condition was particularly attended to by his generous captain. Berrington once visited his hammock, but could not draw a single word from him. When nature, however, was again tranquillized, he received a summons to the bed of affliction, and immediately repaired to it. The soldier raised himself with extreme difficulty; he feebly desired none would be near to him, except the captain, whom he told, with a ghastly expression, that he was dying.

Berrington started, and looked more earnestly in his face; where there was a white and frightful conviction, that death was placing his invisible standard on the poor conquest of human life. Philosopher! where shall you be found, whose eye can contemplate a scene like this, and yet shoot forth the rays of tranquillity? The page that records your fortitude contains, at least, one lie; and if the whole of it were immutable truth, I would not call on virtue to put her studded crown on your head.

Berrington shuddered, as he gazed on the changing matter of which he was composed; and the hand of the soldier sent coldness into every well-supplied vein that ran thro' his arm. The sick man, tho' his end was so near, could still articulate distinctly; and he begged his captain to sit by his side.

"You have given me, sir," he cried, "what every other person in the world denied me; you have bestowed compassion on one, who can be no longer thankless. I have heard it in your words, and seen it in your eyes. Dying, I render you my gratitude—Dying, I call on my offended God, to bless you for your worthiness. It was my intention to go, unknown, out of the world, which I might have adorned, but which I only contaminated. The means of virtue are given to every man: I used those of vice, in preference; and, behold, what a wretch I have made of myself. I intend to tell you what I have been, and who I am. But most of my actions are tainted with villany, and my name can never be spoken with respect. Curses will be piled on curses by my fellow beings; and, by the ministers of God, every thing that,—Oh, shelter me from the wrath that gathers in the angry heavens!—Your consolations once sounded like mockery to me: I almost despised you for offering them; and when your name has been mentioned, I have wildly exclaimed, Perdition to the soul of every man who bears it!"

"And why did you so?" enquired Berrington.

"Ask not the madman why he mutters to the moon. I did it, and own the crime. I would recal the blasphemy; but what access can I expect to the registry where it now remains? The winged centinel would oppose me with his arm; and I should fall to my doom, with his javelin in my side. But—I parch—my mouth blisters—Water, water!"

Berrington put a liquid to his lips; his throat, however, could not receive it, and his head sunk down again despairingly.

"Death approaches still nearer," he cried; "I hear the rattling of his bones, and see the beckonings of his hand; his compulsive, irresistible motions. I must away, for there is no appeal. And yet, I shiver at the chasms and torrents over which I am soon to be borne—into which, perhaps, he will exultingly hurl me! He may still further appal his victim, with loud shouts and laughter, which the hollows shall make more strong and terrific. I burn and freeze alternately. Let me touch you—I want to be convinced that I have not yet passed the verge of the world."

"Be composed, and look for mercy. If you have any thing to communicate to me, do it as soon as possible, lest——"

"I understand you: Lest— That is a pause of horror. I will give you a short, but corrupt history, and trust to your prudence for the rest. I once held a station in the army, superior to your own, but was expelled on account of my vices; and after a thousand vicissitudes, and many years of pain, I should have died in want, had I not claimed the bitter bread on which I have for sometime past existed."

Berrington afterwards learned from him that gaming, seduction, and blasphemy, had been his early vices. He confessed he had ruined many a wife and daughter—derided the plaints of fathers, and of husbands—subsisted, both in France and Germany, by the means of a dishonest gamester; and once franticly plunged into the horrors of murder!—The wretch gasped, and Berrington viewed him with terrified eyes. He afterwards, tho' in a faint and dying voice, pursued his story; then he reverted to some preceding events; and Berrington, while holding his head, learned that he had been listening to the accursed vices of his own father.

A loud shrill shriek tore its way up the throat of the son, who, riveted by horror, had not, at first, sufficient means to separate himself from the object that thus affected him. The all-subduing power was now twisting the features, and nearly reversing the eye-balls of the wretched being. His hand appeared to be feeling for something that could not be found; his head lay motionless on the breast of Berrington; and he still faintly called for water.

The last struggle now came: A strong convulsion dashed him on the hammock; and the released Berrington fled wildly from the groan, and threw himself, speechless, on the neck of the astonished Westdale. Clouds seemed falling on his head, and a frightened sea to swell around him. He shivered, as if a northern storm were pelting him; and his countenance would have served a delineator for a picture of insanity.

Fearing that his brain was really injured, Westdale looked on him with terror, and urged him to speak. Those who were in the cabin, and saw this strange conduct, were filled with astonishment. Berrington took the hand of his friend, and led him out; several other people were following him, but he begged them to remain in their stations; and then returned, accompanied only by Westdale, to the spot he had so wildly fled from.

The hour was still early, and Russel had not left his bed. The fineness of the morning induced all those who were at liberty, to go on the deck; and a few soldiers only were found near the corse. These Berrington sent away: He then put his hands on the body, and exposing the white face, desired his surprised companion to look at it.

Westdale gazed on the deceased, yet could not account for the extraordinary agitation of Berrington, till he laid his head upon his shoulder, and, nearly suffocated, exclaimed, "It is my father! It is my father!"

The wonder of Westdale almost confounded him; and a repetition of the words was necessary, to fix his belief on a story that seemed so incredible. There were not many who, professing friendship, could make the exercise of it so noble, so lovely. With the most simple words, he could not only shew the natural tenderness of his heart, but also express the generous, the soothing, and beautiful sentiments of his mind. In this respect, he had the power of doing much; and in order to secure the peace of a friend like Berrington, he would have invoked angels to plead, and supplicated Omnipotence to listen.

He led the agitated son from his father's body, and took him on the deck. The air, tho' somewhat sharp, was refreshing; and while his body regained vigor, his mind was, in a great degree, tranquillized by the kind attentions and simple philosophy of Westdale. They were bound together by confidence; and Berrington, as he sat at the helm, whispered the story of his wretched father into the ear of his companion, who, knowing the prejudices of proud society, advised him neither to disclose any part of it, nor to suffer his emotions to turn towards discovery.

The verge of the ocean, and its white boundaries, were then faintly in view. He commanded that the body of his father might not be given to the waves; and as the deceased had been known under an assumed name, he felt himself secure. His extreme agitation had excited some curiosity; but this Westdale undertook to appease, and easily succeeded in his attempt.

This was a day of trial to Berrington; he had to fight against his most obstinate passions; and, after all his exertions, he could scarcely be called the victor. In the night, he contrived to visit the body of his father, without exciting any particular notice. He chose an hour when his friends and most of the soldiers were asleep, and but few of the seamen on the deck. The corse, according to his orders, had not been removed; and the beams of the pale moon now broke in the hatch, (which had been raised for the necessary circulation of air,) and fell on the lengthened visage of the deceased.

The object, the hour, and every thing around, served to fill him with strange sensations. Those who were on board had not been so quiet before, since their embarkation. The breeze that blew in the morning had fallen, and brought down the sails. Motion was scarcely felt; and the voices of a sullen pilot and drowsy watch-boy, alone broke the silence of nature.

Berrington looked at the body, and touched it: He almost stiffened into horror; and with that forgetfulness, which the sluggard passions only can chide, he looked above him, and railed at Heaven for its connections. His breast was filled with violent pain; and he was unable to disunite what God had joined together.

His recent discovery seemed almost an incident of romance; and he wished to persuade himself, that his imagination had merely been played upon. But this would not be: There could be no such deception, even for a moment; and he looked on the murderer of his mother, till he believed he saw the eye-lids opening. He sickened with the knowledge he had obtained; and feeling a faintness, which he feared would overpower him, he went on the deck, in order to meet refreshment from the air. It was not long before his body acknowledged its benefits; and tho' peace did not wholly return to him, the oppressive emotions subsided, and melancholy succeeded the grief that had lately been violent. Still the image of his father was before his eye: He saw it by his side, and in the rippling water, and almost believed that his ear was, a second time, receiving the guilty tale of the deceased.

Early in the following day, the vessel was anchored at Deptford;* and the soldiers joyfully saluted their native land. They were, on the ensuing morning, to march to a town, which led thro' London. But the patience of Berrington was not to be sported with; he set off for the capital immediately, leaving Westdale and Russel to accompany the troops.

Previous to this, he consigned the remains of his father to an undertaker, with whom he deposited a sufficient sum of money for a decent funeral. His eyes, for the last time, traced the features of the deceased, but his tears soon blinded him. He was alone: He threw himself on his knees, and exclaimed, "Forgive him, Almighty Father! Pardon his vices, his many sins, and drive not his sorrowing spirit from the gates of Heaven."

And now he turned from a painful, towards a most pleasing object,—his wife, his truly loved Lorina. At the time of his leaving England, his boy was just beginning to make known the nature of his first simple ideas; and when the door of the house in which Lorina lodged was opened to him, he saw his rosy son by the side of the servant.

Nature had been filling his breast with the most exquisite emotions, some of which now broke forth; and while he sent his quick kisses to the blooming and beautiful pledge of Lorina's love, his joy became almost stronger than his reason. The child looked with that peculiar bashfulness, which follows the caresses of a stranger; but he smiled, not less sweet, to the eye of Berrington, than Heaven itself, and shaded his glossy forehead with his arm.

The girl was assured that her mistress's husband was returned; and, with a countenance of joy, she was running out of the room. Berrington knew what her intentions were; and, fearful of the effect her intelligence might have on Lorina, he stopped her at the door, and enquired of the boy whether his mother was at home. Having received a lisping affirmative, he tied a miniature of Lorina around the neck of his little informer, and desired him to go and shew it to her.

The fairy messenger of love departed, in search of his mother, whom he found in her chamber. "Look here!" he cried, exultingly: "See, mother! How pretty!"

Lorina gazed, and, with a shriek of joy and apprehension, exclaimed, "Oh God! How came you by this?"

"There is a gentleman below; a fine, handsome gentleman. He has kissed me a hundred times; and he kissed this fine toy, before he hung it on my neck."

Nearly confounded by rapture, agitated, and almost breathless, Lorina flew down the stairs, and leaped upon the neck of

Berrington. She fastened her lips on those of her speechless husband. Her boy had followed her: She caught him franticly in her arms, and again gave both herself and him to the bosom from which they had been so long estranged.

"Berrington!" she cried, "my husband, my beloved Berrington! Do not regard these as the actions of a mad woman. My joys must work on me, as they please. O, how I rejoice in your preservation! And blessed; blessed be the power, whatever it is, that sends you again to my happy bosom! You are not much altered. Look at our boy—the rose of our true love! Kneel down, my child; kneel at the feet of your parent; and remember the instructions which I have given you every morning and night."

"Bestow on me your blessing, father!" said the lisping boy, putting himself in a supplicatory posture.

"Forbear!" cried Berrington: "This is too much, my Lorina, for endurance. I had reckoned on my joys, but they now make my estimate poor and unequal. Take up the boy, and put him again in my arms; for your tenderness pervades my body, and robs it of all strength. Who shall dare to say, that the happiness of man is never complete? Let those who affirm it come hither, at this moment; and while I clasp my treasures, they shall be compelled to acknowledge their errors."

Their pleasures ended not here: But imagination may finish the scene, and tell of the many raptures that ensued.

Berrington was obliged to join his regiment on the following day; and short as the notice was, Lorina resolved to accompany him. From this he was little inclined to dissuade her; they accordingly went from London together, and left the servant to follow with their trunks. The fate of his father occasionally weighed on the mind of Berrington; but he wished it not to interrupt the happiness of his wife, and therefore not only kept her ignorant of it, but also endeavoured to pass it from his memory.

He felt great pleasure, when he presented her to Westdale, of whose peculiar merits she had been previously apprised; and tho' the young officer expected to find her an amiable and interesting woman, yet her person, and sweetness of disposition, excelled what he had fancied, and drew forth his admiration.

She esteemed him, on account of the friendship he entertained for Berrington; and for the kind attentions he had shewn in the hospital, she now sincerely and most feelingly thanked him. Gratitude flowed as well from her eye, as from her tongue; and she dropped a tear on the hand of him, who had served to raise the sinking mind, and soothed the bodily pains of her husband.

When she was introduced to Captain Russel, she believed that she had come to the knowledge of another very valuable character. She conceived Berrington to have been peculiarly fortunate in his friendships, and expected to join, in future, an amiable and interesting society. The past evil she sunk into the present good; and in her undoubted security, fell every recent prejudice and apprehension.

She was not singular in either of these thoughts or actions: Like the greater part of the still imperfectible world, she called not always on philosophy to bring her happiness; but took it as it flowed to those who were virtuous, without being deeply speculative. She, therefore, was no longer distracted by the station of the man, in whom love had almost placed her life; nor did she, tho' she had been so ardent at a former period, attempt to turn him from his employments. At that time, she had traced him, with the eye of imagination, wildly flying, with streaming wounds, from the murderous weapons of fleeter foes: But now, she saw him move in paths unmolested by war; and while she roved with him, and was supported by his arm, the very outlines of the picture that had frightened her disappeared.

After remaining a short time at a town in Essex, orders were received, to remove the regiment to York; to which place Lorina, accompanied by her child and servant, soon followed her restored Berrington. The manner in which she travelled was productive of no fatigue; and at the end of her journey, she found that comfortable lodgings had been prepared for her. The recent distresses of her mind, and the sorrows of her heart, made her more sensible of the felicities that now awaited her; and the eyes which she had, slowly and despairingly, fixed on her poor boy, shed on the face of him and his father the unclouded rays of peace and pleasure.

On Westdale and Russel she was accustomed daily to smile. She delighted in their society, and formed a comparison between them and several other officers, the result of which was highly honorable to her new friends. Lorina had a love for literature; and she soon discovered that both Westdale and Russel were admirers of genius. Neither of them was a street-lounger;* neither attached himself to the intoxicating bottle, or the ruinous card-table. The one frequently displayed uncommon taste and feeling; and the other was distinguished by a continual flow of strong and elegant sentiment.

Westdale not only pointed out the best written works of imagination, but also read them to her, while she was at her little employments; and with an effect, which may be compared to the fine speeches of a dramatic poet, made still more beautiful by the judgment of a Kemble.* The tones of Westdale, when passion was concerned, were exquisite. Perhaps, in some passages, he felt more acutely than the composer of the tale; and for sorrow, love, and heroism, he had a finely varying voice. Nature was attentive when she featured his face; and if she stamped not beauty on every part of it, she caused a noble expression to rule the whole.

The person of Russel was not at all inferior to that of Westdale; and he was generally spoken of as the handsomer man. His eyes were darker: his mind seemed ever sitting on his visage; and his calm dignity frequently yielded to a smile of irresistible softness. He had an ardent love for women, and attempted not to screen his gratifications. He was not attracted by the lures of common wantonness. Those who were accessible, without being flagrant in their propensities, were preferred; and it had been said of him, that he walked with dignity in his pursuits of pleasure. Tho' his habits were well known, no stigma had ever been placed on him. He despised the garrulity of libertinism; his participations were not spoken of, even to his most intimate friends; and in the presence of modest women, he was polite in his manners, and chaste in his sentiments.

The possession of a good fortune, independent of his profession, favored his inclinations; and he was as judicious in the application of his money, as in the selection of those on whom it was to operate. It was but seldom that he spoke of his gallantries; and when he did discourse on them, it was not vauntingly. He ever professed a sincere esteem for modest women, as well as a desire of being in their company; and he had none of that awkwardness, which generally attaches itself to a man of irregular pursuits, and sits upon him, when he changes the grosser for the purer object. He could carry ease, sentimentality and smiles, wherever he chose; and it was not difficult for him to appear such a man, as even a scrupulous woman would call on, for a friend and protector.

Berrington saw his attentions to Lorina, and did not discourage them. He had long known the virtue of the one, and the honor of the other: A suspicion, placed on either, would have degraded him. His love was pure and unalloyed, and the slightest feeling of jealousy had never interrupted his marriage joys.

Lorina was soon introduced to several ladies of reputation, who resided in the town; in some of them she discovered good breeding, and in others agreeable talents. Her heart, however, found among them no dearly connected friend; and she could boast of nothing more than an acquaintance. The pride of the capital is less than that which springs up in country towns, where women of small fortune, and the wives and daughters of professional men, are ever seen, fluttering with the airs of quality. Their vanity is increased by the tameness of the despised; and their silly consequence grows strong, on the wretched humility of those who render themselves contemptible, by the acceptance of insult.

Lorina entered into several private societies; partook of a few public diversions; and was amused by some of the characters she met with. It was surprising to many young ladies, that Mrs. Berrington, who had so much youth, gracefulness and beauty, should sometimes come to a ball room, and not dance; enter into conversation with old women of fifty, on the dull subjects of literature and morality; and turn indifferently, if not rudely, from their own interesting descriptions of an annual journey to London, a new head dress, or a handsome Baronet that was going to be married to a little, ugly, rich spinster.

She was frequently placed in situations extremely vexatious.

Though she did not pretend to any very superior understanding herself, she was surprised by the total want of it, which was often displayed in the dull prolixities, stupid details, and excessive triflings of children inflated by the trailing of a long gown. From the gaieties of the ball room, the allurements of the card table, and the querulous strains of affectation, Lorina frequently absented herself, in order to enjoy the calmer pleasures of an evening walk, in which she was generally joined by her husband and his two friends.

Young William was also often of the party, and Westdale, who was very fond of the child, sometime bore him on his back, and ran with him down the little grassy hills. Lorina had a love for rural scenery. The vivid green of spring, the darker shade of summer, and the yellowness of autumn, were always beautiful to her; nor did she think nature was to be viewed without admiration, when that universal goddess went forth, in the serener days of winter, robed in her spotless ermine, and directing the faint sun-beam across the trackless country.

The muse never speaks so sweetly to us, as when we meet her abroad, in vallies, in fields, or in groves. The infusion of her spirit is then felt. She fills the heart with sympathies; raises the worshipped images of the mind; and pointing to flowers, to hills, to streams, and to the many-coloured heavens, tells us that these are the themes of which she has so softly sung.

A sentiment like this, Lorina once expressed to Russel, on whose arm she was then leaning, while her husband and Westdale walked at some distance before her. It was on a spot nearly three miles from the town; quiet, green and woody. Lorina spoke with fervour, and her smiles were soft and exquisite. Her sensations passed to her companion; and the eyes of Russel turned, with a mild but full expression, on the face of the enthusiast.

"How fortunate," he cried, "how truly happy am I, in finding a disposition so congenial to my own. The hour that first brought you to my notice, I shall never cease to remember; for how strangely do most of those women who live among military characters, differ from the wife of Berrington. Whenever any one of our officers married, I found that either fortune, or beauty, had been his aim. Of intelligence of mind I seldom made any discovery; and, to my regret, if the object of his choice possessed some degree of wit, it was not long before it ran into flippancy:—If she brought with her a little store of sentiment, it was soon routed, by the loud laughter of those who, not knowing how to appreciate it, considered it as an impediment to the pleasures that were to be found at her husband's table. I have ever loved the mind, that could fly from the common concerns of life, and soar above gross conceptions. Yet, with the poetical character I have rarely met: perhaps it is my profession that makes me a stranger to it; for there is a modesty in it, which will ever keep it distant from every thing that is conceived to be obstreperous."

"The pursuits of Apollo and Mars," continued Russel, "are materially different. Knowing them to be so, they attempt not to associate; and the former can scarcely believe, the strings of his lyre capable of giving any pleasure to the ear that so often turns to the trumpet, and to the neighing war-horse. I have, indeed, occasionally met with those, who would talk of poetry, and write verses. Still they were not what I looked for: The body was not to be distinguished, and its thin shadow only fell across my path. A thousand rhymes may be linked together, and sent abroad in a splendid quarto;* but, in spite of the leading capitals, the measurement, and the regular jingle, the whole may be nothing more than intoxicated prose in masquerade. O, I have seen men, aye, and women too, plucking at the amaranths* of Parnassus!* And they have been so strangely beautiful, and withal so sweetly simple, that they *did* pleasure me when they *did* sing."

Lorina smiled at the quaintness of the last sentence, and Russel proceeded——

"While our new philosophers are sturdily pushing forward, and fitting our ideas to *new* sounds, some of our most eminent poets are turning backward; and through the medium of their flights, the knowledge of Chaucer and Spencer will soon become general. A little volume printed without a name, and in black letter, would really be a prize for the antiquarians. Eccentric and fond of innovation as our present writers are, yet the wreathes which are woven for some of them, will not soon loose either their fragrance or bloom. From my boyish days, and tho' I voluntarily entered the army, I have not been insensible of the charms of our british bards. I have perused their pages with rapture, and taken their richer feelings into my own soul. The enjoying of the turn of an epigram, or reading a little tender tale with a serious countenance, implies no real poetical taste. I would see the fervor of the mind forcing its blaze out of the eye, and producing such an expression, as we may suppose to have come from Shakespeare, when he was delineating the savageness of human nature;* or from Milton, ere blindness placed her hand on his face, and when his vast brain was engendering the terrific chief of the rebels, who met with defeat in Heaven. The seeds of poetry, if they be not cast in the hot-bed of enthusiasm, will seldom produce any thing except weeds; or if a flower should, here and there, lift its head, it will be as only one pale primrose growing on a bank, which is crowned with clustering roses. I once had a friend, and I wish you had known him—a strange, wild, melancholy, amiable being! Few noticed him, while he lived: He died at the early age of man, and his body now rests among the undistinguished graves of peasantry. I have viewed him, as he went forth slowly in the morning—as he stood on the margin of the scarcely-moving river, for a while believing it the mirror of eternity—and as he traced the white clouds, which were hurrying over the moon, and wildly flying into darkness."

"I see him now," cried Lorina, shading her eyes with a delicate hand.

"Some verses of his," said Russel, "are in my possession; and I will shew them to you very soon." Westdale and Berrington now joined them, and they afterwards walked home together.

The gaiety of the town, as well as the acquaintance of Berrington, was increased by the arrival of a regiment of horse, which was to be stationed there for a considerable time. Berrington was sitting one morning with Lorina, when his servant informed him that Lady Heyland was below, and desirous of seeing him. He was in no small degree surprised; for tho' he had heard the name, the person was wholly unknown to him; and he concluded that there was some mistake, on the part of her ladyship.

He knew that Colonel Heyland was in the newly-arrived regiment: Him he had only once seen; and whether his visiter was the mother or wife of the Colonel, was still to be explained. Giving Lorina time to retire, he desired that the stranger might be shewn up stairs. She soon after entered, ran up to him hastily, and began to express great pleasure in seeing him again. He immediately found in her, his former friend and benefactress, Lady Augusta Hartley; and, with gratitude springing into his breast, he kissed the hand which she held out to him, while he expressed such a degree of wonder, as convinced her that he had been ignorant of her marriage.

The personal charms of her ladyship were increased, rather than diminished; and she smiled enchantingly on the young officer, to whom she explained those things, which seemed somewhat mysterious, speaking, at the same time, with such familiarity as was highly flattering to him.

"You will remember," she cried, "that when I last saw you, I was preparing to return to my favorite country; and in the course of a few weeks after our separation, I found myself again in Naples, where I meant to reside two years, if the adventurers of France did not compel me to fly before their victorious army. Almost immediately on my arrival I met with Colonel Heyland, who had come thither for the recovery of his health, which being greatly improved, it was his intention to return to England, in the course of a few months, in order that he might rejoin the regiment to which he had belonged. Tho' some severe troubles had then lately—— Berrington, we became familiar, and, consulting only ourselves, very soon married."

"And let me express a most sincere wish, that the union has proved, and will long continue, a source of unalloyed pleasure to my first and best of friends! To you, madam, who raised me from obscurity, and insured me honor and prosperity. May you be eternally happy!"

Her ladyship heard this, with a countenance falling into seriousness; and, for a minute or two, she continued silent. "I am greatly obliged to you for your good wishes," she afterwards replied, "but if you desire to be better acquainted with me, you must not bear so strongly on the theme of gratitude. You will probably be known to Colonel Heyland, before I shall have an opportunity of introducing you to him; for owing to some little peculiarities of—— Is Mrs Berrington at home?"

"Yes, she is, madam."

"Then pray bring her to me. Tell her that one, who is unceremonious in her manners, wishes for her society. And your boy—let me see him too; for while I continue here, I shall claim regard from all of you. I arrived only last night, when I was highly gratified, by finding that you and I were to meet again."

Berrington left the room; and in a little while he came back, with his lovely wife in one hand, and his child in the other. He led them towards Lady Augusta, who rose to meet them.

"This is my Lorina," he cried, "and this my boy! The one has often heard your name; and, (suffer me for once to disregard your late injunction,) many times blessed you for your actions: The other will, hereafter, appreciate your merits, and praise you for being the promoter of his father's welfare."

Lorina, always beautiful, was now made more charming, by the bloom that spread upon her cheek. Her loveliness was noticed and acknowledged by the stranger, and Berrington's boy was not less admired. Lady Augusta congratulated her on the safe return of her husband from the fields of war, and expressed a desire of having much of her company, since she had been brought to her acquaintance.

Lorina was greatly pleased with the person and manners of Lady Augusta, who had been reared in the school of fashion, without receiving any taint from its many affectations. Though she had resided so much abroad, she still shewed that she never forgot her own country; and the English character was very rarely disguised by her. She had an understanding, which would have eminently distinguished her, had she been more careful in exercising it. But her judgment was often too precipitate; her passions sometimes burst forth in violence; and the love of pleasure frequently led her into serious dissipation. What she further was, will be hereafter developed; and it will, in this place, only be said, that she greatly approved the wife of Berrington, and prevailed on her to take an airing, in the carriage that was waiting at the door.

The invitation was too flattering to be declined. Lorina went to her chamber; and in the few minutes of her absence, Lady Augusta spoke to Berrington. "I find," she said, "that I have not known enough of you; and you must not be displeased with me, if I sometimes deprive you of the company of your wife—a deprivation which some men would not, perhaps, regret. The acquaintance of this morning almost convinces me, that conjugal happiness is not what I suspected it to be: And do you know, Berrington, I have of late considered it as a mere chimera."

"But, I most earnestly hope your ladyship has not actually found it so."

"Why, as to that—But come, I will not be grave with you at our first meeting. I must speak to you hereafter; for I approve your heart and mind, and shall look for a friend and counsellor in you. But, before I go, I must give you one little caution: I have never been accustomed to judge of a man, either by his title or his fortunes. His natural qualities I have generally examined; and tho' I have been once mistaken—wretchedly mistaken!—yet I think I was not deceived, when I determined on *your* composition. The best motives of the heart are frequently misconstrued; and why I did this or that self-commended thing, will be explained, by the sagacious many, in a manner perhaps not merely mortifying, but also very injurious. I made you a soldier: And if the king were personally to thank me for it, his dignity would not be hurt. Our actions lose their richness, when we make them our boast. What I did with so much pleasure for you, I never divulged to any person, except my agent, whom I was obliged to employ in the business; and I have earnestly to entreat, that you will not make known what I have so cautiously concealed. Since I saw you last, I have acted with extraordinary folly and inconsiderateness; and my situation at this time——"

Lorina now returned: The serious face of Lady Augusta brightened into instant gaiety; and taking the arm of her new friend, she led her to the carriage, and left Berrington to reflect on this strange interview, and inexplicable conversation. That she was unhappy in her union with Colonel Heyland, he did not doubt; yet her early confession of it appeared very singular; and he was deep in his reflections, which were soon interrupted by the entrance of Westdale and Russel, to whom he spoke of his late visiter.

Colonel Heyland on that day came to the military dinner; and Berrington now regarded him particularly. The Colonel had sufficient qualities to form a very fine gentleman—such an one as frequently starts from the modern school, exacting admiration from the initiated of both sexes. His face was not unhandsome, and his figure was fine. He drank deep, swore deep, played deep, and had an infinite fund of that kind of wit, which the new comedies bring within the walls of our Theatres Royal.*

There was, occasionally, a looseness in his language, which went some way in explaining the half-expressed sentiments of Lady Augusta; and Berrington concluded, after the bottle had freely circulated, that the Colonel was no observer of the marriage vows. He frequently addressed himself to our young officer; and in the evening, when cards were called for, asked him to play: But Berrington declined, and was a sober looker-on; while the Colonel, heated with wine, and often with anger, threw about the cards and lost his money.

It was late before Berrington left the party; and when he returned, he found that Lorina had spent the whole day with Lady Augusta, of whom she spoke with warmth and pleasure. She had promised to call on her ladyship the following morning; and Berrington accompanied her, at the appointed hour, when his wife was introduced to Colonel Heyland by his lady.

They were found at the breakfast table; and the coming in of visiters appeared a very agreeable interruption of an acrimonious tête à tête. The Colonel's eyes were fixed on Lorina, with infinite pleasure, for she was a new object—a beautiful young woman—and though he did not loudly speak it, he muttered to himself, "she is an angel!"

The intimacy, thus formed, was continued several months, and Lady Augusta and Lorina spent a great part of each day together. The Colonel was not much at home; and his absence seemed more pleasing to his wife than his society. When they met, happiness seldom joined the party; for there was, evidently, a mutual dissatisfaction, and the coldness of their looks was frequently followed by a great asperity of words.

Still Lady Augusta seldom spoke to Lorina on the subject of her discontent: She was too mild, too gentle, to be the adviser of an injured wife; and entertaining the idea, Berrington was preferred as a confidant. One morning he found her alone: She looked anxious—unhappy—and pride seemed almost unable to restrain her tears.

"Sit down, sit down," she cried, drawing her hand across her forehead: "I was wishing to see you, when you came in. Did you meet Colonel Heyland?"

"Yes, I saw him below."

"Then, Berrington, you saw a man whom I despise, and from whom I am determined to separate. Soon too—very soon——"

"Dear Lady Augusta! you are agitated—What is the occasion of this?"

"I have been too much abused to be calm any longer; and it is time I should remove myself from my injurer. You start—But I have formed my project, and will execute it. You know that my marriage was precipitate: It was an act of passion, and reason had little concern in it. The Colonel wished not to remove my fortune from my own power. Our happiness was not of long duration; and I had been but a few weeks in England, when I found that the man, with whom I was connected, had neither feeling nor sincerity. I was very sensible of my own defects, and therefore strove to look on his with patience. He neglected me for other and newer objects, and many nights did not come to my chamber. My temper would not always be tame: I spoke upbraidingly to him, and was answered with grossness and indecency. To tantalize, to mortify me, seemed to give him pleasure; and, in order to shew his complete disgust, he removed my servant from me, and acknowledged himself the lover and protector of a girl, whose intellects scarcely placed her above the brute creation. Had I not in this cause to complain?"

"You had indeed," answered Berrington.

"And yet, perhaps the recollection of my former errors, and my insincerity, ought to have made me more passive. Berrington, you are a moralist; still I will dare to speak openly to you. I call on you to be my friend, and implore you never to become my open accuser. Nature put free spirits into me; and the little discretion I had, was not to be improved by either the words, or actions, of those into whose acquaintance I fell at a very early age. There is a person in Italy, whom I wish to receive the entire benefit of my fortune. I have employed a trusty agent in London to prepare my will: and, in case of my death, I wish you to act in my concerns, according to your own judgment."

"And who is the person to whom your ladyship alluded?"

"Oh, Berrington!"

"Madam, lift up your head: You look faint: Lean upon my shoulder."

"It is my child—My natural daughter!—My secret now rests with you; and tho' it must sink me in your esteem, do not let it drive me entirely out of it. The father of my girl is an Italian, whose fortunes are mean, but whose genius you would admire. We are separated for ever—for ever, poor Bellinzona! Tho' it is my intention to return to Italy, I go not to meet my former lover, but to see my child, whom I wish to have educated in England. Heyland has agreed to a separation; and the hour in which I bid him farewell, will be happier to me than that of our meeting. But you look serious, my friend: I know your thoughts: You wonder at my confidence, and despise me."

"Oh, no indeed! I would only reconcile you to your destiny."

"And persuade me to live with Heyland? I declare to God I will not! I have often very seriously accused myself, for imposing on him as I did; yet in spite of my errors, I would have been to him a faithful, and an affectionate wife. Oh! you know not to what I have submitted—You know not how often, when I smiled on you and your friends, what a painful heart I carried in my breast. Would you believe Heyland to be capable of brute violence—of savageness, which is to be found only in those whom men should be ashamed to call men? Gay, hypocritical villain! Look at this arm!—"

"Good God!—It is black with bruises—Who did this mischief to you?"

"Heyland. He dragged me on the floor—griped, beat me. He could not have more abused the vilest strumpet of the town."

Lady Augusta's arm was remarkable for its loveliness; a statuary could have formed nothing more beautiful, whatever might be his art, or wherever he sought for his composition. She drew up the sleeve of her morning dress, and exposed her injuries. The heart of Berrington was full of pity and indignation; and, scarcely knowing what he did, he first looked, most expressively, on the face of his weeping companion, and then pressed his lips on the bruised and discoloured flesh.

At that moment Lorina entered; and a spectator could not have determined, in which of the party there was most confusion. Lady Augusta was in tears: The face of Berrington was alternately red and pale; and Lorina almost stiffened with astonishment. Lady Augusta saw the true situation of the petrified wife, and in order to save her own reputation, she called for the aid of hypocrisy, and said, that she had just received a very violent contusion, by one of her arms getting between the closing door.

Lorina, tho' she possessed a truly tender heart, had, on this occasion, no pity to bestow. She disbelieved, at least, a part of the tale; for the finesse of the sufferer was very ill supported by the awkwardness of Berrington, who received a most reproachful look, from those eyes which had so long beamed on him with love.

The interview, at first, occasioned a considerable degree of embarrassment to all of them. Lorina's prejudices grew strong; but she wished it not to be supposed, that the circumstance particularly affected her. She, therefore, attempted to be lively in her discourse; and Russel soon afterwards coming in, she asked him to accompany her to the library; when curtseying, with an air which she meant to be expressive of gaiety, but which, in fact, discovered all that she strove to conceal, she hastily retired.

Lady Augusta and Berrington could have very little conversation after her departure; for the Colonel was returning with company, and her ladyship, in order to avoid him, hastened to her dressing room. She had only time to say to her companion, "I know your wife is thinking unjustly, both of you and me; but her good sense will, I am persuaded, very soon tranquilize her. My secret! Oh, for God's sake, never divulge any part of the mystery!"

Berrington avoided the Colonel, for whom he now felt an abhorrence. Indiscreet as Lady Augusta had been, the treatment she received excited his pity; and the services she required of him, he resolved to grant, in case the proposed separation should really happen.

He was somewhat concerned, by the apparent misconstructions of Lorina, but did not suppose that there would be any difficulty in altering her opinions. He found, however, when they met, that she had regarded the affair very seriously. She discovered much anxiety and restlessness; and spoke, in a tone of painful irony, of Lady Augusta's arm.

Berrington was distressed by her uneasiness; but not being at liberty to divulge any part of the mystery that fretted her, he strove, by raillery and his usual kindnesses, to divert the thoughts which troubled her. Lorina's little jealousy sprung from a great source of love. She would have renounced every thing, before she gave up the affection of her husband; and, from a trifling anecdote, related by Russel, as he was accompanying her to the public library, she feared that Lady Augusta had not been entirely disinterested in her former actions.

Still she placed not her reason, on the wings of her passions. She could not, for any very considerable time, be insensible of the endearments of Berrington, who was not long in removing some of her prejudices, tho' a few remained in obstinacy.

Within a few days after, both the regiments received marching orders; and they were to go together, to a large sea-port town, at no small distance from York. Anxious to break the chain that harrassed her, Lady Augusta, at first, protested she would take a last farewell of the Colonel, and immediately depart for London. But Berrington, still hoping to effect a reconciliation, earnestly persuaded her not to act so precipitately; and as the business, in which she wished to make him concerned, was still incomplete, she altered her designs, and followed the army.

Lorina was her travelling companion, but not her former affectionate friend. The one was busied, in her own serious plans; the other, at intervals, perplexed by her suspicions; and they were both more polite and punctilious, than they had been accustomed.

Lorina was happy when her journey ended. She found Berrington ready to receive her, with smiles and tenderness, and really was, in some degree, concerned for Lady Augusta, when she saw the chilling and contemptuous looks of the Colonel.

A very mild winter had just gone by; and spring was impatient to rear her flowers, to catch the smiles of the sky, and to make the fields and trees green and blooming. Lorina preferred lodging on the skirts, rather than in the centre, of the town; and she was accommodated in a neat dwelling, which, on the one hand, commanded a prospect of an agreeable diversity of rural scenes, and, on the other, a boundless view of the sea.

Lady Augusta resided at some distance from Lorina; but they often met; and the latter endeavoured to remove the prejudices, that sought an establishment in her bosom. Her's was no common jealousy: It was rather a tenacity for the thing she loved; and tho' she frequently tantalized herself, she was never reproachful or invective.

Berrington was, for some time, the same she had ever found him; yet, she afterwards thought that his tenderness decreased, and that his affections were really inclining towards the suspected object. His interviews with Lady Augusta were certainly more frequent; but her domestic inquietudes, and anxiety to be released from her abhorred connection, were the principal causes of them. Her spirit was too great for querulous complaint: To Berrington she had confessed her indiscretions; and to him alone, would she speak of the troubles of her mind, and of the pangs of her heart.

From an obscure situation, and from the adversities of fortune, she had generously raised him, to the station which he then maintained. He had heard, and read, that gratitude was no virtue; but it rose spontaneously in his breast, and he found a pleasure in keeping it there. Though many parts of the conduct of Lady Augusta appeared to him very censurable, he found her not undeserving of pity. The Colonel's want of worthiness was evident to him: His sensualities and debaucheries had scarcely a gauzy veil to cover them; and when he was heated with wine, he talked of her with a degree of grossness, which was too disgusting to be relished by any person.

Berrington, tho' the subject was so peculiarly delicate, once ventured to touch on it, which he found to be productive only of mirth. "Most valorous knight!" cried the Colonel, ironically:—"Redoubted champion of the red plume, and lady-wrought scarf! I cannot listen to thy arguments; and my lance has got a damnable crack in the middle. But I tell thee what I'll do. Thou shalt have the damsel—or call her what thou wilt—Have her from this hour—have her for life—but on condition, that the peerless Lorina be made my prize. And by all the knights and squires that ever roved in the world, nay, by the husband of Teresa Pancha,* and his renowned Dapple,* I swear, that if thou wilt not accede to my terms, thou shalt have her—without any stipulation at all."

The uselessness of offering argument to such a man was palpable; and Berrington now believed, with Lady Augusta, that a separation could not be too early effected. Some difficulties, however, still remained, in regard to the business which she had alluded to on a former occasion; and finding that the assistance of Berrington was not to be dispensed with, she thought it better to remain for a while in her present state, distressing as it was, than to fly from it, and by that mean, lose the aid of her friend and counsellor.

Lorina was not unacquainted with their many meetings, and she misconstrued every word and action. Scandal was abroad, and the loving but apprehensive wife, had listened to the artful whisper, the malignant insinuation; and tho' she concealed the wounds which she had received, she could find nothing healing to apply to them. Ashamed of her own weaknesses, she spoke of them to no person; and Berrington, who believed that the little impression he had once noticed, was entirely worn away, looked with a serious concern on her fading cheek.

She pleaded indisposition as an excuse for not meeting company; and her chief gratification was in strolling thro' the fields, or on the beach, with her playful boy. Berrington frequently accompanied her; Westdale was also an occasional associate; but with Russel she now very rarely met. Sometimes she saw him in her rambles; and, estimating his fine qualities, it gave her great pain to observe how strangely he was altered. His spirits were depressed: The sallies which had amused her, and the sentiments with which she had been charmed, she heard no longer. The wit, the moralist, the poet, the philosopher, the dignified soldier, was sunk into a quiet and dejected man.

In a solitary mood she met him a few times on the shore, when she talked on some of his favourite subjects, without seeing any of his former ardour. It was common for him, to fall into a 'strange perusal' of her face, and to seem on the point of speaking of something, which was important and troublesome; but then, he suddenly withdrew his eyes, talked of things very unconnected, and left her with abruptness.

One evening Lorina went abroad with her son; and after a long ramble, he complained of weariness. The day had been fine, and the earth had no moisture in it. Lorina, therefore, seated him on a bank, where there was a profusion of primroses; and while he recruited his strength, and plucked the flowers, his mother stood, silent and reflectingly, by his side. Her mind was serene and unpainful, dwelling alternately on the beauties which were around her, and on the power by which they were produced and arranged.

Neither the leaves of the trees, nor the grass of the meadows, had yet felt the scorchings of the sun; they were brightly green, and every black-thorn bush was teeming with a thousand unopened sweets. The prospect, tho' narrow, was delightful. There was splendor in the skies, freshness in the air, and melody, varied melody, in every shrub and hedge-row. Lorina felt no gaiety; not a single sorrow, however, then pressed on her heart; and she was giving freedom to her imagination, when she heard a footstep, and perceived Russel by her side.

She had not seen him before for several days, and his eyes

now broke on her with evident sorrow. He expressed a pleasure in finding her well; but it was a joy that faded in a moment, and ended with a most oppressive sigh. Lorina regarded him with great tenderness: All her sympathies were immediately awake, and she timidly asked, why he had absented himself so long, and what was the occasion of his late and present distresses.

Russel started; the colour of his cheek grew strong, and faded again; and he looked pensively on the face of the enquirer. "That I am unhappy," he cried, "I will not deny; but you must not enquire into the cause of my wretchedness. It is absolute and irremediable; I call on every power to oppose it, yet still remain in single feebleness. I have not a hope to rest upon: My prospects are dark and desolate; and my expectations have fallen into sickness. Human misery cannot be described more strong than it really is: I once thought it possible; but my agonised heart has since convinced me of the errors of my judgment. Yet I have your pity! The pity of one, whom I might call an angel, without fearing the reproof of Heaven. I see it in your eyes—it rises in your gentle bosom. Oh! there is something in your compassion, which——"

"Had I the means of lessening your inquietudes," said Lorina, "God knows how joyfully I would employ them!"

"Your words delight, yet almost distract me; and your compassion, for one moment, soothes and solaces me; but, in the next, it proves as destructive as the sword. I am not one of those men, who would ease their sorrows by complaints, and become less miserable, by robbing their hearers of tranquillity. I can suffer deeply and still be silent. Mine are not the griefs of a morbid sensibility; they arise from serious perplexities; from passions which weaken even reason in combat—from a lacerated and self-reproving heart. Yet I am now entering into a strain, which, in the last minute, I contemned. Good God! you weep for me—I see the holy tear in your eye, and will complain no more."

"Indeed, indeed I feel most sensibly for your sufferings, whatever they are."

"They are past—they are gone—I will disclaim all knowledge of them. Let us walk further; and you shall see how gay I can be.

Flora's pillager* shall have a ride in my arms. Sweet, rosy fellow! I can almost believe that it is Cupid in disguise."

The boy climbed up the knee of Russel, whose neck he clasped with one of his hands, while the other grasped a bunch of flowers, some of which afterwards fell into his mother's bosom. Lorina was greatly pleased to see the brightened face of Russel, and to hear his occasional laugh; but after walking about half an hour, and on their return to the town, despondency again sat in his face, and his fine features were shaded by a still deeper melancholy.

He did not go home with her; but stopping at some distance from the house, he asked her to call on him the following morning, to examine some little elegancies, which he had received from London, among which there were several new books and prints. She promised to come to him, and they then separated. Russel kissed the boy, and left Lorina to ruminate on the unexplained distresses of a noble mind.

When she reached home, she found Berrington and Westdale in the parlour; and soon after Lady Augusta came in, and proposed to spend the evening with them. She appeared in better spirits than Lorina had observed for some preceding time, and was so friendly in her manners that her late censurer could not repulse her. She was, by turns, gay and thoughtful: she frequently looked with a strong expression on Berrington, to whom she whispered once or twice; and she pressed the hand of his wife very frequently, without speaking of the cause of her present feelings.

She could not be attentive to any particular thing; she took cards, but threw them about at random; she began several songs and tunes, without finishing any of them; and her whole behaviour was, for awhile, at least to Lorina, singular and unaccountable. But in the latter part of the evening they retired to another room; and then Lady Augusta confessed, that her present satisfaction arose from the certainty of being, in the course of four days, for ever separated from the Colonel. The deeds were arrived, and to be signed immediately. The business could not now be impeded; and the long-desired hour of emancipation was nearly come.

"You look on me with surprise," she cried: "You think it strange, perhaps indecorous, that I should talk in this manner. Still I must go on—still rejoice that my wishes will be so soon accomplished. Where there is happiness, I can well believe that the married state is, under Heaven, the most enviable and felicitous: But when disgust steals into the place once occupied by love, and grows great in it, I would prefer death to such an unnatural association. The world knows of my wrongs, and of the baseness of Heyland. Yet, my friend, I have of late imagined, that *you* were very little concerned for me."

"Indeed, I have"—Lorina stammered, crimsoned, and hung her head in silence.

"I cannot tell what you *would* say, but certainly know what you *might*. Trifling as my character may appear to some people, and perplexed as I have been by my own concerns, I have not failed in many of my observations. I am not unacquainted with your recent sentiments; and I have looked into your heart, tho' you strove to hide it from me. I have often said to myself, this woman, (meaning you,) degrades me in her opinions, and is a severe censurer of my actions. She knows of my disappointments, and unjustly thinks I would remedy them, without adhering to the niceties of honor. She fears that I should rob her of her husband's affections——"

"Oh! for mercy's sake, let me hear no more of this," cried Lorina, in shame and agony.

"She wounds me in the tenderest point," continued Lady Augusta;—"yet, I can forgive, and still be her friend! Oh, Mrs. Berrington! let the tears which are now drawn from my stubborn eyes, speak further for me, and shew you the extent of my misery. It was the loathing of my husband, that made the friendship of Berrington dearer to me than it otherwise would have been:—It was the fulness of his disgust that caused me to look for sympathy elsewhere; and I was happy in finding a man, who could give the dues of misfortune, without being forgetful of the honor with which they ought to be rendered. For the rules of my own conduct, I seldom look into other women. I judge for myself on most occasions, dispensing with form and agency. Many there are who would have contemned you, on account of your prejudices; but I will now only smile at your past deceptions, and bid you, for the future, be perfectly secure."

"I see my unworthiness—Blush to look at you."

"Nay, now you are more serious than I wish you to be. Let us return to the men; and when you cast your eyes on the worthy Berrington, pray shew not so much anxiety as you have of late worn in your face. He deserves an eternal smile, love, confidence, the noblest exertions, and the tenderest concern, that are within the capability of the best of women. Come, my friend; for by that neglected, and almost forgotten name, I again can call you."

They went back to Berrington and Westdale. Lorina was, for some time, embarrassed and ashamed of herself; but finding Lady Augusta's behaviour kind and encouraging, she became more easy; and the remainder of the evening passed very agreeably.

In the course of the night, Lorina looked into herself, and discovered many imperfections, of which she had not before been sensible, but which she then resolved to correct. She now pitied and admired the woman, for whom she had long harboured a dislike; and tho' there were some singularities in Lady Augusta, which she could not sanction, yet she believed that her heart was good, and her honor unimpeachable. She had certainly treated the subject of their last conversation with an admirable openness; and there appeared, to the other party, something noble in her manner of discussing a point, which would have filled most women with petulance and anger.

Lorina's mind did not soon turn from this affair; and she strongly hoped, that the eyes of Berrington had not been so active as Lady Augusta's, in searching for the degrading cause of her past inquietude. During the night she obtained but little repose; for after she had reflected on her late interview and conversation, her thoughts turned towards the solitary Russel, and the unexplained cause of those sorrows, of which he had so pathetically spoken.

The interest she felt in this respect was very strong and sincere; for she had long looked, with the eyes of esteem, on the wanderer, who ever shewed her the most delicate and flattering attentions, whether he found her alone, or in the crowd of society.

There was something uncommon in the traits of his dejection—a pensiveness, wildly disturbed.—His melancholy was interrupted, and changed into acute anguish, by the impetuosity and force of thought. His features were very much like those which painters have given to Roman characters, and a rich colour generally broke thro' his olive complexion. His face was such as sorrow could make more beautiful than pleasure; and viewing his distress, it was impossible not to admire the dignity with which he supported it.

Lorina would not attempt to decide on the cause of his unhappiness; this, however, lessened not her commiseration; and she frequently hoped that she should again, and in an early season, observe the returning smiles, and listen to the free voice, of so amiable a being.

She did not forget the appointment she had made; and on the following morning, she went alone to the lodgings of Russel. He was evidently pleased with her punctuality; but they had scarcely spoken to each other, when a servant entered, and told his master that the Colonel was below, and wished to see him for a few minutes.

Begging that Lorina would allow him to be absent, for a little while, he pointed to a piano forte, and left the room. She touched the keys, and turned over some old sheets of music; but finding nothing particularly interesting in them, she took up two or three books, which were lying on the instrument. One of them contained political tracts; another the history of a statesman in the last reign; and the third a beautiful poem, which had been recently published.

Lorina retained the last, and began to read it with a kind of intellectual epicurism.* It opened with sweetness and harmony. The imagery found a free way into her mind; and the sentiments had the warm approbation of her generous heart. She did not now consider herself alone; and she removed not her eyes, till she came to the twentieth page of the volume, where she found a loose paper, on which were written some lines, evidently by the hand of Russel, with which she was well acquainted.

Thinking it might have some connection with, or be a critique on, the verses she was reading, she laid the book down, and perused the little manuscript; in which she found the following stanzas, traced in loose and very irregular characters.

SLAVE of passion, and of pain,
Your complaints are idle, vain:
What avails it if you rove,
Murmuring, thro' the noiseless grove—
If you talk to seas and skies,
Of woman's magic form and eyes?

This is censuring what I do,
Oft, Lorina, oft for you!
Loathing my unquiet bed,
Bending low my troubled head,
Nightly I your name repeat,
In some lone and still retreat.

Ye are fair, ye clouds! I cry—
Yet, while your scattering fleeces fly
Across the moon, a face I know,
White as Siberia's tufted snow!
Then, speckled fugitives, you ne'er
Can boast of being half so fair.

And still a sweet, perennial rose,—
The world no lovelier boasting—blows
Upon the unprophaned cheek
Of that lov'd being, whom I'd seek
Wherever earth is found, if she
Would give one generous smile to me.

What, tho' the wint'ry wind be loud,
And storms descend from ev'ry cloud,
Harsh, frantic storms!—I, *then*, can trace
Eternal summer in her face;
And, viewing charms combined there,
Mock the white horsemen of the air!

But, wretch presumptuous, wretch forlorn!
Whose life is like the clouded morn,
Which promises no golden day,
Drive, drive your racking thoughts away,
And crush the adder in your breast,
That was a blooming love, carest!

In woodlands wild and intricate,
Hurl the curse at ruthless fate:
Or let your heart all joy forego,
Where broad and sullen waters flow;
Hid in the loneliest rocks, repine,
Despairing say—She is not mine!

E'en now the maniac's part I play,—
Lorina, blessed be each day
On which you open your mild eyes!
And, tho' a sated husband flies
To one less fair———

The last verse was unfinished. Astonishment fell heavy on Lorina. The beginning of the poem revealed a mystery, that filled her with pain and shame; the conclusion made her nearly frantic. Her hand lost the paper. She attempted to rise, in order that she might immediately quit the house; but she sunk down again with faintness, and saw Russel wildly rushing towards her.

His face was like that of a man labouring under distraction; his eyes quick and fiery; his action hurried and alarming. Passion, not prudence, was his guide. He threw his arm around the waist of Lorina, who could not disengage herself, and pointed to the paper that she had been reading.

"I can be no longer concealed from you," he cried: "You have discovered the nature of my malady, the disease that preys on my life, and will consume it. Oh, I could eternally curse the mischance, which led to this detection! I was wretched, and no hope told me I should be otherwise; yet I wished to shut up my misery in my own despairing breast, and never to confess the cause of it to any person. But my griefs are still to multiply! I have seen the pity of your countenance—heard the compassionate tones of your voice—But now, the one will be changed to indignation, and the other, perhaps, will execrate me, for harbouring those feelings, which God himself made the free properties of my heart."

"Let me hear no more," cried Lorina: "I must be gone: Russel, detain me not."

"I charge you not to leave me in this state. Merciful Heaven! You seem as if you were dying! I am the occasion of this; and, perhaps, hereafter may have cause to say, that I am your murderer! Look up, revive. Rest yourself upon my breast. Your situation terrifies me; and I must summon some other person to your assistance."

"Hold, hold!" exclaimed Lorina: "Remember who and where I am. Sir, Berrington is my husband!"

"Speak not of that to me!" cried Russel, franticly, "for, from the knowledge of that, arises the most insufferable misery. Every hour of my wretched life, I tell myself he is so. This thought is busy in the night, as well as in the day: My endeavour to expel it from my mind, only secures its establishment; and, after all my efforts, if I were told that my passion for you is unholy, what further could I do, what more forcibly convincing, than to point towards the supposed locality of the power from which it is derived. My head burns, Lorina! Turn not from me in anger. I ask you not, loving as I do, I *dare* not ask you for your love. But let me have your pity: Deprive me of that, and darkness and horror will hang over me eternally."

Lorina was still speechless and incapable of rising. She continued to look on the strangely varying face of Russel, and her terror increased.

"If I am now the object of your hatred," he continued, "I shall not long continue so. You may yet weep for me: And when you hear me spoken of, by those who shall know me, after you have sent me into wretchedness, sent me unpitied too, compassion shall be no longer a stranger to your bosom; and you shall mourn for the sufferings, which were too many for my endurance. I cannot be guilty in my love, tho' I am unfortunate. It was imposed on me: I called on reason to check it—strove to bear myself with virtue, and with honor; my thoughts and actions were strong and absolute compulsions. I had not known you a single day, before I esteemed you; the cherished sentiment grew into love; and I could not prevent myself from deeply cursing the destiny, that gave you over to Berrington."

"Then cease to curse it now," said Lorina, striving for fortitude: "Be your former self, and well consider the moral obligations, which are on the side of either of us."

"Cold, freezing philosophy! My warm, impetuous bosom would melt in an instant. If there are men, who can sit down, and calmly reckon the most serious misfortunes of life, I will not boast of adding to their number. No, no. My lonely lamentations must continue. Still must I heap the sharp invective, on what I have so often execrated—still trace the vision that will not fade, while the fillet of death shall be kept from my eyes. Oh, Lorina! Lorina! May you never know any of this wretchedness. You cannot participate my sorrows: You are deaf to my complaints: You contemn and abhor me."

"Indeed you are deceived in thinking so. But, in regarding you, I must not be forgetful of myself. You have alarmed and agitated me. These verses——"

"I thought not that they would ever come under your eye, nor believed they were to divulge the secret, which preyed on my consuming breast. The resolution of privacy, could not prevent me from communing with myself. There was a charm in your name: I thought I could not repeat it too often; and it has been frequently obliterated, by the weakness of my eyes—by the tears, the obstinate tears of a soldier. Laugh at me, ye insensible, and I shall be still unabashed. We must separate, and immediately too. Forget that I exist—forget all that is contained in the paper you have been reading; and bear your husband's well-dissembled contempt, with the fortitude which has of late distinguished you."

"My husband's contempt!" cried Lorina: "Oh, I have all his love! I am ever sensible of his uncommon tenderness."

"Vile, hypocritical Berrington! You have found, at least, one easy instrument to play on. By Heaven! it was, in part, your undeserved wrongs, which added to the strength of my love. Yet, why should I tear the veil from your eyes, when deformity stands before them? I have seen your patience and humanity, and wondered at them. Madam, he does not boast of continence abroad; and if he did, he is too well known to be believed. He may still treat you with apparent kindness; but where there is weariness, love must soon become a sluggard. I have observed him closely; and noticed him both abroad and at home. He would have walked the stage with some success; for his habits are close, and he has great powers of versatility. In one hour, he is the domestic, the smiling husband; and in the next, the gay, licentious, shameless adulterer!"

"This is the worst of calumnies!" exclaimed the agonised wife.

"It is the most melancholy of truths. Tell him of all that I have said, to his very face; and tho' his unsheathed sword be in his hand, I will repeat it. By some extraordinary means, I have a better knowledge of him, than any other man; and the baseness, the sycophancy and guilt of Lady Augusta, are as familiar to me, as things pertaining to myself. I do not thus decide, on any other opinion; my assertions are grounded on the evidence of my own disgusted eyes and ears. Oh, for God's sake, beware of that vile woman! She is deserving of the name, and almost of the station, which Milton has given to the mother of Death.* There is wickedness in her smile, and her heart is corrupted even to the core. She has, indeed, a brutal husband, to whom her commonness, tho' it is known, gives no disturbance. I go from you: We must not meet again. I am still alarmed by your agitation, and would have you endeavour to quiet it. Remain here for a while, dearest, best, and most unfortunate of women! I will watch without, and prevent all manner of intrusion. Farewell! I could not go into perpetual exile with an heavier heart. Whatever sentiments you entertain for me, may the blessings of every power that has the means to bless, whether it be such as claims supremacy in Heaven, or dwells in the noblest being of the earth, fall like the showers of spring upon your head."

Russel took the hand of Lorina, and pressed his lips on it; she attempted, with all her strength, to withdraw it; but he held it securely, and afterwards snatched a kiss from her glowing cheek. It was evidently an act which he himself condemned. He rushed immediately out of the room, and left Lorina in a situation, of which, for a few minutes, she was nearly insensible.

Fearing her senses would entirely fail her, and finding a most oppressive suppression of breath, she staggered to the window, and lifting up the sash, as high as she possibly could, seated herself in a place, where the current of the air came freely upon her face. This greatly revived her. Her strength and reason returned; and she soon rose, in order to quit the house, in which she had suffered so much pain and mortification.

The last action of Russel not only offended, but also alarmed her; she was apprehensive, lest he should again appear and repeat his freedoms. She, therefore, walked down the stairs with quickness, and thought herself fortunate, when she entered the street, without interruption. It was now absolutely necessary for her, to call all her energies into action; for, on her way, she was accosted by several military saunterers, and their usual train of expecting widows and wearied spinsters. She was entreated to join the party; but she excused herself, and hurried home.

Berrington was not within, which was somewhat satisfactory to Lorina, who went directly to her chamber, and yielded to the emotions, which she had with so much pain and difficulty suppressed. Her thoughts were many, impetuous and confused. She bound her clasped hands upon her forehead, and tears rushed into her painful eyes.

It was a considerable time before she received any interruption; at length, however, her servant came to inform her, that her husband did not dine at home, and to assist her in dressing. Lorina, not intending to change her clothes, dismissed her; but previously desired that her son might be sent to her. The boy soon appeared, full of frolic and sport. His mother caught him in her arms: his father's believed baseness now racked her imagination, and she could not prevent her anguish from growing strong and noisy.

Discretion may associate with love, while it continues an affection; but a desertion is always the result, when it becomes a passion. Lorina's heart was no cold composition of nature: It contained embers, which were easily fanned into heat and brightness; and a long continued association had damped none of the ardor of her first connections. She had, till within a few months, looked on Berrington with the eyes of enthusiasm. The charm, however, that bound her to him, was, in some degree, affected by her original doubts; these had been banished by the evident frankness and virtue of her suspected rival; and now they were excited again, strengthened, and corroborated, by the bold assertions of Russel.

Offended as Lorina was, by one particular action, she did not long entertain any anger when she thought of this man. He soon appeared to her more unfortunate than criminal. She repeated his words; remembered his looks and gestures; and it was not long before her resentment softened into pity and concern. She had too strongly admired his genius and qualities, to fall into sudden dislike. She owed him some mental obligations, and had not remarked his talents, without obtaining advantages from them. She believed that no man, who had so forcibly endeavoured to cultivate and improve the understanding, would ever design to corrupt the heart.

Had it not been for the untoward incident of the morning, she doubted not but that the secret of his misplaced affection would have been for ever in the sole possession of himself. She certainly had witnessed neither libertinism, nor gallantry; and many of the sentiments of Russel she could not condemn, tho' she dared not openly to approve. The honor which he still seemed to profess, and the manner in which he spoke of her situation, were Lorina's safeguards; and she resolved to avoid him for the future, tho' she lamented the necessity of doing so.

The subject of his passion, was not that on which she most deeply ruminated: A hundred times did she repeat the disgusting words of "a sated husband," and as often wish to be informed, by what particular means, the guilt of Berrington and Lady Augusta, became so well known to Russel. His accusation had been strong and peremptory: He had seen their foulness, and heard of it. Berrington might have spoken of his success; spoken proudly of it, and——Lorina was thinking this, and growing almost wild. The destroyer of domestic peace—Jealousy—Accursed jealousy! had entered, and barred itself within her breast.

The time had been, when she would have very severely reproved the conduct of any woman, acting as she herself then did. She would have contemned her impetuosity, and illiberality of mind, and thought the self-imposed vexations of such a person, wholly undeserving of pity and concern. She was, however, unconscious of her own precipitance and folly; for the hand of reason no longer guided her, and the poison which Russel administered, diffused its pernicious qualities, and found every part alike susceptible.

She lamented that prudence would not allow her to meet her informer again. It was risking too much, to put herself in the way of the impassioned Russel, of whose further remarks she was craving, tho' the preceding ones had wounded and nearly distracted her.

She went early to bed; but Berrington did not return till midnight, when he was informed that she was very unwell. He flew to her, and with his accustomed tenderness lamented her indisposition. For the first moment she thought him sincere; in the next, however, she viewed him as a suspected hypocrite, and turned away from him, coldly and without speaking. Berrington felt the force of this, and was offended. He believed caprice was her only malady: His love was wounded; his concern lessened; and he did not address himself to her again during the night.

The heart of Lorina was almost broken by this neglect, which she conceived not to be the effect of her own indiscretion. When he rose in the morning, she counterfeited sleep; and as soon as he had left the room, she opened her eyes, and tears gushed out of them. She continued in her chamber the greater part of the day. That any person in the world was more truly wretched, she did not believe; and, in order to alleviate her anguish, she spent nearly two hours in composing a letter, to apprise her mother of her fancied situation. This, however, she soon gave to the flames; she loved her parent too dearly to afflict her seriously; and she had still a hope of being reconciled to Berrington.

She wished for, yet dreaded his appearance, and felt much inclined to acknowledge her fault, and entreat his forgiveness, when they should meet again. But so inconsistent was she become, that she had scarcely formed this intention, before she despised herself for it. Her wrongs resorted once more to her mind, and she grew vindictive, rather than conciliatory.

Berrington beheld this conduct with amazement, with pain, and with anger. More than once he said to himself, "Can this be Lorina!" and, lamenting as he did this serious interruption of their happiness, (which he had believed would never be disturbed,) he wished her to return to reason without his guidance.

Westdale dined with them; and soon after the cloth was removed, Lorina left the room, and went to her chamber, where she endeavoured, for a while, to amuse herself with reading: But the shell of poetry no longer was filled with sweet sounds; and the song of genius was heard without applause. Having fretted herself into extreme weariness, she wished to take her accustomed ramble; but the dread of meeting Russel abroad prevented her.

The day was closing with uncommon beauty; the air thin; the sun went to the west with unclouded splendor, and the tranquil sea was beautified by his partial decline. From each side of the room a wide and sweetly diversified prospect was presented to the view of Lorina. The western, however, she regarded more particularly, and looked from the green turf of the meadows to the dark brow of the cliff, and from thence, obliquely, to waters so still and sparkling, that the eye of poetry might have traced in them, the gorgeous deity of the element and his sportive train.

The occupier of the house was a man of an active and mechanical genius. Many curious instruments, of his own construction, were in the different rooms; and an excellent telescope was placed in the apartment to which Lorina had retired. She frequently pointed it toward the numerous objects which moved distinctly before her, and served to fill up the wide and long-extended scene.

Looking out at the window, she saw what she supposed to be a large fleet, breaking the uniformity of the sea; and, applying her glass, she found that she had conjectured truly. What had before seemed fit only for the aquatic sports of Titana and her fays,* now appeared such as might have borne the legions of ancient Rome down the Tiber. Her mind was for a while diverted; but, altering the position of the instrument, she examined the rocky shore; and a figure of some interest came within the focus.

This was a man, sitting on the basement of a cliff, and in an attitude melancholy and dejected. He was dressed in military clothes; his head rested on his palm; and his hat and plume were lying by his side. He was at a considerable distance; yet the glass was so excellent, that Lorina was enabled to judge of the person; and tho' she could not wholly trace the minuteness of his features, she knew that they were those which she had lately gazed on with painful emotion, and that she now contemplated the form of Russel.

It was not vain for Lorina, after what she had recently seen and heard, to suppose that she might then be the object of his meditations—that he was cherishing a passion, which honor bade him extinguish, and lamenting a destiny never to be averted. She could do nothing more prejudicial to herself, than by giving him her pity. She sent her compassion to him, and instantly found she had been too generous for her own interest.

Perhaps there is nothing more delightful, tho' it may sometimes be dangerous, to turn our eyes from a person, of whose esteem we suspect ourselves to be wanting, and to fix them on another, of whose love we have strong assurances. It was, at least, so to Lorina, who thought with pain on the strangely misconstrued words and actions of Berrington, and was fascinated by the external sorrows of a man, many of whose equivocal opinions she made her own.

She remembered all he had said, on the preceding day, as well as the greater part of the poem; and the number of her censures very considerably decreased. She was, however, still virtuous: To an audacious love she would have replied with scorn and resentment; but the sentiments of Russel were of a different nature. She would have contemned herself for giving them encouragement; yet he had already convinced her, that it would be criminal for her to despise him, on account of the declaration into which he had been hurried.

There had been a time, perhaps, when Lorina would have examined those things in a different manner: When she might have suspected, there was no small degree of sophistry in what had been advanced, and more earnestly considered what was due to Berrington, and to the dignity of her own virtue. But a heavy cloud hung over the summer of her love; and it had gathered so quickly, that the clearness of her reason was no longer to be admired.

Russel kept his position a considerable time; but at length he arose, and traced the sands, still coming nearer to Lorina, whose eye seldom lost sight of him for a moment. His figure, as he advanced, became more distinct; and she believed, that she could really perceive a great degree of concern and uneasiness in his face. This, however, was an unwarranted remark; and it was not long before the wanderer totally disappeared.

Lorina afterwards went to the parlour, but found that Berrington and Westdale were gone into the town. On the return of the former, and when she was alone with him, she felt awkward and embarrassed. But he smiled on her with his usual fondness. His words were as kind as they had ever been; his conversation tender, affectionate, and domestic.

Lorina was nearly overpowered: She despised herself for her late conduct, and while her husband played with her laughing boy, and occasionally put him in her arms, she murmured inwardly, "God, what a wretch I have been!"

She became herself again—just such as she had been, before the interruption of her happiness. Every doubt was put to rest; she believed that she had been imposed on, and also that she had imposed on herself; and since her union, never had she known a happier night. In the morning she arose as gay as if she had yet to experience the first sorrow of human life; and Berrington was delighted by the alteration.

In the course of the day she saw Lady Augusta: Lorina trembled when she took her offered hand; but she was soon composed, and her heart discarded al its prejudices. If this variableness of disposition appear unnatural to some, those who have been actuated by love and jealousy, still free from the damning proof, will think differently of it. Lorina forgot all the insinuations of Russel; and tho' she ceased not to remember him, her sentiments were certainly much altered.

Lady Augusta was to depart on the following morning; she had taken a last farewell of the Colonel, who went out of town, as soon as he had put his name to the deed. The parting, on his side, was callous and indifferent; on her's it was apparently cold and formal, tho' she was glad to escape from notice, in order to relieve her overcharged heart.

The object that Lorina lately despised, she now very sincerely pitied; for, tho' Lady Augusta had recently said, that the hour of her separation would be joyful to her, yet her pale cheeks, swoln eyes, and often interrupted voice, shewed the strength of her present afflictions. She threw her arms around the neck, and wept on the bosom, of Lorina. Even with Berrington she did the same; and his wife strove to raise and comfort her.

Lorina had already been apprised of some of the designs of Lady Augusta, and others were now imparted to her. It was probable that they would never meet thereafter. The late enemy of the abandoned wife, now looked on her as a pensive and unfortunate exile, and the party continued in the most serious mood.

The visiter spent the greater part of the day with Berrington and Lorina; and as she had desired that the chaise might be ready for her at six the next morning, she arose, in order to bid them adieu. She kissed the boy, and tied her own picture around Lorina's neck, begging that, if the original were worthy of remembrance, she would sometimes look on it. Such actions and words as these, had a powerful effect on the heart of Berrington's wife; and she returned the embrace of Lady Augusta, whom she never saw thereafter. She really lamented the fate of her ladyship; yet she was, afterwards, somewhat pleased with the idea of her being asunder from Berrington.

The present joys of the enthusiast, compensated for all the pangs she had endured. Every thing looked clear and sunny. The time was a free holiday for happiness; and amid her regained delights, Lorina wondered that she had ever missed them. Nothing could be more gratifying, to her almost adoring husband, than her looks and behaviour. He pitied her past delusions; and, not having the power of speaking of them, without leading toward a subject, in regard to which he could not be explicit, he strove, by the tenderest assiduities, to increase the number of her smiles.

The peace of Lorina was never interrupted, except when she thought of the recent declaration and behaviour of Russel, who was now become a stranger to the house. Few people could have heard him complain, without being affected; for there was such a beautiful expression in his face, and so much softness in his cadences, that neither the eye which saw, nor the ear which listened to him, could forbear to admire and approve. That he was strangely deceived, in respect of Berrington's infidelity, she had no longer any doubt; and she believed his opinions had been as illiberal as her own. Still she had reason to think he was no common slanderer; and, tho' she now censured his precipitance, she did not suppose he had been actuated by a vicious disposition.

Berrington was not a little surprised, that Russel should discontinue his visits to a place, where he had confessedly found much pleasure. He had still daily intercourse with him; and tho' all his invitations were declined, he could discover no breach of friendship.

Westdale laughed, when this singularity of temper was mentioned to him; for he supposed that Russel was employed in some new gallantry, and that the object of his present pursuit was the occasion of his frequent rambles abroad. But whenever Berrington spoke of it to his wife, it was with extreme difficulty that she concealed her embarrassment. She was always anxious to point the discourse some other way, and desirous of appearing indifferent, even when she was seriously interested.

She did not see Russel, except when she made use of the telescope, during the month which succeeded their serious interview. One morning, however, she met him in the town. Berrington was with her. Russel could not possibly pass them, in silence, without extreme rudeness; and on coming up to them, he bowed to Lorina, and made some enquiries concerning her health.

For a moment, her distress was scarcely to be endured. She withdrew her arm from Berrington, lest he should ask the cause of its trembling; and it was fortunate for her, that her veil concealed the colour of her heated cheeks. But the conduct of Russel soon restored her. He addressed her with a serious composure; and his formality served to quiet her perturbations.

Berrington requested him to turn, and walk with them, and he accordingly complied. Very little of his conversation was directed towards Lorina: He talked to her only on indifferent subjects; and she believed, that he was not only ashamed of the confession he had made to her, but also convinced that he had spoken unjustly of her husband.

Perhaps it may be thought, by some readers, that Lorina ought to have shewn strong resentment, to the man who had offended her delicacy, and aspersed the conduct of her husband. But her character is not intended to be drawn as a perfect one; nor is it meant, in all respects, as an example for those, who have the desire of acting in a manner which the good and prudent may approve.

The principles by which she was directed, arose from purity and honor; her judgment, however, sometimes proved a weak nurse to them; and while she viewed the beauties of human nature, she searched not for its spots and corruptness. With an abhorrence for crime, she had a pitying eye for error; and she seldom with-held her pardon, from those who neither committed premeditated wrong, nor called on design to fashion their bad actions.

She had never hesitated a moment, in detaching Russel from criminality; and she could lay no very heavy blame on many of those sentiments, of which her own had been quick precursors. The present behaviour of Russel was so gratifying to Lorina, and shewed such a return of discretion, that she was pleased to hear Berrington invite him to dinner. This he was on the point of declining; but when she joined in the request, he held out no longer.

He promised to be with them at five o'clock, and punctually observed the hour. Westdale met him at the table, where harmony and good sense presided. Russel was the most serious person of the party; but he occasionally smiled at the volubility of Westdale; conversed on military and political topics with Berrington; and spoke to Lorina with a calm voice.

He was convinced, by her behaviour, that her marriage confidence, in spite of the recent shock, was unimpaired; and before he left the house, he seized an opportunity of making a recantation. This he did, while Berrington and Westdale went out to look at a horse, which the former was contracting for. Russel had seen it in the morning; he therefore did not join them, and Lorina had no excuse for leaving the room.

The door closed, and the officers were almost immediately observed to be passing the window. Lorina found her situation very unpleasant; and her distress increased, when she glanced at the changing countenance of Russel, and found him preparing to speak to her.

"By your conduct to-day," he cried, "I am still further assured of the excellence of your heart, and the nobleness of your mind. Prejudice lives in neither of them: I have found the one a depository of quick, but generous feelings; and been convinced, that reason seldom becomes a wanderer from the other. I have given you pain, and very serious offence. Acting as I have done, I shall for a long time abhor myself; but, however I may contemn the deed, still am I left to a melancholy examination of the impulse. Madam, I dare not say much on a theme like this; and I will become the martyr of my feelings, rather than speak of them again. In some degree I have been a conquerer; and in those resolutions which I believe to be virtuous, I will persevere. There has been much toil, much difficulty. On the benefits that may arise, I have not yet ventured to calculate."

"They will come to your heart without reckoning," said Lorina, "and to your mind with——"

"Hold! hold! I cannot yet listen to promises of good, without fearing deception. But all that is necessary for me now to do, is to apologize for my late rudeness: Calling it so, however, is a misnomer—I ought to have used the word insanity. To forget, to regard you with indifference, will be impossible. But I swear—In the present hour of penitence, I solemnly protest that I will respect your peace, and never dare to give it the least disturbance. I have injured Berrington too——"

"You have, indeed," cried Lorina, with quickness: "my heart long since assured me of it."

"My meeting him here, on the terms of friendship, shews I have been in some manner deceived. I spoke too freely of him, and examined him too nicely. The gaieties of his disposition seemed to me so peculiar, that I could not avoid noticing them; and, as to those gallantries, which were, perhaps, allowable——"

"Sir, he had no gallantries. You were mistaken; led away by the idleness of report. There is a singleness in his love, of which I should be unworthy, were I to put an ungenerous suspicion on it."

"May you enjoy it till the last hour of your life! And let infamy fall on the woman, who attempted to rob you of it. The dissimulating, the wanton wife of Heyland, is gone from hence; and never may she return, to corrupt fidelity, or to stab the bosom of virtue."

"This is most cruel and illiberal," cried Lorina: "Did I not believe your prejudices to be rooted, I would endeavour to convince you, that she is——"

"I *am* convinced, that nature never put into a female more corruptness. She has smiled on you, and called for your sympathy. Patience! the arts of that abominable hypocrite would make me mad. But let me mention her no more. In your presence, I ought not to breathe the name of a woman, who had the effrontery to declare to her husband, that she entertained an illicit passion for another man—For one, too, who had solemnly sworn, before God, to love you in every season; to solace and bless you as long as he existed!"

"Good Heaven!" exclaimed Lorina, "what are you talking of? Surely you have lost your senses!"

"I frequently wish I had parted with them for ever: And there are times, when meeting an idiot, I feel a desire to transfer to him the properties of my mind, and to become the possessor of his steril brains. But, see, your husband, my friend, returns. Oh, madam, I implore you not to despise me! With-hold not your confidence from me: It will serve as a guide, to lead me back to reason; and you shall find, that I will perform nothing short of what I have promised."

Lorina was discomposed by this conversation; and fearful of trusting herself any longer in the room, she left it as soon as Berrington and Westdale entered. She found that she was not become an uninteresting object to Russel, many of whose words nearly led her again into the dangerous paths, which she had but recently quitted.

His information, in regard to Lady Augusta, for a while had a strange effect on her. After a considerable time spent in reflection, she believed it was only calumny, and did not think it very improbable, but that Russel had been credulously listening to the gross slanders of a vile and libertine husband. She was conscious of the horrors of her late situation, and dreaded lest she should fall into it again.

But she struggled with, and conquered, her passions. She still answered the smiles of her husband, with which she never failed to meet; and she looked on the delusions of Russel with pity and concern.

His renewed visits were more numerous than they had ever been, and Lorina wished to see him less frequently. Whenever any other person was present, his behaviour to her was reserved and respectful. She was seldom alone with him; for, tho' he introduced not the topic, that tended both to distress and displease her, yet there was an expression in his face, which she could not misunderstand, and a melancholy tone in his voice, which was not to be heard without seriousness and commiseration.

His dejection was remarked, as well by Berrington as Westdale: each of them endeavoured to trace its source; and by frequently enquiring of Lorina, what she suspected to be the cause of it, they drove her into such confusion, as was with difficulty only concealed.

Colonel Heyland returned the day after the departure of his

wife, on whom his thoughts seemed not to dwell, even for a moment. Not only by report, but also by a paragraph in a morning paper, Lorina soon learned, that Lady Augusta had been seen publickly in London, but that she continued in the capital a very short time, and had since quitted the kingdom.

Berrington frequently spoke of the woman to whom he owed his present prosperity, with a feeling heart; and Lorina, entertaining scarcely one of her former prejudices, mentioned her in similar terms, and wished that she had experienced a better and more gentle fate. She joined not with those babblers, who were noisy in her ladyship's concerns. She heard, with extreme disgust, that the Colonel was the foulest of her censurers; and tho' she no longer strove to make a proselyte of Russel, she thought him very illiberal, and somewhat malignant.

The visits of this singular man began to be truly distressing to Lorina; and she sometimes blamed herself severely for continuing to meet him. Tho' she was pained by his attentions, it was scarcely possible to be seriously offended by them. He was, apparently, the greater sufferer. His character was changed, his person altered. He had no longer an inclination for mirth; his sentiments lost much of their strength, and the former peculiarities of his genius were not, in many seasons, to be distinguished.

Had he disregarded the promise he made to Lorina, of not renewing the subject that had pained and offended her, she certainly would have entirely declined seeing him. But, silent as he was in that respect, his conduct still conjured up many fears and vexations; and she was greatly alarmed, lest his actions might be observed by those who were around him, and particularly by Berrington.

While her husband was present, Russel did not often look at her face; but, in his absence, his eyes fixed on her, with a wild, terrifying expression; and she sometimes feared the desertion of his reason. He was frequently desirous of reading to her; and she could not always decline hearing him. His selections were beautiful and pathetic: His languid mind, on those occasions, would recal its former powers; his voice rise with the words of anguish, and sink with those of despair; and in his eyes there was a tear, ever in readiness for the sentiment that claimed it.

Lady Augusta had been gone two months; and Lorina and Berrington were living in a state of happiness, which met with no interruption. The conduct of Russel alone was unpleasant to the former. She was now more guarded against his private visits, and much concerned to meet with him one evening, at some distance from the house.

Berrington had dined from home; and believing that Russel would be of the party, she took her boy in her hand, and strolled thro' the fields, which were soon to be covered with the snows of winter. Russel came upon her very unexpectedly. She was apprehensive of the tenor of his discourse, and, in order to avoid it, almost immediately proposed to return. But this he protested against with vehemence. His voice, however, instantly fell, and he supplicated her not to leave him.

She was alarmed by his accents: The strangeness of his countenance also agitated her; and she trembled while he continued to hold her arm. "Captain Russel," she cried, "I entreat you will allow me to go forward, and never again insult the wife of a man, whom you call a friend, by speaking to her in the manner to which you have of late accustomed yourself."

"Insult you!" exclaimed Russel, pressing his lips on her hand.

"Sir, I have said the word; and, indeed, it has been too long with-held. Even your present conduct is cruel and unjustifiable. I must be gone: I will not be detained another moment."

"How you may determine hereafter," said Russel, with a voice hurrying from solemnity to wildness, "shall be no concern of mine; but now, I could bend myself as low as the earth, and implore you to hear me.—Nay, did not that avail, I would grasp you fast in my arms, and bid you look upon the frantic wretch, whose compulsions you could not resist!"

"Merciful God! Do you retain your senses? You alarm me—you frighten my poor boy!"

"Fate sent me into the world, among her curses and terrors. But, listen to me: I repent for what I have done, and promise to atone for it."

"Let me see you at some other time: in some other place."

"You must hear me now—on this very spot. You have avoided me, as if contagion had put her filthy garments on my back; and I have watched for you, with many serious disappointments. At home, you regarded me, sometimes with coldness, and sometimes with apprehension: and abroad, you have shunned me as studiously, as if you believed nature had deviated from her old courses, and given to a tyger the form of man. Why was this? Why, why, I say?"

"Sir, I am a wife, proud of her first-placed affections, and not forgetful of the covenant she made before her God!—I would neither turn into the path of error, nor tamely listen to the insulter of my love."

"Insulter! And that name applied to me? Oh, most unjust, most cruel and unnatural! Look in my face, and sink the appellation. Where is the fire of my eye—the flush of my cheek—the high, imperious spirit of my breast? One of them has been blighted by sorrow; the thievish hand of affliction has snatched away another; and of the third I have lost all knowledge. Madam, I have not now many words to use; yet I could wish not to be a creature so abhorrent to you. I sought for this interview for a few purposes only. It was chiefly to tell you that the man, who is hateful to your eyes, will soon remove himself from them for ever. I am compelled to fly from the post of honor and distinction, and have contracted for the disposal of my commission. A corroding passion drives me from the station, which glory would have me maintain; and when I shall fix myself in a private one, what will there be to console me?"

"Reason: the largest gift of a mighty bestower! which, depending not on localities, you ought to exercise here, and in all other places; at this, and every other time."

"Such a reply I expected from you. Prejudiced as you are, you must ever be amiable. Were I a boy, with a mind infested with romance, and heated by a fantastic love, I should deserve this treatment. But such I am not: The idleness and follies of youth are not my guides. I am the powerless victim of an uncontrollable sentiment; I search for energies which I have not; and, however you may chide me, I shall cease to blame myself, because I am fully convinced that I have been, and still am, virtuous to the extent of all my capacities. You start—you frown upon me—Your eye reproaches a suspected immorality. I will only make one little request of you, madam; and if you accede to it, I will instantly depart, and never give you disturbance again."

"Captain Russel, pray do not ask me to act unworthily. You know my situation."

"Yes, and pity you—Deep as my own distresses are, by Heaven I pity you!"

"Now you are still more incomprehensible."

"Let me remain so: I have only to entreat, that you will take this paper, and read it at your leisure. Surely you cannot object to this, when I inform you, that we are to meet no more. What! For ever—Silent and unknown for ever! Yes, sacred virtue, I swear it shall be so! You will, hereafter, have nothing to fear, and little that is contained in this packet relates to me. Must I see the person whom most I esteem, unconsciously beset by dangers, and not point them out to her? You spoke of your situation—Good God! I am terrified when I think of it; and more so, when I calculate the unseen evils, which are pressing towards you."

"What do you mean!—Why are you ever disturbing my tranquillity?"

"Let me have no questions now. Will you take the letter?"

"No. My present thoughts do you no honor, sir. Artifice shall not persuade me, that I have any concern in this."

"Oh, cruelty and insult!—But I was born to suffer. I must teach myself patience, and not struggle to break the chain, that was made purposely to bind me. For myself I have no further care; but when I think of you, I am almost hurried into distraction. You are guided by error; that *poisonous*, *black*, *insinuating worm* partly twines around, and partly buries itself in your heart, still allowing an exterior beauty to the worst of your actions. Do you not understand me?"

"No. But you have the means of frightening me. Why is this mystical language addressed to me?"

"You hate me for speaking, and despise me for remaining with you. Does not the smile which we bestow on vice, constitute criminality in ourselves? Does not the soft, approving countenance, make us as base, as if we had lent our hands, for the performance of the villain's deed, and applauded him with voices which might be caught even by the ears of deafness? Here my sweet boy! Carry this to your mother; and at the same time say to her—'If *you* can tamely suffer wrong, let me not live under the eye of dissimulation and perjury, and find, when reason shall have grown with my years, that I am tainted by the precepts of the foulest tutor.'—Farewell, poor child! My love for you is only answered by the indignation of your blinded mother."

He departed precipitately. Lorina, nearly fainting, seated herself on a bank, and her boy stood by her side, holding the paper. She snatched it from him, and put it into her bosom. No longer could she doubt but that there really was an important mystery. She hurried home, and, retiring to her chamber, broke the seal of the packet which she had before rejected.

She was devouring the words which Russel had written; and the following were the first that met her eye.

"I have for several days looked for an opportunity of putting these papers into your hands. Regard not, for the present, what I have written below. Read the enclosed; and do not suffer your injuries to overpower you. You have a thousand virtues, and may they all give you support."

Lorina put aside the envelope, and with trembling hands took the enclosure. It was directed to Mr. Saville, at the post-office. The characters were those of Lady Augusta Heyland: Lorina knew them to be such; and she traced them with sickness and terror. The epistle was couched in the underwritten words.

"Still, my dear Saville, must I trouble you with my complaints—still talk to you of my mind's inquietude, and my heart's afflictions. They are many and deep; but they may, hereafter, be otherwise, tho' there is nothing cheering in the prospect on which I am now looking.

"I am writing to you on a bed of sickness: I have really been very ill; and the heats of fever are still lodged in me. Perhaps you will be greatly surprised, to find that I have not left England; but my indisposition has been too serious to allow of a removal.—After our separation, I continued some little time in London; and stove to banish my gloomier thoughts, by entering into the gaieties of the town. This, however, was not within my power. The women of fashion could not lead me into pleasure: The insects of stronger wings flew around me, unregarded; and I found myself too weak to bear the glance of the *knowing*, and to remark the closing and opening eyes of the insinuative.

"I resolved to retire immediately, and cared not whether I was ever seen thereafter, to be remembered. I, therefore, procured a paragraph to be inserted in a morning paper, which you probably either saw, or heard of. Then I left London, and, under an assumed name, took a small lodging for myself and my servant near Blackheath.* Indisposition came upon me immediately; but I have been well attended, and the danger that threatened me is past. My present situation, however, is gloomy and uncomfortable. What can be more distressing than lying, unable to rise, upon a sick and loathed bed, which no solacing friend ever approaches!

"Saville, I never felt myself an outcast, till I came hither. My good spirits are fled; and not possessing the virtue of resignation, I will not take to myself the vice of boasting of it. Friend! My best, my only friend, why are you not near to comfort me? Could I see you for a single hour, I think I should be better. I have something new to say to you, which relates to my little girl, the hidden pledge of my secret, unavowed love. I dare not write to you on this subject. You will be a kind father to her, and bestow on her as much affection as you give to your boy—of this I feel assured.

"And is it impossible for us to meet again? Have you any inclination, and can you contrive to come to me for a few days? Invent something ingenious: Do it, however, without exciting the curiosity of your wife, with whom I would not have you bargain for a long absence. What I have already written, has been with pain and difficulty. Should you take the journey I have proposed, you must enquire for Mrs. Stanley, at the house of a mason, whose name is Bolton—My energies are quite spent. Adieu, my friend; and if I am not to have the happiness of seeing you, deprive me not of the pleasure of hearing from you immediately."

Lorina read this, and became most wretched and indignant. Her quick imagination supplied her with that which she conceived duplicity wished to with-hold; and, impatient to know more, she hurried on to the continuation of Russel.

"What I desired you to peruse discovers, I think, no small degree of baseness and hypocrisy; and if the writer of it be ill, as she represents herself, the tear of pity would be worthlessly bestowed on her. Do you not see thro' her poor artifices and designs? Is it not evident she has already obtained many private gratifications, and is impatient for their renewal? I have no doubt but that this letter was designed for, and received by, your husband. He dropt it at my lodgings, a few days ago; and I think the nature of it, will prevent him from making any enquiry concerning his loss.

"You have nursed this beautiful serpent in your bosom, and censured me, when I warned you of its with-held sting. It is now darting forth—It will shoot itself into your heart, and fill you with the most deadly poison. Wicked, corrupt, infamous woman! I would have her stript of her exterior garb, and, with all her deformities in view, given to the notice of scorn and derision. How shamefully has Berrington disposed of his honor and integrity! They must have been acquainted at a former period; certainly before her marriage with Colonel Heyland. The child she speaks of is, perhaps, nearly as old as your boy; and while Berrington might have joyfully regarded the promised fruit of a married love, he was, probably, engrafting a scion, on an apparently beautiful, but corrupt, tree."

Lorina uttered a faint scream; and, in order to stop her voice, she threw herself on the bed, and placed her face on the pillow.

In the course of a few minutes, however, she arose, and read the concluding part of the letter.

"I should have returned the enclosed, without making myself acquainted with its contents, had it been properly directed. But of Mr. Saville I knew nothing; and not being assured that it was actually the property of Captain Berrington, I thought it not improper to unfold it. I found the equivoque* paltry; the characters and intentions of the parties plain. Tho' I was convinced, you could not come to a knowledge of the vile affair, without being pained and mortified, yet I resolved to apprise you of it, in order that the natural child of your husband, might not be imposed on you, by any stratagem of its guilty parents.

"Perhaps Berrington is wearied by his many pleasures, and has no longer a relish for them. If such be the case, Lady Augusta will not have his consolations; but should the appetite of adultery be still craving, he will neither decline her invitation, nor want a well-sounding excuse for his journey.

"Madam, your peace and happiness are most dear to me. I sincerely pity you. Berrington has my contempt; and Lady Augusta Heyland my detestation. Whatever gives you pain, must be the occasion of concern to me; and as I am so soon to tear myself from a woman, who inspired me with joys which, in an early season, changed to the most corrosive of sorrows, I am truly miserable, that I must depart, while she is surrounded by smiling enemies, and deceived by atrocious falsehoods. It will not become me, openly to resent the conduct of your husband: But I shall regard him with a secret horror, and be suspicious of the friendship of that man, who transfers his love from a virtuous wife, to a woman in whom there is nothing but vice. And that woman is Lady Augusta, who will probably put aside his legitimate son, in order that room may be made for his natural daughter.

F. RUSSEL."

Lorina's agony increased; her thoughts corresponded with those of Russel; and she again believed, that she had been assailed by perfidy and dissimulation. Her doubts of error were few, and those were soon converted into certainties of a different nature. She referred her memory to particular periods, and concluded that Berrington—the faithless, smiling Berrington!—had been indifferent to his vows, before Lady Augusta went to Italy.

The absurdities of this supposition were not perceived; for she was blinded by passion, and racked by increasing jealousies. The lately subdued monster rose again, with ten-fold strength; and she scarcely dared to trust herself in the presence of the alternately beloved and detested Berrington.

She was, at intervals, inclined to talk to him, with the loud voice of resentment; but her courage failed her, when she thought herself most strong; and her tongue had no power to express the sufferings of her heart. Had perfidy placed a seal on his forehead, it could not have added to the conviction of Lorina. She regarded herself as the weariness of Berrington, and the ridicule of Lady Augusta. The fondness of the former now filled her with disgust, and she turned from him saying, indistinctly, "hypocrisy! detestable hypocrisy!"

The third day after she had received the letters from Russel, her husband spoke of an intended journey to London. On hearing this, the gentleness of her nature wore away. Rage rose within her breast; but she resolved to confine it there, and also to teach herself to be as indifferent to his pursuits, as she wished to be in regard to his person. She did not oppose him: She asked no questions. The alledged cause of his absence appeared to her very satisfactory; and never, till his departure, did the smile of malice disgrace her lovely features. Her cheek was not withdrawn, when he offered to kiss it. She sarcastically waved her hand to him, when he rode from the door; and as soon as he was beyond her sight, she franticly beat her breast, and tore the hair from her head.

Lady Augusta, previous to her separation, had agreed to write to Berrington, substituting the name of Saville for his own. He was much surprised to find her still in England, and greatly concerned, when he was informed of her serious indisposition. To alleviate her distresses was his desire, and he resolved to undertake the journey which she had proposed.

Culpable as some of her actions had rendered her, he was not without a considerable degree of esteem; and there was a plaintiveness in some parts of her letter, which, added to her deserted state, called for all the pity of his heart. The loss of it made him for awhile uneasy; but believing that, on account of the precaution which had been taken, and the want of real names, it could be productive of no mischief, he soon became more quiet and satisfied.

The peace of Lorina was always of the highest importance to him. Tho' she possessed a mind in many respects excellent, he knew there was still an imperfection in it, which was apparently unimprovable. Perhaps he loved her rather more for her tenacity. He never saw in her the fretfulness and spleen of common jealousy. The fancied injury seemed to strike at her heart; and, suffering deeply, she sought no remedy in the usual loquacity and murmurs of a deluded wife.

His present domestic state was so calm and happy, that the least interruption would have seemed dreadful; and he meant to dedicate only a few days to Lady Augusta. He flattered himself, that the excuse he formed for his journey was very plausible; and the counterfeit of Lorina was so complete, that neither pain nor suspicion troubled him.

He made not the least delay on the road, and found no difficulty in discovering the retreat of his correspondent, who received him with tearful eyes, but with a joyful heart. Berrington beheld her with pity and surprise; affliction had greatly altered her; and the big spirit that once resided in her breast, seemed wholly subdued.

The motives of Lady Augusta might not, perhaps, be thought sufficiently important for her request; for she had little, that was new, to say to Berrington, and had written to him, when the wish to see a true friend was strong in her heart, and when she apprehended that disease would return, and more seriously molest her.

While Berrington was consoling the afflicted, Lorina was alternately falling into dejection, and raving with resentment. A mighty blow had been struck at her peace: A hundred times in every day, did she read the detested letter of the destroyer of her happiness; and, instead of avoiding Russel, she freely admitted him, believing that he was the sincerest friend she now retained. He was her counsellor and guide: That he loved her still was evident; but he suffered his passion to feed on him; and, tho' his wretchedness was great, he seldom complained of it.

From him Lorina learned, that Westdale was well acquainted with her husband's propensities, and the principal assistant in his amour. After having heard this, she loathed the sight of him. She avoided the amiable looking hypocrite as much as possible, and wondered that deceit could ever be found, where there was such an appearance of sincerity.

Berrington had been gone ten days, before Lorina heard from him. He promised to return within that time; and now she received a letter, which informed her that, in consequence of a fall from a horse, it would be impossible for him to travel till the end of the ensuing week.

Lorina, for a moment, believed the accident had really happened; and her concern shewed that she could love him still. But when she put the letter into the hands of Russel, he gave her another, which he had just received from London, and by which it appeared, that Berrington and Lady Augusta were living together, and under one name, in elegant lodgings in May-fair. Russel entreated her to be calm. His sentiments were tender and impressive; and his tears frequently mingled with those of the unhappy wife.

The time passed away, and she still looked for Berrington: But she received another letter, which contained, as she supposed, a repetition of a most odious lie; and she resolved not to send any answer to the despicable fabricator. There were times, when she felt as if she were growing mad; and, almost fearful of trusting herself alone, she was now always happy when Russel came to her.

One evening he continued with her till an unusually late hour. He contrived to make his discourse most interesting; and the countenance he wore was admirable and fascinating.—Lorina, where was your reason straying, and whither had your guardian angel fled? Your face had ever been the emblem of innocence; and nothing could be supposed more pure and virtuous than your lovely bosom; yet—Oh, let the tear of sorrow mingle with that of indignation! Lost! Lost Lorina! you have committed a crime, which ever was your abhorrence—you have done a deed that, if fate cut you not off, will make your death-bed a rack, and your soul dreadfully fearful of eternity.

The adulteress, with eyes instantly opening to the crime, made the more conspicuous figure. The foul and impetuous passion fled from her breast, leaving a wide space for the entrance of horror; and the burning blush of shame covered her face and bosom. She released herself from the arms of Russel: For a few minutes she remained speechless, with one of her hands pressed on her forehead, and the other on her agonised heart. But, roused from this state, she franticly threw herself on the floor, and beat away the arm that attempted to raise her.

"Leave me here to perish!" she cried; "for such is the fate I deserve. Oh, I am so full of wickedness, that I dare not look upon myself! Continue no longer with me, or you will make me really mad. Berrington! Husband! May my eyes be closed by death before your return."

Russel was alarmed by her violence and grief. His efforts to quiet her were unavailing, and he knew that his continuing alone with her any longer, would beget suspicion among the servants.

Some person knocked at the door, to which Lorina went with affright. She there found the girl who waited on the child, and learned that her boy was awake, and sobbing for his mother to come to him. Desiring her attendant to shew Captain Russel to the door, she rushed up stairs, and took her child to her bosom. He soon became quiet, and slept again. The girl returned in a few minutes; but Lorina dismissed her, and spent a night of horror and repentance. She strove not to justify the act: She had fallen, rather than walked, into vice. Still she believed that none more guilty than herself was in existence, and was tempted to do an act of violence, which would have accelerated the doom she trembled to think on.

Russel felt neither pain, nor remorse. He was enraptured with his present success; and, in spite of the grief and upbraidings of Lorina, he calculated joys which were to follow.

Let shame rest heavily on those, who would teach the unskilled to respect the amiable exterior of vice. In the reading of fictitious history, the pleasure is small indeed, if we cannot, for a while, really bring ourselves to love the good, and despise the bad characters which support it. Should any one have examined the portrait of Russel with an approving eye, or applauded any of his sentiments, he is now called upon to detest the former, and to execrate the duplicity of the latter.

He was, most truly, a villain—a crafty, cruel and despicable villain! When he first came to a knowledge of Lorina, he was filled with brutal desires. He marked her for his prize, and at length obtained her. He suited himself, on all occasions, to her disposition, and of her principal failings took every possible advantage. The verses she found in the book, had been purposely put into it. Artifice instructed him to wear those looks, which afterwards excited her pity; as well as to speak in those tones, which seemed to issue from the breast of sorrow. He forged the letter that had been last shewn to Lorina, and became the most corrupt of liars. The accomplished villain exulted in his success. He was proud of those capabilities, which made him the possessor of a beautiful woman; and the violation of decency, as well as every humane and moral thought, was sunk and forgotten in the gratifications of his corrupt heart.

On the morning which followed Lorina's apostacy,* he presented himself again before her. She was afraid to refuse him admittance; but when she came to him, she clasped her hands in agony, and wept aloud. Her boy was at the other end of the room; he was, however, surrounded with toys, and did not notice the extreme agitation of his mother.

Russel endeavoured to soften her grief; and, for awhile, he put aside the looks of triumph, and assumed those of tenderness and sympathy. But Lorina's anguish was not to be appeased. She accused herself of being the most guilty wretch, that was then living under the eye of God; and protested that she wished her life to end, before the return of her injured husband.

There was something dreadful in her looks and voice: A fearfulness that must have filled every observer with terror; and a wildness which seemed to spring from insanity. Horror, remorse and despair, had the possession of her alternately heated and shivering breast. Russel admitted, that passion had carried him too far; but he professed an ardent love for her, and entreated her to elope, and put herself entirely under his protection.

"What!" exclaimed Lorina; "shall I fly from my child, my—I would have said my husband?"

"Is it, as you have acted, more honorable to stay with him?"

"Oh, madness! Madness! As I have acted? Cruel, unfeeling man! Boy, do not turn your pretty eyes on your disgraced mother."

"Why do you cry?" said the child: "I do not know what you mean: I thought you had been my *dear* mother."

"Do you hear him?" cried Lorina, hysterically: "Do you hear him Russel?"

"For God's sake, for mine, and for your own, release yourself from these terrors."

"Oh, my soul! My perjured, condemned soul! I have disgraced the virtuous woman who bore me: Still more disgraced the man who once loved, and, perhaps, even now loves me; and proved the lasting shame of my tender child. In the world, I shall meet with no more respect; I shall find no mercy in Heaven!"

Her despair was too deep for the reach of comfort, and Russel's efforts were unavailing. He continued with her about an hour, when he was compelled to go to the parade, and to leave the penitent in severe affliction.

Berrington returned in the evening of the same day, and folded his loving arms around his wife, who started from him with horror. But she attempted to conceal her feelings, and after the first moments of their meeting, to put on a necessary disguise. She first considered him as a wretch, unworthy of her notice; her own crimes, however, rushed upon her memory, and she dropped speechless in a chair.

Berrington, terrified and almost distracted, clasped one of her hands, and laid her giddy head against his breast; while, with a hurried voice, he enquired the cause of her extreme agitation.

"I am ill," she replied; "dreadfully ill—sick almost to death. Send the girl to me, and let me be led to my chamber."

He took her in his arms, and carried her up stairs. She could not resist the action. He laid her gently on the bed, kissed her cold lips, and hung over her with sorrow. This conduct was agonising to the guilty Lorina; she filled the ears of her husband with a shriek, and sank into a frightful swoon.

Berrington called up the girl, and ran for medical assistance, by which Lorina was brought to a recollection of her dreadful situation. The first object she saw, was the man whom she had injured. She was sensible enough to perceive, that his eyes were filled with tears, his cheeks bloodless; and that his whole countenance denoted love and misery. "Is he guilty?" she said inwardly: "Oh, God, I cannot believe it!" She hid her face in the pillow; and, not knowing what she did, imprinted her nails in her beautiful bosom.

As soon as she could speak, she declared herself better, and wished only the servant to continue with her. Berrington accordingly retired; but, before he left the bedside, she took his hand, and pressed her lips upon it. He was amazed and agonised by her actions, which seemed almost to arise from madness. He returned often to the room, in order to look at and speak to her; but every time he found her more disturbed; and while he called her by the tenderest of names, he could hear nothing, except exclamations of pain and sorrow.

At length she became silent, and continued so nearly two hours. She then enquired of the girl, whether her master was alone, and being informed that Captain Russel was with him, she quickly left her bed, and wrote a short note to him, which she desired the servant to put into his hand, when he should be leaving the house. The person Lorina now employed, tho' illiterate and ignorant, had some degree of cunning. She was very fond of those things, which she called fine clothes; and Lorina gave her a gown, which she had long admired, in order that she might be more particular in the business.

Lorina had formed a desperate plan; and convulsions tore her bosom, while she waited for the departure of Russel, and the reappearance of her agent, who, at length again entered the chamber, and informed her mistress, that she had privately given the note to the person to whom it was addressed.

Lorina shivered at her own enormities: Berrington soon came to her; and when she told him she was better, he raised his hands and thanked God. He desired the girl to retire, and prepared to undress himself. Lorina, still dwelling on her own defilement, hastily raised herself, and entreated that she might be suffered to sleep alone. He was not immediately agreeable to this; but she renewed the request, and in the course of half an hour he withdrew to another chamber; and the girl went to a sofa, which had been placed in the dressing room.

The horrors of the sleepless Lorina, throughout the night, could be but feebly described. In the morning, however, she declared herself better; and at an early hour she received an answer from Russel, who had given it, with five guineas, to the agent of the former concern. The bribe seemed inexhaustible; and the mystery of the correspondence was destroyed, by the anticipated pleasures of dress and playhouse amusements.

Lorina read the note. Her countenance changed: She shewed a transitory satisfaction; and then her sighs almost deepened into groans. Recollecting what she had promised to perform, she thought it necessary to try her strength; and, leaving her bed, she giddily staggered to the window, near which she was discovered by Berrington, who viewed her altered form, and death-like cheeks, with most painful emotions.

She could have met his frowns, but his smiles nearly killed her. His looks were anxiously tender. He said he must insist on bringing a physician to her, and implored the great bestower of health and life, to raise her from the affliction into which she had fallen.

"The ear of God is deaf to your supplications," cried the wild Lorina; "He has looked searchingly into me; and I can expect no mercy. Oh, Berrington! You know not what it is that plucks at my heart."

"Compose yourself, my love," said the affrighted Berrington: "You have fever: Go to your bed again."

"To my grave—To my grave! But leave me now; and do not come to me till the afternoon, when I will tell you—No matter what—Go, go; and let me see you again in the evening."

This was all he could draw from her; and he was obliged to retire. He afterwards came repeatedly to the door; but she refused to admit him, and was not to be prevailed on to see the physician.

She now resolved to break a vile engagement she had formed: To confess her crime to her husband: To put her beloved boy for ever from her bosom: To write a last letter to her mother; and then to go into some other part of the country, and struggle no longer for life.

Her servant was officious and troublesome; and Lorina, pretending she was infinitely better, sent her out with the child, previously telling her how long she might be absent. It was now about four o'clock, and Berrington soon after came into the chamber; but Lorina, in a peculiar manner, repulsed his fondness; and she appeared to him no less awful than strange.

"You have some knowledge of this letter, sir?" she said.

"Good Heaven! How came it to your hands? It has, I suspect, been the occasion of your present illness."

"Perhaps it has. But I can make no accusation: I cannot say, to the breaker of God's commandments, why have you done this, or that. But you have been to Lady Augusta. You deceived me with an odious untruth, in order that your licentiousness might receive no interruption. You are the father of the child, whom she here speaks of?"

"Oh, Lorina, Lorina! How have you been deceived. Though there is a mystery, which I vowed never to reveal, you shall be in ignorance no longer. But first let me, bending my knees, and raising my eyes to Heaven, solemnly swear, that my acquaintance with the unfortunate writer of this letter is, in every respect, honest and most truly virtuous:—That, since the day on which I took you as a wife from the altar, I never had commerce with your sex, except such as I could have commanded you, and all the world, to look on, without any violation being offered to decency. See, I am still kneeling! If I speak not true, let the arm of my incensed Creator sweep me into instant perdition!"

"Dreadful! Horrible! These are pangs indeed."

"My mistaken, beloved wife!"

"Oh, my agonised—my mangled heart!"

"Lorina!——"

"Come hither and triumph, all you who delight in human misery! Berrington, we separate this day; nay, within this very hour—and separate eternally. I loved you, Berrington, oh, how dearly did I once love you! But, since you left me, some devil prompted me in wickedness, and I——"

"What?——"

"I have been false to you, and unmindful of the words of God. I have given myself up to shame and ruin; and Russel, the smiling, villanous Russel, has triumphed over the virtue of your wife!"

"Have a care—Have a care, Lorina!—"

"I will guard against nothing; and all my enormities shall be known to you. I will not force an abhorred thing upon you, nor take advantage of your ignorance. Bless me no more: No longer put a loving arm around me; for I am sinking beneath the weight of crimes and perjuries. Mercy!—How dreadful has been my fall!—I must fly from my husband and my child, and become the contempt, and derision of the world."

"Dare you confess yourself an adulteress?"

"I do confess it—Hear me—I am such: Foul as contagion itself! Wicked as those whom God has abandoned. Oh, infamous Russel!—To-morrow night I was to have acceded to the elopement which he proposed. Berrington, let my miseries be now ended by your hand. I loved you once, perhaps no less than the Almighty. But my oath is broken—I have stained the marriage bed—My soul is sinking into perdition!"

"Let it fall—Let it still fall! Your words have put madness into my brain, and fire into my breast. Wretch! May an eternal night hang over your accursed head."

"It gathers!" cried Lorina, madly: "The clouds even now are collecting. I see my mother's lips trembling with a curse!—Horrors, the blackest of horrors surround me. My deeds——"

"Silence! Neither shall you speak, nor will I hear of them again. Your deeds!—Shameless obscenity!—This shall determine all."

A bar of iron, which was used for securing the window-shutters, was by his side. He snatched it up, and hurled it at his wife. It struck her head, and the bone yielded. Death was in the blow: She fell: No groan escaped her. She was still—horribly still—and her murderer, frozen and senseless, looked on the bloody works of his own hands.

For some minutes, a stupid insanity weighed on his brain: and he knew not what he had done. But his recollections soon rushed back again; and he threw himself by the side of the corse, which was so maimed and frightful, that he almost instantly hurried on his knees from it, and pressed his face on the floor. His antics were like those of a madman, who has been long accustomed to a dungeon and chains.

He raised himself on his elbow, first fearfully, then with confidence. An unmeaning laugh twisted his features, while he looked on the lily which had been defiled, and cut down by the scythe of ruin. "This is brave!" he cried. He lifted the unnerved arm of his wife, and, letting it fall, said again, "This is brave and excellent!"

He had just enough reason left to make madness more dreadful. A terrible repentance filled his breast: He had never felt any thing like it before: It was strange, confusing, petrifying. A mist seemed to encompass him, and shapeless shadows to flit around. He looked on the murdered joy of many years, and put his lips to her mouth; but he drew them back with affright, in order to wipe off the blood they had collected.

He still had power to act with such cunning as is often attached to the distracted mind. He laid his wife on the bed, bound up her clotted hair, and put her in an attitude of sleeping. On the stained part of the carpet he placed one of her gowns; every thing soon seemed well arranged; and then he sat down, and laughed, and wept.

He had continued in this state about a quarter of an hour, when he heard a knocking at the door. He arose instantly, and enquired who was there; his child answered him, and he let the boy come into the room. He began to tell his father of the pleasure he had enjoyed, in riding with one of the officers and a lady in a curricle;* but Berrington put his hand on his mouth, and desired him not to talk so loud.

"Look at your mother, boy!" said the murderer.

"How sound she sleeps, father: I'll tickle her, as I did in the morning, with a feather, and that will wake her, you know."

"No, no. Do not disturb her: Only go and kiss her—Yet stay!—Touch not pollution with your cherub lips. Come hither, immediately—Do you hear?"

"Lord have mercy! How angry you are now. I am sure Captain Russel never frowned upon me so."

"Ha, Russel!—Damnation!—Come hither, you tormenting imp! I'll beat you into jelly, if you do not obey me."

The child burst into tears: Berrington caught him in his arms, and pressed him franticly to his breast. He did not release him for nearly half an hour; he kissed him nearly a thousand times, and his head grew more wild, as it lay on the boy's velvet bosom. For his brutalities he cursed himself, and could scarcely be persuaded that he was still a man. His eyes were turned towards the bed, with extreme horror; the light of day was fading; and in the course of half an hour, the child sobbed himself to rest on his father's shoulder.

Berrington carried him down softly to the servant. He desired she would take care of him, and, on no account, either go to, or suffer any person to enter, the chamber of her mistress, who was much indisposed, and desirous of procuring some sleep. Altho' the girl perceived something strange in his manner, yet it gave her no great concern. She knew how dearly he loved her lady; and, supposing that his agitation was occasioned by her illness, she merely took the boy from him, and laid him on a couch.

Berrington returned to the dreadful chamber, and gazed on his wife. He touched her, and was chilled: He smote his breast till he bruised it. In his agony and distraction, he rooted his hair from his giddy head; and, with his nails, attempted to empty the sockets of his eyes. His moans were like the wind, when it is dismal, without being loud; his words few, but shocking even to his own ears.

Since God first created man, no one had ever looked with

more frightfulness, or felt severer torture. He seemed to be plunging in the glooms of chaos, and buffeting the muddy waters of death. His imagination became still more extravagant. He thought an angel, with a sword of flame, was menacing him; and he ran round the room, fancying that the weapon of the wrathful minister was cleaving his scull. He fell down near the window, and, with difficulty, shut up his shrieks.

Soon he heard voices, which he could still remember, and looking thro' the glass, saw Russel and Westdale near the door. A loaded pistol lay on the table that stood by his side. He snatched it up, gently raised the sash, and levelled the instrument at his foul enemy.—But he did not discharge it. A thought rushed into his mind, and suspended the action; and, putting forth his head, he saluted the officers. Though the night was young, the moon shone with uncommon lustre.

"In the name of every thing that is wonderful," cried Westdale, "what are you doing in a place like this?"

"Calculating eclipses," replied Berrington; "and comparing the brightness and purity of Heaven, to the darkness and corruption of the earth."

"Well said, misanthrope! But I entreat you to finish your almanack business, and to come down immediately."

"For what purpose? Where are you going?"

"To the ball-room, which will be crowded with all the beauty that can be found in this part of the kingdom. I am in an excellent mood for the evening! Mercury has lent me his heels, and my ears are already filled with the measures of Orpheus.* I hear the exhilarating sound, and can almost believe that the graceful train is, even now, sporting around me. Come down, philosopher, and for awhile dispose of your gravity."

"I shall not go with you."

"I have before declined accompanying him," said Russel: "Is Mrs. Berrington well, this evening."

"O, in excellent health! Her blood is temperate, and her pulse steady. But whither are *you* going. I never saw so fine an evening, in the latter part of the year. Will you walk on the shore with me?"

"Nothing can be more agreeable."

"I will be with you in a moment," said Berrington.

He ran towards the bed, but turned from it instantly, and rushed out of the room. He locked the door; repeated his orders to the servant; kissed, and whispered a blessing over, his lovely boy, and then went to the officers. Westdale, finding he would not go to the assembly, and seeing the unfitness of his dress, wished him good night, and departed. The "good night" that Berrington returned to his amiable friend was emphatical.

Berrington took hold of Russel's arm, and led him from the house. His mind was now in a singular state. Reason yet opposed madness; at intervals, however, it was driven from the throne that was most difficult of ascent. He was haunted by a strange idea, which he could scarcely for a moment banish. He believed that he was then grasping a venomous serpent; the poison seemed to swell in his veins, and he thought the reptile deserved no other fate, than that of being cut in pieces by his own arm.

Russel found there was something much amiss in the mind of his companion, who talked in a desultory manner, and answered at random. It was a night in which God had made the heavens so beautiful, that the atheist, in regarding them, must have banished his disbelief, repented, and adored. Russel could always be eloquent, and so he was on this occasion. His companion was sensible only of half the words that were addressed to him; but those which he understood gave strength to his designs, and fire to his unloosened rage.

As Russel proceeded, he began to observe his associate more seriously, and also to be alarmed by his horrible moodiness and incoherence. He was, however, ashamed of his fears; and tho' the hand of conscience smote him, he continued to ramble, with the fiend-tormented murderer, on the margin of the sea. Berrington now became silent; he walked with his hand spread over his forehead, and suddenly stopt on the brow of one of the cliffs.

"It may be so," he cried; "yet to this point I swear I will stand!"

"My friend!" said Russel, "what point?"

"That a woman, who turns from the breast of a loving husband, and riots with a deceptious paramour, ought not to be wept for when hell demands her."

"Berrington!"

"Westdale?——"

"He is not here:—You are not well:—Your hand is hot, and your eye wild. Take off your hat, and lean upon my breast."

"There—Now there is comfort for me! The bosom of a friend—the cygnet can furnish nothing like it! This is a pillow, on which descended angels might recline, while they looked without regret towards Heaven. My pangs subside; yet I shall soon be melted to infancy. Am I not favored beyond all other men? God's own Son never found so sweet a resting-place as this! Oh, that I could extract the corruptions of this infamous, this inhuman world!—Oh, that I could make all men, like you, honest in their professions, virtuous in their desires, and tender in their consolations! I should, then, be proud of that which I now blush to look on—I should, then, hold forth my arms to every one, saying, 'Brother, my soul longs to meet you!' But, at this time,—Pray lend me your handkerchief. My head is as hot and heavy as a thunder cloud."

"What is the meaning of this agitation?" said Russel: "Speak, tell me the cause, I entreat you." Considering many of the actions of Berrington, he thought himself secure when he asked these questions.

"My wife is false!" cried the maniac: "False as infamy and wantonness can make her! I'll rave it forth—Shriek it every where. I'll take her by the hand, drag her thro' the streets, and join in the derision and laughter of the mob. There is, among the vulgar, a custom—perhaps you have heard of it—of assigning their wives in public. What an excellent plan! By Heaven, I will pursue it. She shall be disposed of, since she is become so saleable."

"You have been led into error," said the shivering Russel; "indeed you have. Allow me to accompany you home."

"Away you infernal villain! I know you are capable of the most damnable deeds. Adultery and murder form sport for you. The light now comes strongly on your face—God!—I shudder at its deceit and ugliness. I tell you, Russel, you have possessed my wife."

"Good Heaven!"

"Talk not to me of Heaven and goodness. Villany! Villany! Of what a growth is villany! It is rooted every where: Its fibres run thro' the whole earth, and still want space: It will make mole-hills of pyramids, and trebly encircle the vast firmament. The stained adulteress of the easy Berrington may laugh at this—No, she will never laugh again! Root her murderer, root him, great power of all motion and inaction! I call on you to fix him on this rock. Let him be made black by your thunders, and to all eyes terrible. My feet begin to rivet; and the bright and unextinguishable lamp, which the Almighty cast from his hand, smiles on and derides my condition."

"You talk strangely, Berrington: Let us return: I entreat you to go back to your wife."

"I have murdered her! I put her to the agonies of death—I made her quiet for ever.—And then—Oh, how I then laughed at my success!"

"This, surely, is not true?" said the horror-stricken Russel.

"By God, by man, by Heaven, and by earth, it is most true! And now accursed wretch! I have an account to settle with you. By you I have been robbed of every worldly happiness. You have bound my struggling soul to an unyielding stake, and shall answer me, when I demand, why did you this?"

The tongue of Russel was immoveable: He was frightened and agonised, by his perilous condition, from which he attempted to fly. But the maniac pursued and overtook him. The strength of the fugitive was unequal to that of his opponent, and he was compelled to yield.

"Villain and coward!" exclaimed Berrington: "In a chase like this, the wind should not press before me. Be still and silent, or you shall not have the chance which I mean to give you. Oh, hypocrite, hypocrite! Mad as I am, I have still some recollections. I have already told you that my wife is dead: that she expired under these hands, which have, a thousand times, raised and supported her with love and ecstacy. These very hands!—Look at them—There is a spot of blood—Here, another—Still more —O——oh!"

This groan was horrible: It shook the soul of Russel, who felt as if he were petrified.

"All your designs and actions are known to me," continued Berrington: "He is the worst of villains who smiles when he wrongs me. You were to have carried off my wife, who, before I put her to death, revealed your previous brutalities. I acted with her most horribly! And, beyond where those stars shine, I must, hereafter, answer for it. I came not hither with the intent of taking your life away, without apprising you of my designs. Still will I be in some manner satisfied: Quickly must it be, for my brain is searing! Nothing can extenuate your deeds: All those who are of any value in the world, will protest against them, and God himself speak of them in a voice of thunder. Roused by a single incautions word—Fired by a rivalry, in regard to a woman whose commonness is known to thousands—Or by the unlucky turn of a card, you would probably resort to your sword for redress. In the present cause there is no frivolity. I call you by the name of villain—monster—brute—And command you to draw in your defence."

"I am unprepared," said Russel; "terror and amazement have taken possession of me. Let us separate now, and meet again in the morning."

"May fiends bear me to the world of horrors, if I consent to this. You have a sword, and, see, mine is ready to meet it. I would not, had I capability, take any unfair advantages; for my love of life is fallen into extreme sickness. But let there be no further talk. Come on! Nay, if you will not be on your guard, you will drive me into murder."

Russel was now compelled to draw, and act for his safety. They fought long and desperately. Berrington received the weapon of his adversary in the shoulder: This only served to increase his madness, and within a few minutes, his sword was driven into the heart of his enemy.

Russel fell. In a few words he confessed his guilt, as well as the justness of his punishment, and sunk into a quick, but agonising death. The victor looked on the body with wildness and savageness. The disturbance of his intellects increased; and, having dragged the deceased behind a large stone, he ran down the cliff, and along the margin of the sea.

He was now at the distance of three miles from the town, and his frantic course was interrupted by a high bank, where the sea turned irregularly. Climbing over this impediment, he saw a man, dragging his boat on the shore, and a boy taking some fish out of a net. The mariners were startled by his sudden appearance; but he quieted their alarm, and asked the elder of them to go with him upon the water.

He put a guinea into the man's hand, and told him that the beauty and tranquillity of the night, alone induced him to leave the shore. The fellow was pleased with the money: Tho' the officer appeared a little strange to him, he supposed that he was merely elevated by wine, and disposed to frolic away an hour in an unusual manner. He, therefore, sent his son to his cottage, which was not far distant, and, desiring Berrington to step into the boat, he began to row from the shore.

The maniac was for a considerable time silent: The blood, unperceived, trickled from his wounds; and he alternately buried his head in his breast, and raised it towards the regions of light and loveliness. When he spoke, it was to desire that the pilot would not keep so near the land, but go further on the sea. The man readily obeyed him: the oar was used with an unwearied arm; and it was not long before the boat was nearly a league from the margin of the water.

Berrington began to mutter his strange thoughts. He spoke in a strain which somewhat alarmed his companion, whose ears frequently caught the words of "Villain, Lorina and murder!" He had lost much blood, but the distraction of his mind kept him from fainting. The wildness of his brain now more strongly appeared: He sent forth a holloo, that went frightfully over the water, and talked of a flame that was scorching him. His companion, no longer doubting his condition, prepared to return; and, with an agitated voice, answered the questions which were put to him.

"The sun will blister us," cried Berrington: "will it not, my friend?—Have you a wife?"

"Yes, sir: I thank God!"

"And is she pure? Is she virtuous?"

"I have no doubt of it."

"She may be foul and vicious, in spite of your opinion. Your belief, however, constitutes your happiness. If she be really such, I will give you all I am worth. Here is gold for you. Take it. Clothe her in lawn and ermine; and think your years well spent, while you are searching in the remotest seas, for pearls to put upon her chaste and loving bosom. Do it: And as the longest period of man's life, is only like the hour of noon, let there be no delay in your business."

"I know not how to answer you, sir; for I have little learning."

"It is better to have none. The slow rotation of mean ideas insures a man more happiness, than the coruscations* of a fervid brain, or that varnished thing, which we arrogantly call a polished mind. Ignorance, be still what you ever have been. We may scoff at the simperings of your unmeaning face; but the acts of your hands cannot draw from us any serious censures.—I did right, however, in begetting a male child! Posterity might have cursed me, for increasing the number of the viler sex. Do I not argue justly, sir? Oh, woman, woman! Those who speak well of you, are either fools, or madmen. I have no words of praise, no commendations to bestow upon your beautified deformities: I have trusted you, and been deceived. While I looked on your faces, I thought I contemplated the smiling Heavens; and I regarded not the ensnaring hell, that burnt in each of your bosoms."

The hand of the terrified mariner could scarcely grasp the oar.

"And all that I have said, here will I prove to be true: Here speak of the wantonness from which I sprang, and by which I have been surrounded. She who bore me, could not keep herself in the ways of virtue—Prostitute!—She who was the mother of my child, ran into the broad path of vice, heated by licentiousness, and fearless of a cheated God—Adulteress—wicked adulteress!—Where are you now, Lorina? Where is your deceitful paramour? Where my boy, my poor, deserted boy! I look on the Heavens for the last time, and now bid adieu to the corrupted world. Sport shall be made of me no longer. I am a man, and will not endure it."

He threw himself into the sea; but the boatman suddenly bent forward, and caught him by the arm before he sunk. The one strove for the preservation of life, and the other struggled for a contrary purpose. The mariner, for awhile, held the maniac; but his limbs trembled with horror, and the edge of the boat was nearly level with the water.

"Release me, release me instantly," cried Berrington.

"For the sake of God," said the mariner, "do not throw away your life thus wickedly! Endeavour to get into the boat."

"What! Am I not yet free from the power of villany? Let go my arm—Take off your hands, this very moment, or I will pull you into death."

By the exertion of his strength, he seemed to be executing this threat; the seaman then released him, and he went down to the horrible bed of the waters, leaving the affrighted man to return to the shore and speak of his melancholy fate. It was heard with pity, terror, and amazement. The bodies of Lorina and Russel were hurried into their graves, and Westdale, with agony tearing his heart, often strove to appease the orphan, while he cried for his dear father and mother.

Lady Augusta sailed from England two days after the death of Berrington, and before she had heard of it. Westdale, tho' his fortune was small, resolved to act like a parent to the child; but in the course of a fortnight, a stranger came, and begged him to resign his charge. This was Robert Fellers, who had seen a dreadful account of the late transactions in a news-paper, and who now, with a voice often broken by excessive grief, told the history of the unfortunate Berrington, which never had been wholly revealed to his late friend.

"Let me have the child," said the villager; "pray, sir, let me have him. I live on a healthy spot, and can support the poor thing, as well as his father was supported. My wife is a good and virtuous woman, and my mother will wholly die with grief, if I return without him—And—she is half dead already!—Oh, what a wicked world is this! I shall go blind with weeping."

Westdale soon discovered the goodness of his disposition, and, after making some arrangements, in regard to the property of Berrington, he consented that the child should, with Mrs.

Gerrald's consent, live with him, till he was old enough to be placed at a public school. Robert thanked him for his acquiescence: He continued in the town several days, in order to gain the love of the little stranger, who afterwards accompanied him in the longest journey that he had ever undertaken; and, at length found a resting-place on the bosom of the sorrowful Mary.

Westdale wrote to the mother of Lorina, and no person could have treated so shocking a subject with more judgment and tenderness. Mrs. Gerrald read it: She began an answer, but—she never finished it!

Adulteress! Should the preceding pages ever meet your eye, be not unmindful of yourself; and let penitence, not confidence, take possession of your breast. If the agent of your crimes has a face resembling the beauties of an angel, believe that he also has the disposition of a fiend.

Your daughters, O, my country! for many ages were admired for their modesty, their virtue, and their continence. Innumerable songs have been sung in their praise, and the moralists of other nations have recorded their chastity. I am startled, therefore, when I hear a thousand tongues affirming, that their minds are seriously turning to folly; their hearts to depravity—That the connubial duties are alarmingly disregarded; and the honor of their husbands, as well as the welfare of their children, more shamefully neglected, than at any former period.

There are many—*Philosophers!*—who would refute these opinions, and make the injured appear the better for the slander. The *injured* such as Russel and Lorina, the *slander* what would once have been called the wholesome reproof of offended virtue. And they would shew the growth of intellect, the expansion of wisdom, the absurdities of worn-out prejudices! I have no power for controversy. If the evil really exist, I must mourn that the clamours against it are just, yet hope my eyes will not finally close on the scenes of the world, before they see it eradicated by Reason.

THE END.

NOTES

PAGE

3 Here, in particular, Summersett refers to the negative reviews of *Martyn of Fenrose; or, The Wizard and the Sword* (1801), which charged the author with blasphemy.

3 *Shakespeare, Otway and Rowe*: All three playwrights were much admired by Summersett. Thomas Otway (1652-1685), Restoration dramatist of numerous popular tragedies. Nicholas Rowe (1674-1718), dramatist who wrote a number of successful tragedies and was also indebted to Shakespeare. Summersett mentions how these authors, who all use a range of curses and oaths, had been admired and praised without censure, both in the act of private reading and in the public arena on the stage.

3 *Periodical Critics*: Those who review new literary works; Summersett had not always fared well in their criticisms of his novels.

3 *Prince of Denmark*: A reference to Shakespeare's *Hamlet*.

8 The disease that Ann mentions could be syphilis.

18 *determine on her insanity*: Even though Ann committed suicide, the coroner's declaration of her insanity would ensure that she would be allowed to receive burial in consecrated ground in the churchyard, rather than on the outskirts of town, the usual place of rest for suicides.

20 *wight*: Archaic; a human being.

21 *rectorial*: Of or belonging to the rector of the parish (*OED*).

22 *would not move my hat*: To doff one's hat as a sign of salutation and respect.

27 *guinea*: At the time that Summersett was writing the novel, the value of a guinea was fixed at twenty-one shillings.

30 *Beattie*: A reference to the Scottish poet and moralist James Beattie (1735-1803). Beattie's *The Minstrel; or, The Progress of Genius* appeared in two volumes between 1771-72.

32 *Westmoreland*: In the north-west of England.

33 *one set of feelings*: The modern poet mentioned is Samuel Taylor Coleridge, who advocates the idea in the Preface to his *Poems on Various Subjects* (1796).

33 *Collins*: William Collins (1721-1759), popular poet. His *Odes on Several Descriptive and Allegorical Subjects* (1747), is referenced here.

33 *war-denouncing trumpet*: From Collins's poem *The Passions: An Ode for Music* (1747), line 43.

33 *Bard of Gray*: A reference to Thomas Gray's popular poem, "Elegy Written in a Country Churchyard" (1751).

34 *Song of Aurora's Eldest Born*: The poem is Summersett's own.

34 *fays*: Fays are fairies.

35 *Hyperion*: One of the twelve Titans in Greek mythology; associated with light.

35 *Astraeus*: In Greek mythology, an astrological deity; God of the dusk.

36 *Louisa*: This is a curious erratum. Possibly Summersett had originally intended Mrs. Gerrald's daughter to be called Louisa in the original draft and then changed it to Lorina, failing to make the necessary name change here. There is no further mention of a "Louisa" anywhere else in the novel.

43 *Titian*: Italian painter (d. 1576).

45 plagued: The 1804 edition reads "paged," which does not make sense in this context.

45 *cant*: The language of roguery.

45 The prostitutes may have purchased wigs because ingesting mercury, a common treatment for venereal disease, caused hair to fall out alongside other grotesque side effects.

45 *the Park*: Hyde Park in London.

48 *pathetic*: Suggesting pathos, rather than the modern usage of the word.

49 *tillers*: A farm labourer who works on the land.

52 *The Task*: These lines are from William Cowper's *The Task: A Poem, in Six Books* (1785), amounting to some 6000 lines. Summersett's quotation, in slightly altered form, is from book six, *The Winter Walk at Noon*, lines 7-10.

57 *Cowper*: This is also from Cowper's *The Task* (1785). Summersett's quotation is from book five, *The Winter Morning Walk*, lines 903-906.

59 *lenitives*: something that softens or soothens; in this context, Lorina is asking for him to take a gentle approach.

63 "*the passion of love . . . smiles or tears*": This quotation is from the

Preface to Elizabeth Inchbald's play *Lovers' Vows* (1798), an adaptation of August von Kotzebue's play *Das Kind der Liebe* (1780). Summersett's own novel *Leopold Warndorf* (1800) is indebted to Kotzebue and Inchbald.

69 *Arcadia*: Mountainous region in ancient Greece. During the Renaissance the place was celebrated as a pastoral haven.

72 *Buffa*: The comic actress in an opera.

73 *vale of years*: Altered quotation from Shakespeare's *Othello* (Act III), spoken by Othello after Iago has raised the subject of Desdemona's supposed infidelity.

79 *Park-lane*: On the eastern-side of Hyde Park, London.

82 *Temple*: Notable centre of law and lawyers in London.

82 *meed*: The *Oxford English Dictionary* defines as a prize given for excellence, in this instance in battle.

88 *gout*: painful inflammation of the joints.

88 *Canterbury*: City in Kent in the south-east of England.

89 *to repel the French in the Netherlands*: On the 18th May, 1803, Britain once again declared war on France after the French refused to withdraw from the Netherlands.

96 *epaulette*: The women are attempting to strip Berrington of the ornamental shoulder-piece that signifies that he is in the army.

96 *Harpies*: In Greek mythology, a horrible winged monster, consisting of a woman's face and body with claws. Often a harpy is depicted as an agent of divine vengeance.

98 *Paternoster-Row*: Infamous haunt for men trying to earn a living by writing, the area was well known for its publishing houses. The suggestion here is negative; that Westdale and Berrington are "hack" writers producing cheap and popular disposable literature. Summersett's own novel *Martyn of Fenrose* was sold in Paternoster-Row.

99 *Mercuries*: Related to the Roman god Mercury; a messenger who brings news.

99 *Idiotism*: If, from the species of poetry alluded to, there can be no such effect, the author, as well as Lorina, is mistaken. [Summersett's note.] Summersett suggests the power of melancholic poetry to influence the reader in an intense and emotional manner.

100 *gnomes*: The *Oxford English Dictionary* defines as a spirit said to inhabit the interior of the earth.

101 *Apollo*: Amongst other things, Apollo is the god of truth, music and poetry.

101 "*an ounce of civet*"—From Shakespeare's *King Lear* (Act IV). Lear, in an agitated state is talking to the blinded Gloucester, asking in vain for perfume to sweeten his imagination.

102 Imogen is the heroine from Shakespeare's *Cymbeline*. The play appears to have been a personal favourite of Summersett's, as evinced by his borrowings in his earlier novel *Leopold Warndorf* (1800).

111 *Deptford*: Deptford is on the south bank of the River Thames, South East London.

115 *street-lounger*: Not recorded in the *OED*. Summersett seems to imply that Westdale and Russel do not loiter in the streets in idleness or hedonistic pursuits.

115 *Kemble*: John Philip Kemble (1757-1823), one of the greatest actors of his age. Summersett admired him for the many Shakespearean roles that he played.

118 *quarto*: Refers to a size of book: the pages in a quarto volume were made by folding a large sheet of paper twice to make four leaves (i.e. eight pages). Summersett's novels were duodecimos (a sheet of paper folded to make twelve leaves) and thus considerably smaller in size.

118 *amaranths*: The *OED* defines as an "imaginary flower reputed never to fade".

118 *Parnassus*: Mountain in Greece; in mythology the home of the muses.

119 *Shakespeare, when he was delineating the savageness of human nature*: Summersett probably has in mind Shakespeare's *King Lear* or *Timon of Athens*.

123 *Theatres Royal*: Suggesting popularity, as there were many Theatres Royal across England at the time that Summersett was writing.

129 *Teresa Pancha*: The wife of Sancho Panza in Cervantes's novel *Don Quixote* (1605). In the novel, Sancho Panza acts as a squire to Don Quixote.

129 *Dapple*: The renowned Dapple is Rucio, a donkey in the same novel.

132 *Flora's pillager*: Flora is the Roman goddess of spring and flowers. The idea is that the young son of Lorina has been stolen away from nature and the goddess, reinforcing his innocence.

135 *epicurism*: Pursuit of pleasure.

140 *mother of Death*: In Milton's *Paradise Lost* (1667), Sin is the mother of Death.

145 *Titana*: Probably a reference to Titania, queen of the fairies ("fays") in Shakespeare's *A Midsummer Night's Dream*.

158 *Blackheath*: Blackheath is in south-east London.

160 *equivoque*: Suggesting that there is a double meaning in a seemingly innocent phrase or name.

165 *apostacy*: The *OED* defines as the abandonment of one's moral allegiance.

172 *curricle*: The *OED* defines as a light two wheeled carriage drawn by a pair of horses.

173 *Mercury, Orpheus*: Mercury is a Roman god, proverbially known for his swiftness. Orpheus was a legendary Greek poet, musician and prophet, well known for his ability to charm all living things with his beautiful music.

179 *Coruscations*: Glittering, or sparkling. Summersett suggests flashes of brilliance from the mind of the individual.

www.ingramcontent.com/pod-product-compliance
Lightning Source LLC
Chambersburg PA
CBHW030531310726
48979CB00010B/1871/J

* 9 7 8 1 9 4 1 1 4 7 1 5 3 *